Praise for the "wickedly titillating"*
novels of Cathryn Fox

"Hot sex in creative places, passion on every page, and erotic writing throughout. Realistic and arousing imagery." —*Romantic Times*

"Humor, sex, science, relationships, and sex . . . a pleasing, prolonged pleasure read." —*Midwest Book Review*

"Sizzling, irresistible, wonderful."
—*New York Times* bestselling author Lori Foster

"Witty, clever, and wickedly titillating. . . . Cathryn Fox is the next Queen of Steamy Romance."
—*USA Today* bestselling author Julianne MacLean

"Fun, sexy, and sassy—a Cathryn Fox book is a must-read great escape!" —Sylvia Day, author of *Bad Boys Ahoy!*

"Wonderful blend of passionate sex and witty intelligence."
—Fresh Fiction

"Hot, enthralling, and simply delicious. Run, don't walk, to the nearest bookstore and purchase this book today. It's a must-read!"
—Romance Reviews Today

"Delightful . . . hooks the audience from the start."
—*Midwest Book Review*

Sun Stroked

CATHRYN FOX

HEAT

Heat

Published by New American Library, a division of
Penguin Group (USA) Inc., 375 Hudson Street,
New York, New York 10014, USA
Penguin Group (Canada), 90 Eglinton Avenue East, Suite 700, Toronto,
Ontario M4P 2Y3, Canada (a division of Pearson Penguin Canada Inc.)
Penguin Books Ltd., 80 Strand, London WC2R 0RL, England
Penguin Ireland, 25 St. Stephen's Green, Dublin 2,
Ireland (a division of Penguin Books Ltd.)
Penguin Group (Australia), 250 Camberwell Road, Camberwell, Victoria 3124,
Australia (a division of Pearson Australia Group Pty. Ltd.)
Penguin Books India Pvt. Ltd., 11 Community Centre, Panchsheel Park,
New Delhi - 110 017, India
Penguin Group (NZ), 67 Apollo Drive, Rosedale, North Shore 0632,
New Zealand (a division of Pearson New Zealand Ltd.)
Penguin Books (South Africa) (Pty.) Ltd., 24 Sturdee Avenue,
Rosebank, Johannesburg 2196, South Africa

Penguin Books Ltd., Registered Offices:
80 Strand, London WC2R 0RL, England

First published by Heat, an imprint of New American Library,
a division of Penguin Group (USA) Inc.

First Printing, November 2008
1 3 5 7 9 10 8 6 4 2

LIBRARY OF CONGRESS CATALOGING-IN-PUBLICATION DATA
Fox, Cathryn.
Sun stroked / Cathryn Fox.
p. cm.
ISBN: 978-0-451-22511-5
I. Title.
PR9199.4.F69S86 2008

Set in Centaur MT Regular
Designed by Alissa Amell

Printed in the United States of America

This book is dedicated to all the heroic soldiers who bravely serve and protect.

And to my sister, Susie Murphy, whose strength, selflessness, and compassion make this world a better place.
I love you.

Sun Stroked

The Sensual Soak

ONE

Danielle Carrigan would gladly give up her fantasy of ever joining the mile-high club if the frigging plane would just make it to the ground safely. Not that she could join the club with her two best girlfriends and one female pilot on board, however. She'd definitely need a man for that scandalous initiation.

But still . . .

Truthfully, at twenty-eight she was too young to die, plus she hadn't done enough good deeds lately to warrant an early pass through the Pearly Gates.

Danielle pinched her eyes shut as the old Cessna tumbled them around like a load of laundry. "Remind me again why we're doing this," she said to her best friend, Lauren Sampson.

"We're doing this because we all need a vacation," Lauren reminded her, patting Danielle's leg in a placating manner, which did little to pacify her under the circumstances. Dammit, she hated flying, especially in a pissant, four-seat aircraft with less horsepower than her Honda Civic. "Now, relax. We're almost there," Lauren added.

With her fingernails digging into the upholstered seat, Danielle pried her eyes open and chanced a glance at Lauren. Suddenly, flying in a small commuter plane to a private island in the South Pacific didn't seem like her ideal vacation anymore. What the hell had she been thinking?

Sitting poolside at a Sandals resort with a menagerie of cabana boys catering to her every sinful need. Yes.

Flying to the O Spa on a Cessna 172 Skyhawk with an engine the size of her old Singer sewing machine. No.

With a nod toward the cockpit, Lauren added in a hushed tone—well, as hushed as she could be and still be heard over the ungodly clatter of the engine—"And we're doing it for her."

Oh, yeah, now Danielle remembered. One last "girls-only vacation" at the luxurious singles spa—a magical spa where fantasies were known to come true—before Abby Benton got engaged. A vacation that, if they were all lucky, they'd walk away from with their deepest desires fulfilled. And maybe, just maybe, Abby would see that her deepest desire wasn't to marry Artie Drummond. Too bad everyone knew it but her.

As for Danielle, well, she just wanted to get laid. Plain and simple. Danielle glanced at the brochure in Lauren's hand and read the boldface inscription: *The O Spa, Oasis of Pleasure.*

She really hoped that O stood for orgasm instead of oasis. Because her deepest desire was to find a man who knew how to take charge of her pleasures and give her exactly what she wanted.

A shiver of desire pulsed through her body, and the convulsions in her pussy reminded her exactly how long it had been since she'd felt a man between her legs. Then again, that shiver could have more to do with the way the plane cut through the turbulence like an injured eagle and less to do with wanting to play out her secret fetishes.

From the front seat, Abby twisted around and smiled at them both. After seeing the relaxed look on her friend's face, Danielle gathered her bravado and, for Abby's sake, presented an outwardly calm demeanor. Danielle was, after all, the one who had convinced the girls to shut down their interior design boutique for two weeks and take off to the exclusive resort smack-dab in the middle of the Pacific. To a place where *real* planes didn't even fly.

She resisted the urge to slap her forehead. Obviously this would require her to yank her fingers off the seat, and that she wasn't about to do.

From where she sat in the cockpit, Abby's face lit with euphoria as she angled her head to glance out the pilot's window. Even facing an impending fiery death, Danielle smiled as she watched her friend's blue eyes glow with excitement.

Everyone knew Abby's soon-to-be fiancé was all wrong for her. Okay, not exactly everyone. Abby truly believed her deepest desire was to marry Artie, a man who fit right into her "life's plan." College, career, a husband by the time she was thirty, followed by a nice little house in suburbia. But seriously, how could Danielle, or even Lauren, just come right out and tell her they thought her boyfriend was a reserved, emotionally distant workaholic and she deserved someone who appreciated her? Someone who wasn't afraid to show his passion, despite Abby's belief that no such man existed.

With any luck during their vacation, Abby would let her hair down, get seduced by their exotic location and forget she was a good girl with a mapped-out future. Then maybe she'd indulge in a wild, no-holds-barred affair with a man who wasn't afraid to unleash his passion, and show her that Arctic Artie—as Danielle liked to call him—was far from husband material.

A sudden gust of wind caused the plane to seesaw, gaining her focus. Danielle cringed and dug her fingernails in deeper. Drawing on her yoga relaxation techniques, she breathed deeply, in through the nose, out through the mouth.

Trying desperately to get her mind off the shaky landing, she took a moment to think more about the exclusive resort and the legend surrounding it. Rumor had it that the owner's private springwater held magical healing powers, and when ingested this "magic elixir" had the ability to help you discover and fulfill your deepest, most coveted desires.

Naturally Danielle planned on supersizing her drink.

And then maybe her most secret desires would finally come true and she'd find herself a man who would introduce her to a world of pleasure, pleasure that she knew existed for some women but that she had yet to experience. Lord knew the men she'd dated thought a little role-playing meant she'd pretend to be a waitress and serve them breakfast in bed while they lay there and basked in the afterglow of sex. Too bad none of them had ever given her anything to bask about.

Bemoan another failed attempt. Uh-huh.

Bask in the afterglow. Uh-uh.

She glanced at the brochure again and read the small print at the bottom of the page. *Where all your desires will be fulfilled* . . . Although she'd heard all about the magic elixir from friends who'd vacationed at the spa, the pamphlet made no mention of it. Truthfully, Danielle didn't put much faith in the legend, but what the hell, it'd be fun to give it a whirl just in case. . . .

The tires hit the runway and pulled her thoughts to the present. When the movement jolted her forward, she gave a silent prayer. As she fumbled the words, she mentally kicked herself, wishing she'd paid more attention in catechism class.

Shit, she really was going to go to hell.

Lauren leaned into her. "Open your eyes. We're here and we're safe."

It suddenly occurred to Danielle that they'd have to ride the old jalopy back to civilization in two weeks. Maybe she'd rethink her deepest desire and pray for a pair of big-ass wings instead.

Nah, she really wanted a good fuck from a man who wasn't afraid of a little bondage play and could satisfy her sexually.

As the plane slowed, her stomach fell back into place. She opened her eyes, gave the cushiony seat a break from her death grip and glanced out her window. Off in the distance she could see a red turret peeking out from the treetops. Strategically located deep in the forest, the extravagant resort was mostly hidden by palm trees, foliage and lush vegetation. Higher on the hilly mountaintop she spotted a waterfall. Ahh, that had to be the Pleasure Pool, as it was called in the brochure. A natural lagoon with an emerald green pool known to promote fertility and social delights, and attract love. She took a moment to wonder what kind of pleasure—or rather mischief—they could find there.

Danielle craned her neck to look out Lauren's side of the plane and was presented with an amazing view of a coconut grove. A brilliant blue, green and yellow parrot flew by, squawking loudly as it foraged for food.

"Wow," Danielle said, her head twisting from side to side as she tried to take it all in. "It's surreal." The place was absolutely gorgeous. An oasis, really. Just like the brochure promised. Maybe the flight from hell had been worth it, after all.

"It's amazing," Lauren agreed, dark brown eyes bright with pleasure.

After the plane came to a full stop, Shana, their pilot, escorted them off. Following her friends, Danielle stepped onto the small, makeshift runway and inhaled the fresh ocean air. She stretched out her fatigued limbs and stifled a yawn. Her body relaxed as the fragrant scent from the indigenous flowers curled through her blood and soothed her ragged nerves. Her gaze panned the vast landscape, taking in its majestic beauty and the sparkling Pacific Ocean. Moisture beaded on her forehead as the blazing November sun beat down on them. Time to shed her winter wear.

The tropical rays immediately warmed her flesh, reminding her that with her pale complexion and fair skin she needed to play it careful and apply extra sunscreen. Either that or she'd burn to a crisp.

Turning her face to the sun to let it melt away her tension, she shrugged off her jacket and wrapped it around her waist. Gathering her long strawberry blond hair, she tied it into a ponytail as she continued to savor the view. Heck, they were a far cry from Chicago's snowy concrete jungle, that's for sure.

"Welcome to the O Spa."

The male voice came from behind her. Damn, she hadn't even heard anyone creep up on them. Danielle spun around and came face-to-face with an elderly gentleman. Dressed in an ankle-length white cotton robe tied with a red sash decorated with intricate symbols, he took a moment to look each girl in the eye. As he studied them, a smile touched his lips and his head nodded slowly, knowingly. There was an energy about him that rushed through her bloodstream and gave her a second wind.

From the description she'd been given by her friends who'd recently vacationed on the island, she presumed the man standing before them was the resort's proprietor. She took a moment to study him, surprised and delighted that the owner of the spa had come to greet them personally. Not much taller than her five foot six inches, he had an intuitive intelligence about him that made him seem larger than life. He sort of reminded her of her own grandfather, minus the white goatee and bald head. His pleasant, amicable smile immediately put her at ease.

After a round of introductions and handshakes, the owner, Mr. Malik, pressed his palms together in front of his chest and questioned in a soft voice, "I take it your flight was enjoyable?"

Not wanting to be rude, Danielle said, "Yes." Her friends nodded in agreement. Mr. Malik narrowed his eyes and cocked his head, giving her the distinct impression that he could read her every thought and knew she'd just told him a bold-faced lie. Then again, perhaps her green skin had given it away.

The look in his eyes compelled her to tell the truth. She kicked at an imaginary rock, the same way she had back in grade school when

Mrs. Beeswanger caught her lying about her involvement in the locker room spray-a-thon. "Well, actually, I guess it was rather rough."

He smiled at her as though she'd just passed his test. "Then you must choose what to say, when to say it and how to say it, my child. There is no ambiguity in the truth."

Alrighty then . . .

She was pretty certain he'd just offered her words of wisdom. Maybe one day they'd make sense. But today wasn't that day, not unless he cared to elaborate.

Mr. Malik turned around and stepped onto a stone walkway. "Come this way."

Another day it was, then, Danielle mused. They grabbed their luggage from the plane and followed him along the path leading to the resort. Abby stepped up beside her.

"I have to hand it to you, Danielle. I was a little skeptical when you suggested this singles resort in the middle of nowhere, but now that we're here . . ." Abby glanced around, her short honey blond hair catching the sun's rays. Danielle followed her gaze, her eyes coming to rest on a beautiful pond full of brightly colored fish. "Honestly, after having to fill out all those personal forms, I wasn't sure what to expect," Abby added.

Danielle leaned in and whispered, "Yeah, I felt like I was re-taking my SATs, except this time, instead of calculating the time it would take for train A to meet train B, I had to say what color panties I'd be wearing for the journey."

Abby grinned, her blue eyes glistening. "It wasn't that bad. Close, but not quite—" Her voice fell off when Mr. Malik turned to face them. He removed three key cards from his pocket.

"Ladies, your cabanas are right through this pathway, each overlooking the ocean, as you requested. Please take your time to look around and familiarize yourself with the facility. If you have any questions, do not hesitate to send for me. I am here to ensure you have a fun-filled vacation." His voice was low, almost hypnotic. After a moment of silence, he pressed his palms together, a movement Danielle guessed was habitual for him, and added, "I would like to invite you all to be my personal guests for dinner."

Danielle smiled, wondering whether he'd offer them the island's so-called magic elixir while they indulged in the local cuisine.

They all accepted their keys and agreed to meet Mr. Malik at the restaurant at seven p.m. sharp. Just enough time for her to take a short nap and shower. As they separated and made their ways to their private cabanas to unpack and relax, it occurred to Danielle as she walked the tree-fringed footpath that she'd yet to see another person on the property. She knew the resort was elite and expensive, but heck, she sure hoped there were other guests—of the male persuasion, to be precise.

A short while later, Danielle found herself all alone, standing inside her gorgeous, spacious cabana. She spun around, cataloging the contents of her room, her designer's eye taking in the earthy colors, the wicker furniture and the beachy décor. Aromatherapy candles and plant oils were placed throughout the room. Fortunately, through her numerous design courses, Danielle was educated in the benefits of fragrances and the way they affected the body, mind and soul. She inhaled the scent of the eucalyptus and peppermint candle, letting the fresh aroma rejuvenate her body. Feeling revived and invigorated, she glanced out her window, taking pleasure in her own personal view of the pristine white sand and warm Pacific waters.

Paradise . . .

A tingle rushed down her spine and she felt giddy with the anticipation of things to come.

With this perfect seaside location, she could forgo clothes and venture out after dark for a decadent moonlit dip.

As another parrot flew by her window, something warm and wonderful whipped through her body. It occurred to her just how powerful, how magical, this exclusive vacation island felt. With its private beach coves, gentle lapping waves, warm pools and exotic cabanas it was the perfect seaside escape. She'd have to remember to thank her friends for turning her on to the place, a place where inhibitions would be shed under the decadent starry nights.

After years of failed relationships and bedroom disappointments, Danielle knew she deserved a vacation where she could just let go. A vacation where anything could happen and fantasies were known to come true.

Unlike Abby, she was never really the good girl, and never liked to keep a guy around for too long. Why would she? Why keep a guy around only to have him bolt once he was sexually satisfied, with no regard for her pleasure? Truthfully, she was hurt by how many times she'd found herself alone.

Danielle certainly wasn't here looking for love. She was merely looking for a once-in-a-lifetime fantasy—a wild, scandalous affair that would fulfill her secret desires. Then she'd return to Chicago, to men who knew nothing about her wants and needs.

As her gaze scanned the beach vista a second time, delight bubbled up inside her, but it wasn't the view that brought on the wave of joy; it was the tall, shirtless, hard-bodied male walking along the shoreline that set her pulse racing, not to mention her libido.

Dayum, he was yummy!

Beginning with his mussed, windblown black hair, her eyes traveled down his long torso toward his finely toned body parts and came to rest on his knee-length swimsuit. Even from a distance she could see his hard pecs, hard abs, and even harder leg muscles. For a brief moment she wondered what they'd feel like wrapped around her.

Arms folded, she leaned against her doorjamb, her body registering every delicious inch of the stranger who piqued her interest. And by the looks of things, he had a lot of inches to keep her interest piqued.

His bronzed skin glistened with perspiration as he made his way down toward the water. She noted that his walk seemed rather rigid, stiff. He favored his right leg as if it caused him great pain to move.

When Mr. Hardbody reached the water's edge, he stopped and spread his feet to shoulder width. He crossed his hands behind his back, palms facing out. Since Danielle's uncle was a military man, she'd recognize that at-ease stance anywhere.

She watched him a while longer, studying his body language. It occurred to her that he looked like he should be addressing the troops, not staring out over a sunlit ocean. But, hey, soldiers needed vacations, too, right?

Lucky for her.

Without warning, he turned around. As though he felt her eyes on him, his gaze strayed toward her cabana, toward her. When their eyes met and locked, she faltered backwards, jolted by the ribbons of need rushing through her veins. Heat bombarded her body and her skin moistened right down to the tips of her toes, but she knew it had nothing to do with the tropical sun.

What was it about him that made her thighs tingle even as he stood thirty feet away? As lust exploded inside her, her thoughts careened off track. Her lascivious mind took her in an erotic direction.

She closed her eyes, imagining what it would be like if she offered herself to a trained soldier, a guy who seemed worlds away from the men in her social circle. Judging by his commanding presence, his disciplined body language and his piercing gaze, she'd hazard a guess that he'd be more than capable, and more than willing, to play out all her secret fetishes with her. Warmth flooded her pussy and dampened her panties as she visualized herself bound to his bed, restrained and subdued while he disciplined her body in the most delicious, most scandalous ways.

Truthfully, it amazed her that one captivating look from a stranger had her hormones squawking louder than the native wildlife.

Danielle drew in air, determined to make every moment of this vacation count. She decided to forgo a nap, slip into her bikini and head out to meet the locals, or rather, that tall, brooding, mysterious man lingering at the water's edge.

When she opened her eyes again, he was gone. Gone!

Vanished.

AWOL.

MIA.

She blinked and glanced up and down the beach for Mr. Hardbody, but dammit, he was nowhere to be found. She suddenly wondered whether she'd imagined him. Had this magical island caused her salacious mind to conjure up the perfect fantasy man for her?

Either way, she needed a swim to cool herself down before her body spontaneously combusted. She peeled off her clothes, pulled on her new itsy-bitsy peach bikini, and strolled lazily to the shore, squishing the warm white sand between her toes along the way. She spent a few moments walking the beach line, absorbing the sun's warmth. Stopping to stare out over the ocean, she gave a little heavenly sigh and noted that even though she'd been out on the beach for only a few minutes, her pale skin had already begun to burn.

She planted her hands on her hips, and her gaze skimmed the aquamarine water as she tested the temperature with the tip of her big toe. It was actually warm, far different from the cool lake waters she was used to. With these tepid temperatures, there was no need to psych herself up to jump in.

Feeling adventurous and bold, Danielle rushed forward and waded out until she was submerged up to her neck. The water felt glorious against her scorching skin and was so crystal clear, she could see right down to the tips of her toes.

At the same time, she saw something swim by those toes.

Holy hell, what was that?

That same something brushed against her leg.

Oh, damn.

Her pulse skyrocketed. She opened her mouth to scream, but no words formed. Arms and legs flailing, she began to tread water.

What had she been thinking, venturing into unknown waters by herself? Lord only knew what kind of deadly sea creatures swam in the Pacific Ocean. Heck, she might be a streetwise city girl, but that certainly wasn't helping her in this situation. She was completely out of her element here. She should have at least invited Abby to join her since her friend had spent her college days teaching water aerobics at their local health club.

She decided to change tactics and stilled her movements. Steeling herself, she scanned the ocean floor for whatever was down there, waiting for it to pounce. After a good thirty seconds, her racing heart began to slow.

Maybe it had swum away.

Taking her by surprise, that same *something* brushed against her thigh and slipped between her open legs.

"Jesus," she cried out as she lost her footing. "What the fu—" Her words came out garbled, drowned in a mouthful of water as she sank to the sandy bottom. Body now completely submerged, she opened her eyes and came face to face with a snake.

A. Great. Big. Frigging. Snake.

An anaconda, really.

And if there was one thing she hated more than flying . . . Sputtering and gasping for air, she tried to regain her footing as the reptile swam closer.

Something tugged her arm. A moment later she found herself upright, staring into the most gorgeous pair of baby blues she'd ever had the pleasure of setting eyes on.

"I've got you."

Oh, God. It was him. Mr. Hardbody. In the flesh.

"I—" She suddenly remembered the anaconda. Her gaze flew to the water as she practically crawled into his arms. "We need to get out of here before we're bitten."

"They rarely bite."

" 'Rarely' being the operative word here," she said, snuggling against him while her body quivered all over. Strong arms slipped around her waist and lifted her clear out of the water.

"Better?" His face was expressionless, and she couldn't tell whether he was amused or annoyed with her.

"I will be once we get the hell out of the ocean."

With long strides he carried her to the shore, except he didn't stop there. With an air of command about him, he took control of the situation and continued right on up the beach toward her cabana.

"It was an anaconda," she whispered, eyes blinking away the salty water. "It had to be at least ten feet long."

"It was a banded sea snake."

"Did you see it?"

"I saw it."

"It was so big."

"It was two feet, tops."

Without censor she blurted out, "I don't know about that. It swam between my thighs, and I think I'd know the difference between two feet and ten feet between my legs."

Mr. Hardbody cleared his throat and said, "I would think so." When she heard the inflection in his tone, she tipped her head to look into his eyes.

Real smooth, Danielle. Real smooth.

Just then she began coughing, the last of the water leaving her lungs. When his forward motion stopped, she angled her head to see him. Protective blue eyes looked down at her with genuine concern.

"Are you okay?" His rich, sensual baritone aroused all her senses and did the most amazing things to her nerve endings.

Was this guy for real? She resisted the urge to pinch herself to see if she was dreaming. Instead, she pinched him. Right on the nipple. It hardened.

Okeydokey, then . . .

"I'm okay," she squeaked out, pressing against him, loving how good it felt to be in his arms and thinking about how much better this gorgeous hunk of man would feel between her legs.

His striated muscles bunched and his brow furrowed as he glanced down at his reddening nipple, but he didn't question her action. He just shifted her in his arms and trekked onward. Danielle's body continued to quiver, but for entirely different reasons now.

As she melted into him, her flesh soaked in his warmth. She inhaled his fresh scent. He smelled like sun, sand, ocean . . . *and man.*

She took that moment to peruse the Greek god who had appeared out of nowhere and come to her rescue. His short hair was damp and slicked back; his face was tanned, cleanly shaven. Water clung to his dark lashes and dripped from his even darker hair. Danielle moistened her already wet lips and bit back a moan of pleasure as she continued her leisurely inspection.

His hand slid closer to her ass, repositioning her in his oh-so-capable arms. As his fingers neared the swell of her backside, heat prowled through her.

Packaged against his rock-hard body as she was, it was easy to tell he kept himself fit and finely tuned. She had to admit that she liked a man who took good care of himself.

His brow was furrowed, and his gorgeous lips were compressed, set in a grim line. Did the man ever smile?

She guessed him to be in his late twenties or early thirties, which was far too young to be jaded.

Although she took him for a well-disciplined military man, she sensed a darker side to him. Underneath that cool exterior, he seemed restless, troubled somehow.

Before she could stop it, a strange gurgle crawled out of her throat and she burped.

"Sure you're okay?" he asked.

"Yeah, just waterlogged." Nothing a little mouth-to-mouth couldn't fix, she mused.

With his lips positioned close to her ear, he said, "I could call for the doctor."

She had a better idea; maybe they could *play* doctor. "No, I'm fine, really."

Alpha that he was, he continued to take charge of the situation and carried her through the door of her cabana. He glanced around and then deposited her in a wicker chair. Strange how she felt absurdly safe in his arms. Back in Chicago she wouldn't dream of letting a stranger into her place, no matter how much he resembled a Greek god. But there was something about this man. Something trustworthy and fiercely protective that put her at ease.

As he inched back, his gaze left her face and skated over her barely clad body. She watched his nostrils flare as his eyes roamed over her mouth, neck, and chest, and lower. She felt her nipples swell under his probing gaze. Dayum . . . the guy was blatantly checking her out.

"You're burnt."

Or not.

She threw her arms up in the air and told him, "I was cursed with strawberry blond hair and delicate skin."

His jaw muscle twitched. "Not cursed."

Danielle wasn't sure whether he meant it as a compliment or not but decided to take it as one just the same. She held her hand out, realizing she didn't even know her rescuer's name. "I'm Danielle Carrigan. It's nice to meet you, Mr. . . ." She caught herself before she added, "Hardbody."

He squared his broad shoulders, nodded his head in acknowledgment and met her handshake. "Ethan Sharpe."

Oh, he of so few words.

She motioned for him to sit. He didn't.

Once again his eyes narrowed on her skin and she could feel her flesh tighten and tingle—although she wasn't sure if it was from his gaze or the impending sun blisters.

"You need after-burn lotion." Before she could tell him that she hadn't brought any, he disappeared into her bathroom and came out with a bottle of green aloe vera gel. Now, how did he know that was there?

He flipped open the cap. "A bottle in every cabana," he said as though reading her mind. She reached for the bottle, but he ignored her. Clearly used to taking charge, he leaned forward, poured a generous amount onto the front of her arms and rubbed it in with the utmost care. She let out a sigh as he tended to every inch of her exposed skin.

Oh, how she loved his attention to detail.

The cool gel felt heavenly against her heated flesh, but not nearly as heavenly as his calloused hands felt. As he rubbed she noticed that his palms were rough around the edges, just like him. Unrefined. Rugged. Bold.

Scrumptious.

She shivered under his invasive touch, enjoying his take-charge attitude. As he worked the gel in, ripples of sensual pleasure danced over her skin and brought on a quiver. She wondered if he felt her body's reactions. She bit back a heated moan as desire twisted her insides.

As she reveled in the feel of his hands on her, her head fell forward. She worked to keep her passion-rattled brain focused on conversation before she ripped off his swimming trunks and forced him to have sex with her. Wild, crazy, earth-shattering monkey sex, that is.

Her gazed roamed to his hard abs and lower, lingering at the juncture between his legs. Wait . . . was that what she thought it was? Her pulse raced with pleasure. Okay, so maybe she wouldn't have to *force* him, exactly.

He walked behind her, moving with confidence and self-assurance. She had to admit, there was nothing sexier than a guy who knew how to take charge.

When his hands touched her back, her body started to tremble almost uncontrollably. Every nerve ending came alive. He began rubbing the gel onto the backs of her shoulders, slowly, methodically. As his thumbs made small circles, her mind took her on an erotic adventure, imagining him stroking another sensitive body part in just such a seductive manner.

As her hair began to dry, it fell into her eyes. Danielle blew a wispy bang off her forehead and shook her head to uncloud it of its delicious meanderings. She cleared her throat, curious about her mysterious rescuer, curious to know what brought him to the exotic island.

"So, tell me, Ethan, what brings you here?" Her voice came out raspy, edgy.

His sweet-scented breath whispered across her neck and made her quake. "My job." Once her back was sufficiently coated, he circled her again, coming to rest in front of her, giving her a perfect, unobstructed view of his crotch. Nice . . .

After a good hard look, she glanced upward.

"Military?" she asked. She knew the spa catered to singles looking for escapism from the everyday, as well as those seeking pleasure.

She wondered which one had brought him here.

Surprise registered on his face, and then he nodded. He snapped the bottle closed. "That should keep the blisters at bay."

With her mind still contemplating that delicious bulge in his swim trunks, she blurted out, "You sure know a lot about burns."

"I've spent a lot of time in the blazing sun."

She examined his bronzed skin, wondering whether his tan had come from his time on the island or his time on active duty. "Have you been here long?"

His gaze shifted, camouflaging his emotions. "Long enough." It occurred to her how little he seemed to like talking about himself.

She clicked her lips. "You're a real talker, aren't you? I guess you're a man of action and not words." Exactly the kind of guy she was looking for.

That brought a smile to his face. "Guess so," he murmured.

She rolled her aloe-vera-covered shoulders. "Then again, I guess I make up for both of us."

"Guess so," he said again, amusement pulling at the corners of his mouth. His gorgeous blue eyes narrowed. "What brings you here?"

"My friends and I needed a little vacation."

He cocked his head and glanced around her cabana. "Friends?"

"Lauren and Abby. They have their own cabanas," she added. "We're here for a girls-only vacation where all your deepest desires are fulfilled, just like the brochure promised."

He made a noise low in his throat. "And I suppose you've heard about the magic elixir."

She nodded. "Have you tried it?"

"No."

She leaned forward. "Is it true? Does it work?"

Skepticism flashed in his expression. "Some would think so."

"Don't you want to know for sure?"

A storm brewed in his eyes and he gave a quick side-to-side shake of his head. Once again he turned the conversation away from himself and back to her. "So, tell me, what desires are you looking to have fulfilled?" He took a moment to peruse her, his dark gaze caressing her barely clad body with pleasure. "You look like a girl who has everything she's ever wanted."

She moistened her parched lips and shifted restlessly in her chair. If only she had the nerve to tell him the truth. "Not everything," she murmured. When she glanced up at him, she noted that his gaze was locked on her mouth. His tongue snaked out and made a slow pass over his bottom lip. The hungry look in his eyes sent a plethora of sensations rippling through her.

She swallowed. Dayum . . .

Something in her gut told her this take-charge soldier, this skilled warrior, a man who would serve and protect to the bitter end, could give her everything she needed, everything she craved.

Probing for information, she asked, "I'm sure you must have secret desires you'd like to have fulfilled."

Naturally, he redirected the conversation. "Where are you from?"

"Chicago. You?"

She took in the tension in his posture. "All over. What do you do in Chicago, Danielle?"

"I'm an interior designer. My friends and I own our own shop."

One brow rose. "Impressive." He toyed with the bottle of afterburn lotion, tossing it between his hands. Wow, he had big, fabulous hands.

The better to spank her with.

Her body shivered with longing when she thought about how he could take matters into those large, capable hands. She wondered whether he worked with them. "What do you do in the military?"

His eyes darkened, and after a moment he said, "Commander, weapons expert."

Danielle sensed a "but" at the end of that sentence. She paused, giving him a moment to elaborate. He didn't.

In need of a cold drink, she climbed from the chair, but Ethan was standing so close, she bumped into him. Her hard nipples scraped across his chest. Ethan's body stiffened, his head lowered and she heard him draw a quick breath. When smoldering blue eyes latched onto hers, sexual energy arced between them. Lust started at her core and traveled onward and outward until coherent speech was nearly impossible.

She saw need, desire and turbulence in his eyes, but before either of them could act on it he stepped back and said, "My fault. I should be going. I have an appointment."

Danielle reined in her lust. "I guess I should be getting ready anyway. I have to unpack and get showered before dinner. Mr. Malik invited my friends and me to eat with him this evening. Maybe I'll catch up with you later."

And maybe he could tie her up and fuck her silly, too.

Ethan's mood changed so fast, it caught her off guard. His jaw clenched. Anger sparked in his blue eyes. "I was invited to join him as well, but I hadn't planned on attending." When she gave him a questioning glance, he continued. "You see, Malik and I don't always see eye to eye." He raised his hand above his head. "And believe me, I've had it up to here with all his cryptic words." Danielle heard the edge of bitterness in his tone. "So help me, if he says one more thing . . ." His voice trailed off.

Geez, provoke the guy and you couldn't shut him up. Who knew?

Ethan moved toward the door, and she could tell he was trying not to favor his right leg. "I know, but I truly believe he means well," Danielle said. "And since you're the first person I met since I arrived, I'd love it if you came." The truth was, she liked being around him and wasn't quite ready for him to walk away. She knew she'd only just met him, but never had a man aroused her so quickly, or had her mind spinning with such wild, erotic scenarios. There was an undeniable spark between them that she'd love to explore further.

When he gave her a noncommittal shrug, she tried to lighten the mood. "Plus I want to make it up to you for rescuing me. You're my hero." She suddenly had a lightbulb moment, a very seductive, very scandalous lightbulb moment. "Hey, I wonder what the island customs are. Maybe I owe you my life now that you saved mine. Maybe I'll have to be your servant."

That caught his attention. Standing in the doorway, he spun back around to face her, his blue eyes brimming with intrigue. Sculpted muscles bunched as he pushed his hair back. In a low, controlled voice he said, "Servant, huh?"

Excited at the prospect, she felt heat coil in her belly. "Yeah, and maybe I'd have to call you 'master,'" she rushed out, shocking herself with her boldness.

His palms flattened on either side of the doorjamb, giving her an erotic view of his gorgeous, naked chest. His eyebrows shot up. "You think?"

She nodded and continued to play, knowing she'd never before had the courage to speak her fantasies to any man. There really was something magical about this island that brought out the vixen in her. "And if I was naughty you'd have to—"

"Discipline you." He cocked his head, the challenging look in his eyes daring her to deny that she wanted him to do just that.

Danielle gulped. Her blood pressure soared. Primal need bombarded her body.

Oh. Good. God. He was so very good at reading her.

Deep in her gut she just knew her man of action and few words would have no problem disciplining her. Her gaze moved to his large hands, hands that were more than capable of giving her a good spanking if she needed it.

And dammit, she was pretty sure she needed it.

Shoulders squared and body stiff from pain, Ethan circled Danielle's cabana, having promised her that he'd think about joining her at the owner's table for dinner. He lied. He had no intentions of dining with Malik and conceded only because he had to get out of her quarters. Fast.

Once he was certain he was completely out of sight, he drew a sharp breath and collapsed against the exterior wall. Grimacing, he shifted his full body weight to his left foot. Fuck, even after all this time, his right leg still hurt like a son of a bitch.

He knew if he'd stayed inside her cabana for one more second, his goddamned leg would have given out on him and he'd have ended up flat out on her floor.

Some hero he was.

Carrying her up the beach had taken its toll on him—in more ways than one—and he needed to take the edge off fast. Nothing short of painkillers would help at this point. With pain blurring his thoughts, he glanced around, strategizing his next move, calculating the quickest route back to his cabana.

His head began throbbing; his joints ached already. Ethan drew on every ounce of strength he possessed, pushed off the cabana wall and started down the walkway. As he cut through the footpath, his mind revisited their playful conversation, recalling her suggestive words, and relishing the way her soft body had felt cushioned in his arms, her heat curling around him, arousing his primal needs.

He growled low in his throat, but this growl was from sexual frustration, not pain.

His cock hardened inside his swim trunks, and his blood flowed hot and heavy through his veins, a reminder that it had been a hell of a long time since he'd held a woman next to him, since he'd smelled her enticing feminine scent.

From her gorgeous curvy body to her strawberry blond hair and sexy, playful demeanor, Danielle was the epitome of sweet perfection. Her angelic yet seductive voice had quickly pulled him under into a current of need and desire.

He'd never met a more exquisite woman, really. Her creamy, flawless skin and fascinating green eyes had mesmerized him. And that lush ass. Jesus, the woman had an ass that erotic dreams were made of. He'd like nothing better than to take a bite and gobble her up like the big bad wolf. Hunger clawed at his insides, urging him to turn back around, go inside and do just that.

There was no denying the attraction between them. He saw it in her eyes, felt the way her gaze devoured him with sexual need. She in turn aroused him to the point of distraction, making him temporarily forget he wasn't the strong, commanding officer he used to be.

Ethan took a moment to indulge his wayward thoughts, imagining what it would be like to explore the sparks between them, to taste those gorgeous plump lips of hers while he sank into her damp heat and lost himself in her body for the remainder of the evening. Moisture collected on his flesh, and his cock grew another inch. Christ, he'd only just met her, but it had been a long time since he'd wanted to fuck anyone the way he wanted to fuck her.

He was intelligent enough to know that her naughty, suggestive words insinuated that she too wanted to indulge in a few sex games with him. He also felt the way she trembled beneath his touch, and the way her hard nipples pressed against his chest, enticing him to strip her bare and have his wicked way with her.

A year ago he'd have jumped at the chance. He'd have gone all night long, giving her exactly what she wanted. And he was pretty sure he knew what she wanted. He saw the fire in her eyes when she glanced at his hands, and when he mentioned *discipline*, her entire body quaked with raw hunger.

Damn, that excited him.

Sure, when she first mentioned a little role-playing, the idea intrigued him, but then reality hit him harder than a predawn sneak attack.

Who was he kidding? He couldn't give her what she desired even if he wanted to. No doubt his fucked-up leg would fail on him and he'd end up making a total ass of himself. Either that or she'd take one look at his scarred, mangled thigh and retreat. The last thing he wanted was to see pity in her eyes. He'd had enough of that. His stomach lurched just thinking about it.

Drawing a centering breath, Ethan banked his desires and trekked forward, working to get the sexy vixen out of his head. Because a bold, feisty woman like Danielle needed a real man, a whole man, a man in control of himself and in control of his world. A man who could give her what she needed, all night long.

What she didn't need was a shot-up soldier who could barely tie his own shoes, for Christ's sake.

Frowning intently, he felt a burst of anger rush through him and worked to control it. He moved forward, each painful step reminding him he'd never be that man again.

As he stepped into the clearing, he spotted Malik sitting on the steps of his temple, deep in meditation, the scent of incense filling the air.

Ethan moved quietly, careful not to disturb him. The reasons for his actions were twofold: one, he had great respect for this man's or any man's need for privacy, and two, he wanted to make it to his cabana undetected, knowing that any exchange between them would be less than pleasant.

"Hello, my child."

Ethan bit back a curse.

He stilled, balancing himself on both legs despite the pain. Malik rose and moved toward him. Dressed in his meditation robe, he folded his hands in front of his chest and nodded. His warm, amicable smile did little to soothe Ethan's ragged nerves or his aching muscles.

"I haven't seen you in days, Ethan."

Annoyance palpable, Ethan indulged him for a moment. He jerked his chin to the right, toward the ocean. "Been busy." He'd been swimming in the Pacific, attempting to strengthen his leg, but didn't bother to elaborate.

"Is your therapy going well?" Malik asked.

Ethan scowled. He was sick and tired of their therapy. He wanted to go back to civilization, back to . . .

Ah, hell, now that his career in the military was over, all he had to look forward to was early retirement. He scoffed and shook his head. Retirement at thirty. That was a first. Ethan had spent the first eighteen years of his life dreaming about serving his government and the last twelve years living that dream, only to be written off. Those fucking insurgents might as well have taken his life when they shot up his leg. Ethan fisted his hands, his anger exploding inside him like shrapnel.

Malik held his hands out in front of him, palming an imaginary bubble around Ethan. He gave a slow side-to-side shake of his head. "You still hold so much anger, Ethan. You need to release your destructive emotions."

Ethan clenched his jaw until the muscles ached. "I'm not angry," he shot back. Okay, so maybe he was angry. Who could blame him? His goddamned government had sent him to this island in the middle of Buttfuck Nowhere to *heal.*

In other words, they wrote him off.

He knew the military mantra when he signed on—if he wasn't deployable, he wasn't employable. So what the fuck was he supposed to do with his life now? He'd grown up in a military family, and even though he'd been disgruntled lately, disgusted and completely fed up with all the bureaucratic bullshit that went along with the job, it was his way of life. It was all he knew.

"Why don't you sign my damn release papers and let me get back to civilization?"

"Ahh, but you're not ready."

"I've been here for two months. I've tried all your therapeutic methods. There isn't anything else you can do for me. All I want is to be left alone to heal on my own." Ethan cursed under his breath, hating that this medicine man had the ability to hold him, along with a dozen or so other injured comrades, until he felt they were healed, inside and out.

Malik stroked his goatee. "There is one more thing I can do for you."

Ethan straightened to his full six foot three. "Like I told you, I don't believe in magic water from your private spring."

Malik bowed his head slowly. "Very well, then, but I planned on serving it at dinner this evening, and it just might be what you need to facilitate your progress."

When Malik turned to leave, Ethan blew a resigned breath, compartmentalizing his emotions. "Look, if I drink it, can I go home?"

Ethan's strongest desire was to feel in control again, of his life and everything around him. And that was never going to happen. Magic elixir or not, nothing would ever give him full use of his leg, and without the use of his leg, he'd never feel in control. And he needed his control. He thrived on it. He was shaped by it.

Malik turned back to face him, and in a soft but commanding voice he said, "Your destiny is in your hands, Ethan."

After a good show of exasperation, Ethan drew a breath and let it out slowly. "Just tell me, if I drink it, can I go home?"

"It's in your hands, Ethan," he repeated. With that, he walked away and returned to his temple, to his meditation position.

Jesus, if he kept talking in riddles, the only thing that was going to be in Ethan's hands was Malik's neck.

TWO

After pulling on a soft, cotton, cranberry-colored sundress decorated with big white flowers, Danielle knotted her long hair on top of her head, applied a light layer of makeup and made her way to Abby's cabana to gather her friends for dinner. Of course, prettying herself up had nothing at all to do with hunky soldier Ethan Sharpe, or those big, deft hands of his. Or all the delightful ways he could discipline her lascivious body with them.

Nope. Nothing to do with that at all.

Flip-flops snapping against her heels, she followed the sandy footpath to Abby's secluded cabana, which was located in a private cove flanked by tall hills and foliage. As she knocked on the door her mind raced, wondering whether her hard-core military man would show up for dinner tonight. It occurred to her just how excited she was at the prospect. Then again, she still wondered whether her mind had simply conjured up the perfect fantasy man, meaning she'd imagined the whole bizarre, yet stimulating, encounter.

"Come in," Abby yelled, pulling Danielle's thoughts to the present.

Blinking her mind into focus, Danielle stepped inside the cabana. She took a moment to let her eyes adjust to the darkness. Squinting, she found her friends sharing a bottle of wine, both grinning like village idiots.

She shot them a questioning glance. "What's up?"

"I think the better question is *who's up*," Lauren piped in. "You're here for five minutes and you have some beautiful sea god carrying you to your cabana. A beautiful sea god who looked like he'd gotten all kinds of things *up* for you. Damn, girl, you work fast."

Danielle couldn't help but grin. She widened her eyes in delight and adjusted the straps on her dress. "So he was real," she whispered to herself.

"Oh, yeah, he was real all right. A gorgeous Greek god straight out of a fairy tale," Lauren added.

Abby grabbed her key card and stuffed it into her beach bag. "Come on, we're running late. You can tell us all about him on the way to dinner."

"Maybe I'll skip dinner and go for a swim," Lauren said, grinning. "I wouldn't mind finding myself a sea god." She frowned and added, "Then again, I'd probably end up with the likes of Hades, overseer of the underworld." She stopped walking and shuddered. "Like I need another greedy man solely concerned about his own needs." She put her hand on Danielle's shoulder. "Honey, I'd give anything to find a guy who sees me for who I am. Someone who doesn't need to be looking at my body to appreciate and want me." She paused to gather her breasts into her hands. "The men I've been with only care about how much they can fit into their palms, or their mouths."

Chuckling at her friend's antics, Danielle nodded in agreement. Too bad men didn't see Lauren for the wonderful person she was. All they wanted was to get their hands on her luscious body. Danielle glanced down at her own chest and was thankful that she was of average size. Getting men to like her for who she was wasn't her problem. They liked her and her body; they just didn't know what to do with it, or how to satisfy her. Of course, she wasn't entirely without fault there. It just wasn't easy for her to tell a man how she wanted it. Honestly, she didn't know how to come right out and ask a guy to tie her up, spank her and have his wicked way with her.

As they walked to the dining lodge, Abby said, "Hey, did you know that not only is this place an elite singles spa; it also houses a rehabilitation center for soldiers injured overseas?"

"Really?" Lauren asked.

Danielle's thoughts raced to her military man.

"Yeah, while Danielle was busy making time with her sea god, and you were busy spying on them, I familiarized myself with the facility," Abby teased.

As Abby and Lauren chatted back and forth, Danielle recalled her conversation with Ethan. He'd said he was here because of his job, but he hadn't elaborated. Obviously he was here because he'd injured his leg, but she sensed there was more to it than that. She remembered the way he tried to hide his injury, and the way he seemed so restless, so deeply troubled about something. And when she'd brought up dining with Mr. Malik, he'd damn near exploded.

Danielle couldn't help wondering about her soldier, and what secrets he held close.

A few minutes later, the three girls made their way inside the dining room. They were greeted by a maître d' and led through the restaurant. Danielle glanced around the dimly lit room, absorbing the romantic ambience and Asian décor while taking note of the patrons, wondering about each and every one of them and what brought them to this magical island.

As she rounded the corner to a private outdoor dining area overlooking the ocean, she glanced at Mr. Malik, who was seated at the head of the table, his hands folded in front of his chest. He'd changed out of his white robe and now wore some sort of ceremonial red kimono decorated with mystical symbols. He stood as the girls entered.

"Welcome," he said, a smile lighting his face. Danielle scanned the table, her gaze coming to rest on the two men already seated. Disappointment settled into her stomach when she noticed that Ethan hadn't shown up. "Please have a seat," Mr. Malik added with a wave of his hand. "I'd like to introduce you to Ryan Thomas and Cody Lannon."

As the girls all introduced themselves, Danielle's gaze panned over the two guys, wondering whether they, too, were military men. She studied Ryan Thomas first, noting that his face seemed pale, making a stark contrast against his dark hair. Come to think of it, it looked like his skin hadn't been touched by the tropical sun at all. He wore mirrored sunglasses, which camouflaged his eyes, but the snarl on his lips spoke volumes. The other man, Cody Lannon, had lighter hair and was sporting a gorgeous tan. He stared off into the distance, as if he, too, had somewhere else to be. Outwardly they didn't appear injured, or if they were, they tried to hide it, like Ethan.

Once they were all comfortably seated, a waitress served crisp greens and bread. The fresh scent of herbs and garlic made Danielle's stomach grumble. After the waitress left, Mr. Malik cut his hand through the air. "Please eat, my children. Enjoy the food that has been prepared for you."

He didn't have to ask Danielle twice. Starving, she grabbed her utensils and dug into the greens. As she chewed, Mr. Malik spoke again. "Tonight is a special night for you all."

Despite her hunger pangs, Danielle stopped eating, excited to hear more.

Mr. Malik held his hands over a ceramic crock carved with foreign symbols. Acting like he was some sort of medicine man, he chanted something incoherent under his breath as though he were performing a ritual. He spoke with his eyes closed, and in a soft voice he said, "It is with great pleasure that I welcome you to this island and offer this drink to you."

Danielle watched him, noting how his actions seemed tribal and primitive.

"You must drink it with an open mind and an open heart. And when you let the magic flow through your veins, your deepest desires, no matter what they might be, will be fulfilled."

"If you believe in such a thing." The deep, hardened voice came from behind them. Danielle spun around and watched Ethan move into the room. The grim line of his mouth and the turbulence in his gaze showcased an intensity about him that was both frightening and exciting to her. His primal essence completely overwhelmed her, derailing her ability to think straight. She drew a deep breath but couldn't seem to fill her lungs.

Dressed in a pair of loose-fitting khaki pants and a short-sleeved dress shirt, he came toward her. His steps were determined, predatory, and from the way he moved, one never would have guessed that he had an injured leg. He pulled out the chair beside her.

She shifted in her seat to get a better look at him. Damn, was it possible that he was even more handsome than she remembered? She took in his thick wavy hair, his deep, tortured blue eyes, and his warm, familiar scent.

"Hi," she whispered as he moved closer, realizing just how badly she wanted to touch him, to feel his body beside hers. Deep down Danielle instinctively knew that if she had the courage to tell Ethan what she wanted—exactly what she wanted—she would undoubtedly experience the best, most orgasmic sex of her life.

So what was she going to do about it?

Ethan nodded his greeting to all those seated around the table and then turned his attention to her. His warrior features softened when their gazes collided. His voice was low, deeply intimate. "How's that burn?" he asked, concern in his eyes.

His deep, sexy cadence curled her toes, and his concern for her well-being touched her. "Fine now, thanks to you," she said, impressed that her lust-rattled brain managed to form a full, coherent sentence.

His gaze shifted to her breasts, to the two big flowers covering each nipple. She watched his throat work as he swallowed. "It was my pleasure," he said, his voice sounding a little ragged.

Oh, no, it was *her* pleasure.

Her gaze roamed over him a second time, her body quivering in delight as she fantasized about losing herself in him.

The mere sight of her soldier evoked a myriad of sinful thoughts. Rattled by the way he affected her, she shifted restlessly and exhaled a slow, controlled breath. When Ethan lowered himself into the chair next to her and offered her a sexy smile, warmth pooled between her legs. She wondered if the others in the room felt the sexual pull between them.

She clasped her hands under the table, fighting the urge to pinch him again, to see if her sea god was indeed real.

"I'm glad you came," she whispered.

He faced her with an intense, intimate gaze and pitched his voice low. "I couldn't let you face him alone."

She lowered her voice to match his, deepening the intimacy between them. "I think he's harmless."

One brow arched. "Then I believe you just might be a bad judge of character, Dani."

She gulped. The sexy way he used her childhood nickname sent shivers of desire racing though her. She cleared her throat and gave a casual shrug, feeling anything but. "I've never been accused of that before."

"Oh, no?"

She saw a spark in his eyes and couldn't tell whether he was teasing her or not. "No," she said adamantly.

"I bet you probably think I'm harmless, too."

Fiercely protective. Never harmless.

"Not even for a minute," she said with conviction.

He grinned and leaned into her. "Smart woman."

Smart woman, indeed.

Battling an internal war, Ethan had convinced himself that the only reason he'd shown up tonight was to drink the damn elixir and appease Malik. Not that he believed for one second that the springwater would magically fulfill all his desires. But the second he looked into Dani's sexy green bedroom eyes, he knew that was pure bullshit. Ever since he'd carried her from the ocean, and ever since he'd felt her lush body in his arms, he'd been unable to get her out of his head.

How the fuck was he supposed to dispel the image of her soft, voluptuous body in a barely there bikini, her sweet scent all over him, arousing him to the point of pain? Jesus, here it was hours later and he was still sporting a hard-on a mile long.

Despite knowing he couldn't give her what she wanted, what she needed, everything inside him craved to sink into her plush heat, melting his resolve to stay away. After just one sexy encounter, Danielle had somehow managed to seep under his skin and arouse a primal need in him.

Malik spoke, bringing his attention back around to their host and jostling his thoughts back to the present. As Ethan's gaze bore into the man, he commanded himself to purify his wayward thoughts.

"It is with great pleasure that I offer you this drink." Malik walked around the table and poured them all a glass of water from his crock.

Ethan watched the way Dani's eyes lit with intrigue. Did she truly believe that if she drank the water all her desires would be fulfilled?

Earlier in the day, after their sexy exchange about servant and master, he realized what had brought her to this island. Intuition told him that underneath that bold, strong, independent exterior existed a submissive woman, a woman hungering to hand control of her pleasure over to another.

Something inside him twisted as he studied the group. Ethan glanced around the table, perusing his fellow comrades. He watched them stare at their glasses with reluctance. He knew they didn't believe in the powers of the springwater any more than he did and suspected that they, too, like him, were coerced into being here tonight.

As Ethan studied those seated around the table a moment longer, it occurred to him that Dani could fulfill her desires with any one of his fellow soldiers. But dammit, he wanted to be the man to remedy her longings. He wanted to be the man to fulfill all her fantasies.

Needing something to occupy his hands, he toyed with his utensils and glanced her way. When she offered him a smile full of sensual promises, his body grew tight with need, sexual tension warming his blood. As they stared at each other for a long, thoughtful moment, he wondered what it would be like to tie the little vixen to his bed, tease her to the point of no return and make her beg for his cock.

A breeze drifted in off the ocean, blowing her delicate scent past his nostrils. He inhaled, wanting nothing more than to dust kisses over her entire body and breathe in all her feminine scents, especially the one between her legs. As her eyes devoured him—the heat in her gaze telling him what she wanted—chaos erupted inside him and his thoughts scattered like a round of gunfire.

He had no idea how he was going to make it through a meal with his libido in such an uproar. Just then the waitress brought bowls full of rice, beef, noodles and seafood. Ethan welcomed the distractions and worked to marshal his thoughts. After the food was served, they all ate while a few made small talk. Malik was talking to the others about some upcoming sailing excursion and exploration of Pearl Island, the uninhabited island to the south of them. Ethan glanced at Ryan, who looked less than interested, which was unfortunate, really, because before his injury, Ryan, with his adventurous side and exceptional tracking skills, would have loved such an expedition.

A short while later, once the meal was finished, Malik stood and extended his arms. "Danielle, Lauren and Abby, please join me at the temple for a tour."

As Danielle rose, she cast Ethan a glance, her tongue moistening her plump lips. Fuck, there was something about her sensuous mouth that drove him mad. The need to feel her lips on his grew to an almost unbearable level. Warmth, need and desire reflected in her eyes when they met his. She leaned forward, the plunging neckline of her sundress affording him a view of her creamy cleavage. His mouth watered.

"Thanks for coming," she whispered, brushing a loose strand of hair from her cheek. "Maybe we'll bump into each other later."

Ethan nodded. Truthfully, Dani had no idea how close he

actually was to *coming*. Sitting next to her for the last hour had played havoc with his libido.

He shook the buzz from his head. "Like I said, I didn't want you to face him alone." Ethan knew a smart, confident woman like Dani didn't need his help. She was quite capable of holding her own, except when confronted with a banded sea snake, of course. Ethan smiled in remembrance.

Eyes alive with curiosity, she asked, "Something funny?"

"We'll talk later," he promised, his words hinting at a deeper intimacy as his gaze moved over her face. "They're waiting."

Dani glanced behind her to see her two friends lingering at the door, waiting for her. When she turned back to him, her eyes flashed with dark sensuality. The way she moistened her lips sent him to the edge of oblivion. He shifted, adjusting his thickening cock. Did she take pleasure in arousing him to the point of pain?

Even though her eyes were sultry, sexy and teasing as they raked over him in return, there was vulnerability in her voice when she spoke. "We'll talk later, then," she said, but something in Ethan's gut told him that she was holding back, that that wasn't quite what she wanted to say to him.

When she touched his shoulder, an unexpected wave of anticipation whipped through him as his cock ached for something far more intimate than conversation. Sexual tension rose in him. Blood rushed to his dick, and he could barely contain his mounting desire. Before he came unhinged, he said, "You'd better get going."

She twisted around, and with a sexy shake of her curvy hips, she sashayed across the floor.

As his gaze caressed her body, a low groan crawled out of the depths of his throat. "Damn," he cursed under his breath, his fingers twisting the cloth napkin in his lap. He was ready to explode from sexual frustration.

"Hey, Ethan, want to go shoot some pool?" Ryan asked.

The sound of his comrade's voice pulled his focus back. He transferred his thoughts to the present. Feeling restless and antsy, Ethan knew he needed to work off some steam before he chased after Dani, hauled her off into the woods and fucked her hard until she begged for mercy. Or better yet, played her master-servant game.

It was damn near impossible to resist her, and the way she looked at him with such need, desire and vulnerability had him thinking about going against his own best interests and giving them both what they wanted.

But what if his fucking leg gave out on him only to bring pity to her eyes?

What if it didn't?

With a disgruntled huff, he tossed his napkin onto the table. "Yeah, sounds like a plan." Ethan glanced at Cody, who was staring out over the ocean, lost in his own thoughts. "Come on, Cody," Ethan said. "You can play the winner."

"Meaning you can play me," Ryan added, tossing them both a cocky grin. Ethan laughed but didn't deny it. Even with his limited vision, Ryan could clean the table in a matter of minutes.

By the time they made their way outside, darkness had fallen. Ethan watched the way Ryan glanced around, orienting himself. Cody remained quiet, lost in his own thoughts, battling the ghosts that plagued him. As a trained sniper, Cody had witnessed some pretty grizzly shit through his scope, which caused him to shut down his emotions, his insides turning to ice, a protective reaction, Ethan knew.

Distressed by Cody's emotional withdrawal and worried that he could snap at any point, Cody's superiors had sent him to the island for emotional therapy and to reconnect with people, but Ethan wasn't so sure anything or anyone could thaw him out.

When Ryan tripped on a step leading to the games room, Ethan resisted the natural inclination to help out of fear of injuring his friend's pride. Ethan knew Ryan had a cane back in his cabana, but understood his reluctance to use it. Ethan, too, had a cane, which sat untouched.

As the three guys made their way inside, Ethan scoffed and said, "I really could use a beer. I'm sick of all the protein and sea-weed shakes they try to pass off as drinks here."

Ryan leaned in and whispered, "I can hook you up."

"No shit?" Ethan asked.

"No shit," Ryan replied, smirking.

Ethan slapped his friend on the shoulder. "You've been holding out on me, pal?"

"Nope, my stash just came this afternoon, by plane. Didn't have time to tell you."

Ethan arched an inquisitive brow and relaxed into conversation. "You've been sweet-talking the pilot again?"

Ryan shrugged and grinned. "It's a gift."

"Just don't let Malik catch you with it."

"Or what, he'll kick me off the island?" Ryan snorted.

This time Ethan laughed out loud. "Right. Give me the key

card to your cabana. You and Cody set up while I go grab us a couple of cold ones. With a little luck, we'll all get kicked off this hellhole together."

A minute later Ethan walked the footpath, deliberately going the long way to Ryan's cabana. Okay, so he couldn't deny that he wanted to catch another glimpse of Dani before he retired for the night. At least then he'd have a sexy image to occupy his mind while his hands were occupied elsewhere on his body. Pleasure resonated through him and his cock throbbed in anticipation.

As he circled the temple, he heard Malik speaking to the girls, spewing cryptic words of wisdom, no doubt. Ethan stepped into the shadows, masking his presence, listening intently as though he was on some sort of reconnaissance mission. As soon as he heard Dani's sweet, seductive voice, his body grew needy for her again. Cool night air brushed against his flesh but did nothing to ease the heat inside him. Dammit, if he didn't do something about the fire between his legs soon, he was damn well going to explode.

Senses finely tuned, he listened to Malik's cryptic message. He was speaking to Dani in hushed tones, reciting words that sounded like "There is no ambiguity in the truth."

At that moment, Ethan considered Malik's words of wisdom to him: *Your destiny is in your hands.* He replayed the words over and over, working at understanding the deeper meaning. He held his hands out to study them.

Ethan was so preoccupied with his thoughts, he didn't hear the sound of approaching footsteps. Before he knew what was happening, someone rushed around the corner and barreled right into him.

"Whoa," Dani yelped, her arms flailing, grasping frantically for something concrete to hold on to before she sailed to the ground.

As their bodies collided, Ethan reached out for her. "I've got you," he said. His palms circled her waist and he caught her in his hands. Suddenly, his skin prickled and Malik's words filled his thoughts.

Your destiny is in your hands.

THREE

Air ripped from Danielle's lungs as she crashed into a wall of rock-hard muscle. She snaked her arms around the man's neck; her lips brushed against his cheek as she clamored to right herself. Despite the darkness, she knew it was Ethan—by the way her flesh came to life at first contact, by the way his muscles bunched beneath her touch.

As he anchored her body to his, awareness flared through her and her nipples quivered in erotic delight. While her knees turned to mush, she drew a steadying breath and tried to find her balance.

"It's okay, Dani. It's me. I've got you." The rich timbre of his voice combined with the masculine scent of his skin aroused all her senses. Her body vibrated, liquid heat rushing to the juncture between her thighs.

Danielle bit back a breathy moan. She inched backwards and worked to formulate a response. "Thank—" Her words died on her lips when she glimpsed the heat smoldering in the depths of his blue eyes. His carnal, wolfish grin triggered a major reaction in her body. The instant flash of desire had her pulse racing out of control.

With her hands slipped around his hard, athletic body, she became hyperaware of his arms sliding around her, his big palms pressing into the small of her back—big, strapping palms made for disciplining.

Her.

Right here.

Right now.

Oh, yeah.

As sexual energy jetted between them, their chemistry became explosive. "In a hurry to go somewhere?" he asked without bothering to release his tenuous grip. Possessiveness flashed in his eyes, and she became acutely aware of the way his body and hands trembled as he pulled her in tight.

Pleasure engulfed her, and she wondered whether he noticed the shiver that stole over her flesh. She felt heat and desire flood her cheeks as her body absorbed his warmth.

She tilted her chin and spoke with conviction. "Actually, I was going to find you."

He looked at her with pure lust. "Yeah?" Ethan dipped his head, his lips coming perilously close to hers. His tongue made a slow pass over his bottom lip, as though moistening, preparing it. Raw, tortured eyes met hers. "Why?"

Danielle drew in air. "I wanted to tell you something." Need colored her voice.

"So, tell me."

With a sudden burst of boldness whipping through her blood, she pressed into him, her actions conveying without words what she wanted, what she needed.

His sweet breath washed over her face. His hands roamed over her back, and his touch felt erotic and stimulating. Blistering heat exploded inside her, demanding attention.

Heart racing, she arched into him and could feel his hard cock. His hands moved urgently over her body. Simmering blue eyes flitted over her. His tone dropped an octave. "Tell me, Dani," he said again, his voice rough with arousal as he caressed her all over. "I'm listening."

"I—" She stopped and stole a glance around the torchlit clearing, noting they weren't entirely alone. Her hands fell away from him and she eased backwards. Reading her hesitation, he cupped her elbow and tugged.

"Come with me," he said, his voice full of tortured promises.

Moving deeper into the shadows, she followed Ethan. He guided her along the gravel path that led to the foot of the rocky mountain. With their strides quick and purposeful, moisture soon pebbled her flesh. A refreshing breeze blew in off the water and helped cool her heated skin.

"Watch your step, Dani. It's damp and the terrain can get rough." He slipped a warm arm around her waist to support her.

She swallowed, noting that his gesture warmed more than her flesh. He really was a man who'd serve and protect until the end. She pulled in a quick breath. By small degrees her body tightened.

He must have sensed the shift because he angled his head and asked, "You okay?"

"Fine," she said and offered him a smile. "It's just that my flip-flops weren't made for mountain climbing."

His sheepish smile tugged at something deep inside. "Right. Sorry about that."

A moment later Danielle found herself cradled in his capable arms. She frowned, worried that her added weight would only aggravate his leg.

Not wanting to hurt his pride, she resisted the urge to tell him she was more than capable of walking. Instead she melted into him, once again enjoying how she felt wrapped in his powerful arms.

She didn't bother asking where he was taking her, knowing she'd be happy wherever they went just as long as she was with him. A few minutes later, Ethan stopped and set her on the ground.

They stood on a cliff at the top of the south side of the mountain. Danielle gazed at the moonlit ocean, taking in the majestic beauty of the island in all its glory. "Wow, this is so beautiful." When she twisted around she noticed the private grass hut overlooking the water. She widened her eyes in delight as she moved toward the hut. "I didn't even know this was here." The minute she stepped into it, the low, soothing sounds of the night life fell silent and she felt worlds away from civilization. Ethan followed her inside and immediately moved close to her. God, she was so aware of him next to her. A shiver raced down her spine as her entire body responded to his proximity.

Standing behind her, he bent his head forward. "Do you want me to light a torch?" he asked, his warm breath washing over her neck.

"Yeah," she whispered, glancing around. The hut felt so rustic, so cozy—the atmosphere put her in touch with her primal, animalistic side.

"What is this place?"

"It's called the mood hut," Ethan answered.

She squinted in the dimness and glanced at the bottles of oils, noting that there were different scents for every mood imaginable. "What else is in here?"

"Candles, blankets, incense, matches . . ."

"Everything you need to set the stage for seduction," she murmured.

"If that's what you're interested in," Ethan replied, his voice as shaky as she felt.

That's exactly what she was interested in.

Danielle grabbed a small vial containing a heady blend of rose, jasmine, and gardenia and handed it to Ethan. "Put some of this in the torch."

She followed Ethan out into the clearing, where soothing sounds of animals were coming to life. As soon as the torch was lit, an exotic scent filled the night air. Ethan drove the torch into the ground, then turned to face her. Warmth and desire enveloped her.

She glanced out over the water once again. "This place is absolutely gorgeous, Ethan."

"I thought you might like it." In a fast motion, Ethan hauled her to him. She held his gaze as his eyes devoured her with raw hunger and his breathing grew labored.

Oh, God, this man did the most wonderful things to her libido. Her hand touched his cheek. "Ethan—"

He cut her off. There was a gleam in his eyes as he focused on her. Without preamble he asked, "What is it you wanted to tell me?"

The torchlight behind him flickered, bathing Ethan in a warm, seductive glow. The magic of the erotic atmosphere, and the alluring scent, seeped under her skin and urged her forward. She tilted her chin and recited Mr. Malik's cryptic words. "There is no ambiguity in the truth."

He softened his voice and asked with a puzzled look on his face, "What does that mean, Dani?"

"Those were Mr. Malik's words of wisdom to me."

"Go on," he coaxed. The perplexed look in his eyes prompted her to continue. He caught hold of her hand and tugged.

"I came here to fulfill a fantasy."

"What fantasy?" he asked, even though she suspected he already knew.

There is no ambiguity in the truth.

Danielle knew if she wanted to experience true passion, she needed to tell Ethan exactly what she wanted. Deep inside she believed he was a man she could tell all her secrets to, and for the first time in her life she didn't feel embarrassed by her needs. It was time to embrace her submissive side and offer herself up to him. When she looked into his eyes, she knew beyond a shadow of a doubt that he was the right man for the job.

The arousing scent of sweet jasmine continued to seduce her senses. The passionate aroma combined with the amazing chemistry between them gave her the courage to go on. "One night. A no-holds-barred affair."

He nodded. "And?" he asked, encouraging her to continue.

"And . . ." She paused to study her soldier. Even though he was troubled and restless, she instinctively trusted him in a way she'd never trusted another. She knew Ethan had integrity, character and a fierce sense of protectiveness. "Just once I want to experience the pleasure of submission with a man I can trust." His nostrils flared while his eyes darkened. He groaned low in his throat. "With my pleasure and my pain," she added, and bridged the small gap between them.

"And, Ethan."

"Yeah?"

"I suspect you're that man."

He gripped her hips. "You suspected right."

Without warning, his burning mouth closed over hers and his tongue slipped inside. His kiss was so full of power and passion, it sucked the air from her lungs. By curling his hands around her body, he absorbed the shiver that ripped through her. A moment later he stepped back and spent a long moment looking at her. She stood there, watching the flurry of emotions pass over his eyes. Her body quivered as his gaze tracked her every movement. There was a suggestive edge to his smile.

He cleared his throat and slanted his head. "I checked into island customs earlier, Dani."

"You did?" Her voice sounded both strangled and excited.

"Yeah, and you were right. Since I saved your life, you now owe me yours."

Oh. Good. God.

"You are mine to do with as I please, and you must obey me at all times. I am your master," he said, bringing her fantasy to life.

She almost sobbed with pleasure.

"Do you understand, Dani?"

"Yes," she whispered. She had to work to get that one word out as her entire body vibrated with excitement.

Ethan reached out and brushed his thumb over her engorged nipple. "Yes, who?" he asked.

She swallowed down a whimper. "Yes, Master."

"Ah, that's better." He placed his hands behind his back and began circling her body. "So you completely understand that I can do whatever I want with you, and you can't protest. If you do, I'll have to discipline you, Dani." He pitched his voice low and added, "And trust me, you don't want any part of my discipline."

Her body tightened; her thighs quivered in erotic delight. It took great effort to speak. "I understand, Master."

Standing behind her, he touched the back of her shoulder. "So if I touch you like this, you won't protest."

She shook her head as her pussy clenched with need.

He slapped her ass. "I can't hear you," he bit out, his voice firm. "Speak up."

A wheezing sound escaped her lips. "No, Master."

"Good." His hand trailed lower, to her ass. He pulled up her dress, cupped her cheeks in his hand and squeezed her to the point of painful pleasure. "And if I touch you like this, you won't protest."

Her heart beat in a mad cadence. With her breathing barely controlled, she whispered breathlessly, "No, Master."

Without removing his hand from beneath her dress, he circled her, his thick fingers inching toward her throbbing pussy. He pulled aside her panties and rolled his thumb over her swollen clit. His gaze slid to her breasts.

Aching to impale herself on him, Danielle bit down on her lip. She felt like her body was going up in flames. She gulped air before glancing into his dark, tortured eyes. She loved that he was playing this game for her.

"*Hmph.*" He frowned, his fingers stretching open her swollen lips while his thumb inched into her slick heat.

Her veins thrummed with impatience for him to go deeper. She flushed. "What is it, Master?"

"I don't remember giving you permission to get so wet."

Oh, sweet Jesus!

He shook his head and gave a heavy sigh. His thumb purposely pressed harder against her clit, coaxing it to come out to play. "I'm afraid I might have to discipline you for your insubordination, after all."

Body throbbing with need, she squirmed against his finger without permission. That action earned her a scowl.

"I also think you need to be disciplined for shaking that hot little ass of yours at me and my comrades earlier." His brow furrowed. "Did you really think you could do that and get away with it?"

His words brought on such a burst of excitement that she nearly erupted right there, all over his hand. Concentrating on the points of pleasure between her legs, she moaned her response.

He pinched her nipple, hard, while his other hand did the most delicious things to her pussy. She adjusted her body, coaxing him to push his finger all the way up inside her. He didn't, letting her know he was completely in control.

"Answer me, Danielle. Did you think I was going to let you get away with that?"

She took note of his dark tone and the way he used her full name this time. She whispered in an unsteady voice after slipping her lids closed, "No, Master."

Ethan stepped away from her and bit out, "Look at me."

She opened her eyes and met his turbulent gaze. He looked so fucking wild, so primal, so sexy. It excited her beyond anything she'd ever known.

His scalding eyes dimmed with desire. "Take your clothes off."

The authority in his voice thrilled her, but she hesitated and glanced around.

Ethan gave a humorless laugh. "What is it, Dani? Are you worried someone will see you? Maybe you should have thought about that before you shook your ass at my comrades." He jabbed his thumb into his chest. "If I want someone else to see your body, they'll see it. That decision is mine. Understand?" Possessiveness flashed in his eyes. "Now, get undressed, and show yourself to me."

He stood there with a riveted expression, legs spread and hands behind his back as he watched her shed her sundress.

"Keep going," he commanded.

Silence stretched on as she unhooked her bra and let it fall to the ground. Wiggling her hips, she lowered her panties, certain she heard a low growl crawl out of his throat.

Once she was naked, his eyes softened, warmth flooding the depths of his baby blues. Without warning, he leaned in and brushed his lips over hers. His kiss was achingly gentle, full of such tenderness that it took her by surprise. Oh, God . . . Out of nowhere a myriad of emotions erupted inside her. Her head shot up. Her voice wobbled. *"Ethan . . ."*

"Back up."

"What?"

With a tense expression on his face, he raised his voice and looked over her shoulder. "Back up against that tree."

Given no time to explore that tender interlude, she stepped back until the tree bark scratched her flesh.

He advanced purposefully and stood before her. She glanced down and could see the huge bulge in his pants. Needing to touch him, she reached out and cradled his cock in her hands. He shook. Almost violently. It excited her to know she had the ability to rattle him.

Jaw clenched, he flinched backwards and growled, his tone clearly indicating his displeasure with her. "I didn't give you permission to touch me." With that he pulled a jackknife out of his back pocket and moved into the woods. He came back with a couple of long, flexible tree vines.

She gulped. He was a regular Boy Scout.

"Put your hands behind your back."

He stepped around her and, using one of the vines, shackled her wrists together, forcing her compliance.

Oh, how she loved his ingenuity, his creativity, his preparedness. Who better to know his way around the woods—or her body—than her trained soldier?

"Now, where were we?" he asked. "Oh, yeah, I remember. I was about to discipline you."

*   *   *

And discipline her he would.

Ethan stepped in front of her and, in a whiplike motion, slapped the vine against his palm. He loved the way her eyes lit with excitement.

A fever broke out on his skin as he took pleasure in the sight of her gorgeous, naked body tied to a tree, his to do with as he pleased.

And boy, oh, boy, did he please.

Sexual need was ruling his actions. He inched closer to her. His pain and injury completely forgotten, life surged through his veins in a way it never had before, giving him strength and power.

He placed the whip between her legs, and with excruciating slowness meant to drive her wild, he dragged it higher and higher on her thighs. He slipped the vine between her pussy lips and stroked her. She shivered under his invasive touch. Her eyes snapped shut. Her head rolled to the side.

"Oh, Jesus," she whispered.

Ethan growled as his cock thickened with need. He clenched his jaw, forcing himself to slow down, to do this right, because if she wanted to play master-servant, dominant-submissive with him, he'd damn well play it for her, and he'd damn well drive her mad in the process.

"Open your eyes," he barked out, struggling to rein in his lust.

When she immediately did as he requested, desire slammed into him. He stared at her, welcoming the power and control she handed him and the way she trusted him so readily.

"That's better," he said, shoving his hard cock against her thigh in search of some sort of relief before he exploded inside his pants. Soon, he promised himself. Soon.

He trailed the vine higher, until he reached her breasts. He whacked her pebbled nubs with the tip. Pink nipples tightened and puckered against his gentle assault. Ethan slapped the vine over her tender flesh a second time, gauging her reactions, so he could give her what she wanted, but not wanting to hurt her just the same.

He stabbed a finger between her legs, feeling her hot, creamy core. She clamped her legs together, holding his hand in place. He could feel small butterfly pulses inside her and knew she was close.

"Please. Fuck me with your fingers. I want to come," she murmured shamelessly.

He wiggled his finger, stroking her G-spot, giving her a taste of things to come. He lowered his voice, and in complete control of her and of the situation, he said, "You'll come when I say you can come, and not before." Her muscles clenched and her waves grew stronger with his words. "Are we clear on that, Dani?"

"Nooo . . . ," she cried out, bucking against his index finger, crazy with need. Her words of protest were lost on a moan when he added another finger to the mix. He finger-fucked her for a moment, stroking deep inside her, and then easing out, bringing her to the brink of ecstasy but never allowing her to tumble over. She whimpered when he withdrew his fingers and turned his attention back to his vine.

Using small whiplike motions, he treated her entire body to a vine lashing, the protector in him taking care not to mar her delicate skin. She shifted and twisted against the tree. Her actions conveyed without words how much she enjoyed it. There was something about the way she trusted him that really got to him.

She tipped her head to see him. When glossy green eyes met his, he ached to hold her, kiss her, fuck her, and possess her.

He shook his head to clear his thoughts, and stepped back into his role. Ethan pushed the vine between her legs until it reached her ass. "This is what you get for not following my orders," he bit out harshly, knowing how she wanted this game to play out. He stroked her clit again, toying with her hard, blood-filled nub until he had driven her into a frenzy of need.

With her backside wiggling, her head fell forward, her hair cascading over her eyes. Ethan fought the urge to brush it away and rain tender kisses over her forehead, her cheeks, her mouth.

"Ethan," she whispered with her green eyes blinking at him, begging for release as he pinched her clit. "It's too much, too intense," she said breathlessly, pleading with him to take her over.

He sent her a look of intimacy and promise. "Shh," he commanded. "I never gave you permission to speak." With that he angled his head and drew one hard nipple into his mouth. Blood pulsing hot through his veins, he sucked hard and long, rolling her pert nub between his teeth, nipping and biting, leaving his mark.

With the vine teasing her ass, his thumb caressing her clit harder and his mouth wrapped around one pert nipple, Dani sucked in a breath and arched into him. Her ragged breath felt hot and erotic against his neck.

Ethan inched lower, his tongue trailing over her flat stomach and her hips until he reached his destination—her hot little cunt.

Sinking to his knees, he positioned his mouth in front of her gorgeous sex.

He gripped her ankles, forcing her to widen her legs. He heard her gasp when he brushed his nose over her pussy, inhaling her tangy, aroused scent. He sat back on his heels, shot her a glance and tsked. "You're a very naughty girl, getting all creamy and wet without asking first." She rolled her hips toward him and he felt a shiver race through her.

"Are . . . are . . . you going to punish me?" she murmured, her words coming out shaky. The hungry look in her eyes urged him on.

"I believe a tongue lashing is in order."

He ran his hands up her thighs and turned his attention to her pussy, where her silky hairs were damp with arousal. "Mmm," he moaned, loving how excited he made her.

His tongue teased her lips open. The first taste of her liquid heat made his head spin, and the world as he knew it suddenly shifted. Dizzy with pleasure, he blinked and worked to shake the fog from his brain.

Driven by need, he swirled his tongue over her clit, stroking her sex all the way from front to back. He slipped a hand around her ass and pulled open her cheeks, his finger gliding over her puckered opening.

Entirely lost in the moment, he licked, kissed, and sucked her cunt, unable to get enough of her. Without fully understanding what was happening to him, he lost control of himself and the situation as he indulged in her sweet center. He drove his tongue up inside her, his thumb working her hot button until her cries of pleasure stirred the night life. Animals scurried around him, birds taking flight overhead.

"So good," she cried out, bucking her pussy against his mouth. "So fucking good."

Who knew one taste of her sweet syrup would reduce him to a mass of quivering need?

"I'm . . . I'm . . ."

"I know, sweetheart," Ethan whispered over her pussy so that his warm breath would bristle her silky hairs and stimulate her clit. He could feel her legs buckle and knew it was time to take her over. He rolled the tip of his finger over her G-spot. "Come in my mouth," he commanded, giving her the permission she was seeking. "Now."

As soon as the words left his mouth, her sex muscles fluttered, powerful waves rolled through her pussy and her sweet cream poured over his chin.

"Ethan . . . ," she whispered.

"That's a girl." Exquisite sensations ripped through him as he lapped up her feminine juices. "Let me taste you." He stayed between her legs for a long time, listening to her ragged breathing.

After she was thoroughly cleaned, he continued to lave her pussy until her juices stirred once again, preparing her for his thick cock.

He slid up her body, crushing himself against her, his cock pushing against her hip. His mouth found hers and he kissed her hard, driving his tongue into her mouth.

"Ethan, please, I want your cock."

"Do you want to suck it?" he asked.

"Yes."

He took heavy breaths and drove his cock harder against her. "Do you like to suck cock, Dani?"

She nodded, and it was all he could do not to throw her to her knees and jam his cock into her mouth.

He growled before racing his hands over her with an aroused edginess. He needed her so badly he ached, and he knew he wouldn't last long if she sucked him. "I need to fuck you first, Dani."

"Oh, God, yes," she cried out.

Forgetting about his mangled leg, he stepped back and stripped off his clothes. He watched the way her hungry eyes devoured him with longing.

"You're beautiful," she murmured, struggling against the vines. "Let me touch your cock."

As he stepped toward her, reality inched its way into his lust-fogged brain. His fucked-up leg was bare, exposed. He stilled his movements. His gut twisted. Fuck.

As her gaze raked over him, he glanced into her eyes, but he didn't see pity there. All he saw was desire. Her expression was filled with pure adoration.

For him.

Warmth and something else, something he couldn't describe, sang through his veins. He stood there trying to remember how to breathe, with the longing in her eyes wreaking havoc on his emotions.

"Condoms?" she whispered, her sweet voice pulling him back.

Oh, fuck, why hadn't he thought of condoms? Ethan swallowed and shook his head, noting the way Dani's breath was coming in small bursts. He touched her face. "Dani, I haven't been with any-one in a long time and I'm clean. I promise you."

"Me, too," she returned, her eyes full of trust. "And Ethan, I really need to feel *you* inside me. No barriers."

Warmth and longing seeped under his skin. He dragged her into his arms and poised his cock at her entrance. She wiggled against him, his cock breaching her opening.

"Fuck me, Ethan," she said. "Hard."

With wild abandon he pushed all the way up inside her, lifting her feet clear off the ground. Their cries of pleasure merged as he drove into her, harder and harder, not stopping to think he could be hurting her. He needed to be deeper, to drive his balls up inside her, to bury himself inside her and stay there forever. He drew air, grasping to understand what was happening to him. He'd never lost control with a woman like this before.

For some reason he couldn't get enough of her. Couldn't get deep enough. He felt disoriented, dizzy. His thoughts scattered like the wildlife. He pounded into her, filling her with his impres-sive girth. She wrapped her legs around his waist, opening herself wider. Stabbing his cock into her heat, he groaned and slammed her body against the tree, taking everything he could get and giving everything he could give. Pain and pleasure mingled into one.

He'd never felt so crazed, so driven by lust, by need. He plunged harder, and each powerful jab edged on painful. His breath came in short, harsh bursts as his whole body shook with blinding pleasure.

He glanced into her damp eyes. Oh, Christ, he was fucking hurting her. "Shit, Dani, I'm sorry," he whispered, slowing his pace. He reached around and ripped the vines from her arms, releasing her.

She wrapped her hands around his neck. "No, don't stop, Ethan."

"I'm hurting you."

She shook her head, her hands racing over his arms, his chest. "Take what you need, Ethan, please. It's what I need, too."

When he hesitated, she bucked against him, encouraging him to continue. Once again he picked up his pace, driving into her with frenzied need, his cock ready to explode as her cunt sucked him in deeper. Her muscles clenched around him; her liquid heat singed his dick. She threw her head back and cried out his name. She rode him hard and long as her orgasm took hold.

An unexpected rush of emotions rolled through him, and suddenly it felt like time had slowed, just for the two of them. Everything in him softened, tenderness stealing over him as he watched her. "That's it, Dani; come for me again," he whispered into her mouth. He loved watching her come, the way her eyes lit, the way her mouth opened and closed, and the way she called out his name with such longing, such passion.

His own orgasm came on the heels of hers. He pushed deep and stilled, letting his seed splash up inside her.

She squeezed her sex muscles, milking him. He growled and concentrated on each pulse of pleasure.

His lips found hers. "Dani, that feels so fucking good."

"So good," she whispered back. "So damn amazing, Ethan."

He buried his face in her neck and held her against the tree for a long time. When her legs slipped from his backside, Ethan stepped away from the tree, hauling her with him. He collapsed onto his back, positioning Dani on top of him and keeping her body off the damp ground.

As they lay there for a long moment, Ethan ran his fingers through her hair, staring at the mosaic of stars overhead.

After a while, he angled his head to see her. She glanced at him, her eyes drowsy, sated. He offered her an apologetic smile. "I'm sorry. That was pretty intense. I didn't mean to get so carried away." He shook his head. "That's never happened to me before."

"Don't be sorry. I got pretty carried away, too, and that's never happened to me before, either. But I liked it." She grinned and added, "A lot."

"Did I hurt you?"

"It's a good hurt," she said, then stretched like a satisfied cat. A long, thoughtful moment later, she teased, "So I guess the elixir really does work."

"Oh, yeah? How so?"

She ran her index finger over his nipple. "Well, the minute I set eyes on you this afternoon, I knew you were my fantasy man. The one man who could take control and give me what I needed."

He chuckled. "Ah, but you met me before you drank the elixir, sweetheart."

She squirmed on top of him, inching upward. "But maybe it was the elixir that gave me the courage to tell you what I wanted." Ethan shifted her against his body. Suddenly, Dani paused and opened her eyes wide.

"What is it?" Ethan asked.

Pulling a face, she eased herself up on her arms. "It just occurred to me that this position might hurt your leg." Once again he glanced into her eyes and saw concern, not pity.

He pulled her back. "You're only a lightweight, babe." After a moment of silence, he said, "I don't think it was the elixir that brought us together. I'm pretty sure I had my mind set on ravishing you anyway."

She laughed and cut her hand through the air. "So you still don't believe in the magic of the elixir, or the magic of the island?"

"No." Then again, after the shrapnel had shattered his femur, he never thought he'd feel like his old self again. He never thought he'd feel in control, and for a while there she had given that control back to him. He pulled her in tighter, so he could appreciate how she felt in his arms. And after he'd buried himself in her tight heat, he'd totally fucking lost control of himself and everything around him. He shook his head in bewilderment. Man, he'd never lost it like that before.

It suddenly occurred to him that losing control didn't seem so scary when he was buried inside Dani.

She snuggled into him. "So what was the one thing you'd want if you could have it, Ethan? What is your deepest desire?"

He chuckled. "Besides fucking you again?"

"Well, that's a given," she teased.

He wasn't sure what compelled him to tell her; perhaps it was the alignment of the planets, or perhaps for the first time since his injury he felt comfortable enough with someone to talk about it.

"After my leg got fucked up, I got sent here to heal. But this island can't help me. My deepest desire is to have my control back and to be back on active duty with my fellow comrades. No magic elixir can make that happen."

He looked into her eyes and felt her warmth and acceptance of who he was, and everything else about him. A riot of emotions erupted inside him. Desperately needing to lighten the mood, Ethan said, "So what was this about fucking you again?"

She chuckled. "Anytime."

"Anytime, who?" he commanded in a soft voice.

"Anytime, Master."

FOUR

Even though Dani had told Ethan that she wanted only one night of uninhibited sex, that one night of fucking had led to many more. Over the past few days Ethan had monopolized all of Dani's attention, barely giving her a moment to spend with her friends. Not that they seemed to mind, Ethan mused. They both managed to keep themselves happily occupied.

It was strange, really. Though he had spent such a short time with her, his well-sought-out solitude suddenly felt like loneliness when she wasn't tucked in beside him.

During the hours they spent together, they ate, slept, showered and played. She even accompanied him to his therapy classes and encouraged him to use his cane. He still hated the damn stick but had come to understand he needed it, especially if he continued to chase Dani up the mountain, tie her up and fuck her senseless.

Honestly, he'd never met a woman quite like her. As he lay there basking in the afterglow of great sex, on this beautiful tropical island, it occurred to him that life as he knew it was damn near perfect.

With Dani lying beside him in her bed, Ethan opened his eyes, pleased to see the bright sunshine after the wild storm that had moved through the night before. He gathered Dani into his arms and pulled her in, glancing at the tangerine candle they'd lit after the power had failed. Ethan grabbed the matches and relit it, letting the sweet scent fill the room with warmth and a sexy ambiance.

When Dani stirred, he looked at her. "Good morning, sweetheart," he said, rousing her with a kiss.

She stretched. "Is it morning already?" She glanced at the clock and smiled when she saw the burning candle. "I think you mean, 'Good afternoon.'"

"So it is, my sweet Dani; so it is."

She snuggled closer. "I've been meaning to ask you. Why do you call me Dani?"

He lazily stroked her strawberry blond hair, taking in the spray of freckles on her nose. "It's cute, like you."

"Cute? I'm not cute." She flipped her hair, feigning insult. "I'm sexy, baby."

He laughed and dropped a kiss onto her mouth. Passion rolled to the surface as her tongue slipped inside his mouth to play with his. He inched back and tore the covers off their bodies. "Show me how sexy you are, Dani. Climb on my cock, and let me watch you fuck me."

She offered him a sultry smile, climbed on top of him, parted her twin lips, and sank onto his cock.

"Ah, Jesus," Ethan moaned, his dick thickening and throbbing deep inside her.

"Are you praying, Ethan?"

He grinned. "I believe I might be. You feel so fucking amazing, you've got me giving prayers of thanks."

"You feel pretty damn good, too." Rotating her hips, Dani cupped her breasts, threw her head back and moaned.

Her scorching heat caused his balls to constrict and his body to quake. "You are so wet and hot, sweetheart."

She writhed against him, thrusting her hips forward. When her hand went to her cunt, to stroke her engorged clit, a burst of possessiveness whipped through his blood.

As he watched her ride him, he began trembling and panting, hungering for so much more. No matter how many times they fucked, he still couldn't seem to get enough. Fever gripped him hard, and the need to take her, all of her, *everywhere*, consumed him.

Driven by extreme need, he gripped her hips, lifted her from his cock and pushed her onto the bed, facedown. He eased a pillow under her hips and climbed from the mattress. She lay before him, her gorgeous ass tipped upward, just begging to be fucked.

He positioned himself behind her and spread her lush ass cheeks. Her beautiful pink puckered hole tightened when he stroked it.

"Ethan, I don't think—"

"Shh," he growled through his haze of passion, and pinned her shoulders to the bed. "I *know* how to take care of you, Dani." Ethan could feel her growing combination of nervousness and excitement.

"But I've never done this before."

Good. He wanted to be the first. "You need to trust me."

"I do trust you," she said.

"With your pleasure *and* your pain?"

"Yes," she whispered.

He felt a fierce urge to always protect her when he heard the emotion in her voice. He dipped into her cunt cream and, with the utmost care, lathered her puckered hole. Once she was sufficiently coated, he pushed one finger into her, opening her tight walls. He stilled, giving her a minute to get used to the sensation. When he began to insert a second finger, she stiffened and tried to squirm away. He held her down.

"Stop it, Dani."

"I'm not sure—"

"You need to trust that I know how to take care of you."

He gave her another inch. When her muscles tightened around his finger, he groaned deep in his throat.

"Now, open up for me."

He felt her body relax. "Mmm, nice," he said and began working his finger inside her ass slowly, gently, stroking her sensitive nerve endings. Soon her cries of protest morphed into small moans of pleasure.

"That's my girl," he whispered. With the heady scent of feminine arousal saturating the air, he leaned over her and said, "I can smell your arousal, Dani."

"It's what you're doing to me. It's making me hot," she whimpered.

"Do you like having your ass fucked, baby?"

"Only if it's by you, Ethan. I would never entrust anyone else with my body this way."

Everything in him softened. Needing desperately to make this good for her, he said, "Get up on your knees for me, sweetheart."

After she climbed to her knees, he reached between her legs and stroked her clit. Her ass muscles clenched around his finger. "Ah, you really like that, don't you?"

He eased his fingers from her ass and coated her with more cream. Aching and trembling to fuck her, he positioned his cock at her opening and worked to control his shaky voice. "I need to be inside you, Dani."

When she nodded, he pushed into her tight hole, giving her only an inch at a time as he spread her wide open. A whimper escaped her lips as he slowly sank his girth between her puckered cheeks.

Jesus, she was tight.

"Oh, my God," she cried out, her fingers gripping the bedsheets.

He pushed deeper, spreading her wider. When a low moan sounded in her throat, he asked, "Does it hurt?"

She nodded as her ass opened for him.

"You like when it hurts a little, don't you, babe?" he asked, showing her how well he knew her. Answering his question, she pushed her backside against him, encouraging him to give her his entire length.

Once he was completely buried in her ass, he began to pump, slowly at first, but when she began grinding against him, his slow pumps became more frenzied, more demanding.

He reached around and dipped into her cunt and knew she was chasing an orgasm. He picked up the tempo, giving her what she needed. When he felt her start to quake beneath him, his whole body went up in flames.

Her voice came out sounding rough and impatient. "I want to feel you come inside my ass, Ethan."

Her words pushed him over the edge at that moment. Teetering on the precipice, Ethan groaned out loud and released his seed high inside her. As his warmth rushed through her, the erotic pulse of his cock brought on her orgasm.

"That's it, baby. Come for me," he murmured. Her sweet pulses milked his cock, draining him completely. He stayed inside until their tremors had subsided.

He pulled out and dropped beside her on the bed. "Are you okay?" he asked while stroking the curve of her ass in a soothing manner.

"I'm better than okay," she reassured him. "I had no idea how good that could be." After a moment of silence she asked, "How do you always know what I need?"

Instead of answering, he brushed gentle fingers over her cheeks. "You're beautiful when you come."

"You think so?"

"Yes. I should make you come every day," he said.

She gave him a playful grin. "At least twice," she said.

Ethan brushed her hair away from her face as they fell into easy conversation. "So, what do you want to do today?"

"Well, I was planning on having a late lunch with Lauren and Abby. If I don't show up, they're going to think I've abandoned them. And since coming to this island was my idea, I'd better get going," she said. "After that I have the hydrotherapy room booked for a long, hot, sea-salt bath. I can use a nice sensual soak after what we just did," she said, grinning.

He delighted in how comfortable they were together, how easily they fell into conversation after passionately charged sex. "Will I see you tonight?"

She touched his cheek. "Whether you want to or not."

He grinned like the village idiot, feeling so damn juvenile. "Oh, I want to, but you already know that."

"So, what are you going to do this afternoon?" she asked.

He shrugged. "I guess it's time to work on the deck."

"Deck?"

"Yeah, it's some makeshift project Malik gave me when I first got here. Something to help me reenter the workforce, I guess, because it'll be a cold day in hell before my superior officers come pounding on my door again." He grabbed the blankets and hauled them up, noting the strange sense of relief washing over him. It hadn't occurred to him until lately just how disgruntled he'd become with all the red tape and bureaucratic bullshit. "I've had a pile of building materials sitting at the back of my cabana for months. I haven't felt like touching it. I think I'll get started on it today, though."

Dani touched his hands and gave him a playful wink. "I always knew you were good with your hands." She snuggled in tighter. "So, where did you learn carpentry work?"

"My grandfather."

"I thought you came from a line of military men."

"I do. That's what Grandpa did in the military." Ethan chuckled and added, "My mom made sure I learned how to wield a hammer. She said the one thing she hates is a man who is useless around the house."

"Same here." Dani grinned. "Where do your parents live?"

"Mom and Dad call Florida home now. But they've lived all over. How about you?"

"My mom, dad and baby brother are all in Chicago. Not far from me." After a moment she added, "You know, Ethan, in my line of work we're always looking for good carpenters. Of course, I'd have to see your finished product first before I could recommend you," she said playfully.

"Why, you . . ." He covered her lips with his.

After a long, thorough kiss, Dani stole another glance at the clock. "I'd better get going or the girls are going to think I've been eaten by the big bad wolf."

Ethan cocked his head and gave her a wicked grin. "Oh, but you have, my sweet Dani, you have. Numerous times."

Dani laughed out loud and threw the covers back. "On that note . . ."

Ethan sat up in the bed and watched her get ready, enjoying the view of a naked Dani strolling around the cabana.

A short while later he showered, dressed and made his way back to his place, which he hadn't seen the inside of in days. After grabbing a bite to eat, he fastened his carpenter's belt and stepped outside to the waiting stack of lumber. He laid his cane to the side, filled his tool apron with deck screws and began sorting the wood.

Time flew by as he cut and tacked together the frame. It occurred to him how good it felt to be doing physical work again. It also occurred to him how much he liked working with his hands, and how much he'd missed it. For the first time in months he felt his restlessness ebbing away, felt the tension ease from his body.

After wiping his brow with the back of his hand, he measured the lumber while his thoughts raced to Dani. His sweet, wonderful Dani who'd be leaving the island in a little over a week, with both of them going their own separate ways.

He paused to consider things further. Shit. How the fuck was he going to walk away from this—this crazy, amazing thing between them? How the fuck was he going to walk away from her? A woman who'd given him back everything he'd lost.

Every time they'd made love, Dani had given him back his control. Of course he always ended up losing it again the minute he sank into her damp heat. But it wasn't totally horrible. Not at all. In fact it felt exhilarating with her. It felt safe. And it didn't make him feel like less of a man.

Dani had never once looked at him as broken, and he didn't see a trace of pity in her eyes when he'd shed his pants and exposed his injury. All he saw was dark desire. She looked at him like he was a man, a man who could give her exactly what she needed. The powerful, virile man he used to be.

Still was, in fact.

He recalled Dani's words the first night they were together: *Just once I want to experience the pleasure of submission.* That one night of wild fantasy sex had turned into many. The way she looked at him with such need and the way she put herself completely in his hands had warmed his darkest corners.

But how did Dani feel? Sure, they were having fun together, but that didn't mean she wanted anything permanent. Maybe when her vacation was up she'd be eager to get home, back to life as she knew it, taking only erotic memories with her.

Ethan grabbed a two-by-six and carried it to the circular saw. He knew what had happened between Dani and him wasn't magic and had nothing to do with any elixir. Although he wasn't a believer in destiny, he was beginning to think that maybe everything did happen for a reason. If he hadn't gotten shot, he never would have been sent to the island and he never would have met Dani. Something told him she was far more important than any control he'd ever had.

He shook his head. What the fuck was happening to him? He was beginning to sound like the medicine man.

And speaking of . . .

"Hello, Ethan."

Ethan watched Malik come toward him. "How's it going?"

"I see you've decided to build the deck."

Ethan nodded. "Yeah, I figured it wasn't going to assemble itself."

Getting right to the point, Malik smiled and held his hands out, feeling the air around the two of them. "Your tension is gone, Ethan."

"I'm doing okay." When Malik glanced at Ethan's cane, Ethan propped his deck board on the ground and leaned on it. "Listen, I know I've given you a hard time the last couple of months, and I'm sorry about that. I know you were just trying to help me."

"How are you managing the pain?"

"It's better and I'm getting stronger." Of course, chasing Dani around helped with the strength building, and also helped him focus on something besides the pain.

Malik's smile widened. "Then I think you might be ready for this now." He reached into his pocket and held out a government-issue envelope.

"What is it?"

Malik didn't speak. After dropping the two-by-six, Ethan brushed sawdust from his hands and then ripped open the manila envelope.

His stomach tightened as he scanned the words.

"Well, I'll be damned," he murmured under his breath. As he scanned the paper again, his surprise segued to confusion. He glanced at Malik. "I don't understand."

"What's to understand? Your expertise is needed, and I'm signing your release papers. You can go back overseas, Ethan. A desk job for now, and then eventually into battle."

"So I'm free to go?"

"Like the letter says, you can leave tonight if you'd like. You see, Ethan, your superiors haven't written you off like you believed. And you're here because they care."

Working to mask his conflicting emotions, Ethan folded the paper and shoved it into his back pocket. He picked up a deck board and carried it to the frame.

Malik folded his hands and studied him. "Isn't this what you wanted and have been waiting for? Isn't this the future you've strived for?"

"Yeah. I guess so," he replied, turning his attention back to his project.

Malik turned around to leave, but before he walked away, he said, "Your destiny is in your hands, Ethan."

Ethan glanced at the screw he'd just taken out of his tool belt and suspected the medicine man was right. He was definitely screwed.

In the span of a few short days, he had learned that the one thing he thought he always wanted wasn't the same thing as what he really needed.

After showering and pulling on a bright yellow sundress, Danielle hurried to meet her friends.

"Well, well, look who's all giggly and glowing," Lauren said as Danielle hurried through the restaurant toward them. Danielle pulled out a chair and glanced at the salad and iced tea in front of her.

"You were running late, so we ordered you a Caesar salad, hold the anchovies," Abby said, her blue eyes twinkling, a gorgeous gleam to her sun-kissed skin. Danielle also took note of the shine on Lauren's skin and wondered what, or who, had put it there.

She momentarily turned her attention back to her lunch. "You two are the best." Her stomach was grumbling, so Danielle grabbed a fork and dug in. "Mmm, delicious."

The three fell into easy conversation, talking about the resort, its luxurious facilities and all it had to offer. Danielle ate her salad, ripped into the fresh bread and washed it all down with her iced tea. As her friends continued to talk, her mind wandered to Ethan and all the wonderful intimate things they'd been doing together.

After a long while, she glanced up at her friends, who were staring at her in wide-eyed anticipation. She dropped her napkin, wondering whether she was exhibiting some telltale sign that she'd been having the best sex of her life. "What?"

"You're smiling," Lauren said.

"I am?"

"Yeah, you are, and we want to know what you're smiling about and what you've been up to for the past few days," Abby piped in.

She gave a casual shrug. "Well, I met a guy."

"No shit," Lauren said. "We want details, girlfriend. Details. Tell us all about this fabulous sea god who's been keeping you captive inside your cabana."

Chuckling, Danielle glanced around to make sure no one besides her friends could hear her. "I think there is something very magical about this island's springwater. My deepest desires have come true."

Abby leaned forward. "Oh, yeah? Do tell."

She gave a long, contented sigh, reflecting on the sexy little games she'd been playing with Ethan and how quickly they had moved from strangers to lovers. She'd never shared herself with anyone the way she'd shared herself with him. And the way he took charge of pleasing her made her pussy ache and moisten just from thinking about it.

"He's very . . . *creative*, I'll tell you that."

"Creative?" both women asked at once.

She arched a brow. "Yeah, creative."

Lauren pitched her voice low. "But the real question is, has he had his wicked way with you?" Danielle suspected her friends knew her well enough to know what she really wanted from a man, even though she'd never come right out and told them.

"He knows what I want, Lauren," she rushed out. "He really, really knows me. I've never, ever been so sexually satisfied in my life." She shivered. "The things that man can do with a vine."

Truthfully, he was everything she'd ever wanted in a man. She loved his commanding attitude, his attention to detail, his protectiveness and the way he always touched her like her pleasures were paramount.

Lauren blew a breath. "Oh, boy."

"What is it?" Danielle asked.

"You've got it bad for this guy."

She smiled as she thought about Ethan and how good they were together. Deep down she knew she'd never find with any other man what she'd found with him. Since he was a skilled soldier and a commander in the military, Danielle expected dominance from him, but what she hadn't expected was the underlying tenderness he showed her. It was that tenderness, and the way he took painstaking care of her needs, that touched her so.

She drew a deep breath and let it out slowly. She certainly hadn't anticipated this turn of events during her vacation and knew there was no sense in hiding the truth. Her friends knew her too well for that.

"Okay, so he's great and I want to keep him around longer." Which, as her friends knew, was something she'd never wanted before.

When her friends grew quiet, mulling over that bit of information, she continued. "I hadn't planned on anything more than a good fuck with a virile warrior. I guess I got more than I bargained for."

Abby reached out and grabbed her hand. "So go tell him. Be honest and tell him exactly how you feel."

"You think?" Danielle glanced at Lauren.

Lauren, being the more practical of her two friends when it came to relationships, frowned and shook her head. "I think you should remember that you both lead very different lives, Danielle, and when this vacation is over, the affair will be over, too. Just keep it about sex. Great sex, by the sound of things." Lauren stood and hustled Danielle out of her chair and pointed her toward the door. "What I think you need to do is go, have a good time and fuck him out of your system once and for all."

Danielle turned back around to look at her friends. "But I haven't heard what you two have been up to." She glanced at Abby. "Abby, are you enjoying your vacation?"

Abby nodded, but Danielle didn't miss the gleam in her eyes. She wondered who had put it there. "I'm fine. Now, go. Tell him how you feel. We'll talk soon. I promise."

With those two very different, nonnegotiable pieces of advice, Danielle rushed from the restaurant and made her way to Ethan's cabana. As she walked the footpath, she spotted Ryan Thomas nestled between the trees at the back of his cabana, sprawled out on a hammock. On closer inspection, she noticed a pink Chicago Bears hat on his head. It looked suspiciously similar to Lauren's favorite ball cap. How interesting . . .

Deciding to investigate later, she rushed to find Ethan. She found him at the back of his cabana, bent over a stack of wood, a drill in his hand. As she took a moment to watch him screw down a deck board, it occurred to her that her warrior was strong and virile, yet the most tender man she'd ever come across.

He reached for another board, his muscles flexing with the movement. Her body stirred to life. Dayum. She had to admit, there was something very sexy about a shirtless guy in a pair of work boots. Unbridled need rose to the surface. He looked good enough to eat. Perhaps that's exactly what she'd do. A sexy bedroom sound rose from her throat, gaining his attention.

When he glanced up at her, his face lit up. "Hey, babe." He walked over to her and pulled her in tight, like touching her was the most natural thing in the world. His lips found hers, and he kissed her with intimate recognition.

He inched back and cupped her face with gentle hands. His eyes were so full of want, her knees liquefied. "I thought you had the hydrotherapy room booked this afternoon."

Her heart pounded in her chest as she explored her desire for him. He brushed his thumb over her bottom lip. Lust exploded through her senses and her pussy clenched, needing to feel him inside her.

"I do, but I thought you might like to join me."

Intrigue registered in his eyes. "Oh, yeah? What do you have in mind?"

"Well, since you're all hot and sweaty, I thought you could use a nice, long, sensual soak." She grabbed his shirt and tossed it to him. After he pulled it on, she laced her fingers through his. "It's time for *me* to take care of *you*." And for her to give him back everything he'd given her.

A few minutes later, they found themselves alone in the hydrotherapy room. She glanced at the state-of-the-art tub, a tub big enough for two, she mused. On a small metal rack next to the tub, the jars of edible body butter sparked her imagination.

When she turned back to Ethan, his eyes were brimming with lust. Deciding to tease him, Danielle walked over to the tub and bent over it to give him a good view of her ass.

As she set the plug and filled the tub with hot water, she heard a low growl coming from behind her. Before she had a chance to stand up, she felt Ethan lift her sundress and push against her ass cheeks, pinning her body to the cool porcelain. His hands spanned her waist and came around to play with her nipples.

He gathered her breasts into his palms and whispered, "Perfect fit."

Physically aware of the way he was stimulating her senses, she grew slick with need but struggled to keep her focus. She turned on the powerful jets and filled the tub with sea salts.

Wiggling slightly, hoping to drive him as mad as he was driving her, she glanced at Ethan over her shoulder. "Grab a bottle of aromatherapy oil on the shelf beside you."

Growling in reluctance, Ethan stepped back and glanced at the small bottles. "What scent?" he asked, his voice ragged, his cock pressing so hard against his jeans, it had to be causing him pain.

Danielle sat on the edge of the tub and watched him move, her pussy clenching and throbbing with desire to feel him between her legs again. "How about lilac?"

He grabbed the bottle and handed it to her. She poured a generous amount into the tub, turned off the running water and inhaled the sensual scent. When she turned back to face Ethan, she came face to face with his crotch.

Yummy!

She reached out and stroked the length of his cock through his jeans. With his body shaking, he fisted her hair and groaned. "Goddamn, girl, I need to fuck you again."

Danielle unhooked his button and listened to the hiss of his zipper as she lowered it. She pulled down his shorts, allowing his magnificent cock to spill out.

"Mmm," she moaned, licking her lips. The scent of his arousal called out to her. She closed her eyes for a brief moment, filling her lungs. Leaning forward, she brushed her tongue over his head and watched the way it pulsed in response. "I need to taste you first."

"Fuck," he whispered, his hands tightening in her hair.

Reaching beside her, she grabbed the raspberry-flavored body butter. She opened the jar, dipped into it and rubbed the lotion over his cock.

"Holy fuck," he bit out, his hips jerking forward.

Danielle moaned, working the body butter over his shaft, making him slick and so damn hard, she was sure he was going to rupture an artery. She licked his slit, tasting the heady mixture of raspberry and tangy male cream. "Mmm, delicious," she whispered. She glanced into his smoldering eyes. "Want a taste?"

"Yeah," he murmured, and bent his head down to meet hers. When his lips crashed down on hers, she slipped her tongue into his mouth, giving him a sample.

A moment later she pulled back and watched him lick his lips. "That is so fucking sexy, Dani." Lust raged in his eyes, and she sensed it took considerable effort for him to speak. "You sure know how to work magic with your lotions and scents."

She grinned and turned her attention back to his cock. She cupped his balls, her mouth taking possession of his shaft, drawing his impressive length in as deep as she possibly could. He began rocking his hips, fucking her mouth. She took her time with him, wanting to pleasure him the same way he'd been pleasuring her over the last few days. Her hands skimmed his sinewy muscles. She enjoyed the feel of his hard, sculpted body and the way his muscles bunched beneath her touch. As she continued to feast on his cock, her nipples hardened, and her pussy lubricated, aching to feel him deep inside her.

"You're so good at this, Dani, I'm not going to last." His voice sounded strangled.

Fueled by her need to taste him, she picked up the pace, her tongue working over his shaft. She stroked and sucked and discovered all the ways he liked her mouth on his cock. His muscles tightened, his shaft filled with heated blood and she could feel it swell beneath her tongue. Ever determined to taste his juice, Danielle moaned and slipped a finger between his ass cheeks.

Ethan moved urgently against her, plunging his cock in and out of her slick mouth. Her own sex fluttered, and she squirmed against the tub, seeking release.

A rumble of pleasure sounded low in his throat, and he pitched forward. "*Yesss,*" Ethan bit out, his cock pulsing in orgasm. Not wanting to waste a drop, she wrapped her mouth around his engorged tip, letting his seed shoot down her throat. She nuzzled his cock and spent a long time enjoying the taste of his cream.

"Hey," Ethan said, breaking the quiet between them.

She glanced up at him. He shot her a scalding look before laying his big hands over her shoulders and drawing her to her feet. He pressed his mouth to hers and kissed her deeply. His tongue moved inside to play with hers. "Now it's my turn to lick your cunt and taste your cream," he murmured into her mouth.

She lifted her dress for him. "By all means."

With a grin, he grabbed the hem from her, inched back and pulled the fabric over her head. She listened to the soft rustle of her clothes as he discarded them. He unhooked her bra and tossed it aside, then sank to his knees. The silky sweep of his hair against her skin brought on a shudder. Then a surge of warmth flooded her veins. He pressed his nose into her stomach, trailed kisses over her flesh and ripped her panties from her hips. She gasped with excitement.

One finger brushed between her thighs to stroke her wet pussy. He breathed a kiss over her quivering sex lips, then buried his tongue inside her. That first sweet touch sent her to the moon and back. The heat of his mouth scorched her sensitive flesh. She gave a lusty groan and slackened against him. Strong hands wrapped around her waist and held her stable.

Her fingers gripped the tub as raw desire seared her insides. He pushed one thick finger up inside her, and her body shook all over. A powerful, mind-numbing orgasm suddenly tore through her, taking her completely by surprise.

Her legs shook, and she lost herself in his touch. "Ethan," she cried out, reaching for him, her hands moving to his shoulders.

"I got you, sweetheart," he whispered from between her legs, his hands spanning her waist, anchoring her pussy to his mouth.

Once her sex muscles stopped spasming, he gathered her into his arms and stepped into the tub. He pulled her on top of him and turned on the jets. The hot, scented water felt luxurious against her skin.

She straddled his waist and he slipped a hand between her legs. Softly, gently, he stroked and smoothed her swollen pussy. She gave a contented moan and brushed a kiss over his mouth.

"Nice," she whispered, feeling completely free with him.

"Mmm, very nice." After a long, comfortable silence, he asked, "So, how was lunch with the girls? Are they enjoying their vacation?"

She moaned and relaxed into conversation. "I think so. They didn't say much. They were more interested in me and my sea god."

As he continued to caress her sex, he asked, "Sea god?"

She chuckled and splashed warm water over her breasts. "Yeah, you looked like a Greek god rising from the water to rescue me that first day. I wasn't even sure you were real."

His finger brushed over her labia and then moved to her clit. "Is that why you pinched me?" His voice was so tender, it made her insides ache.

"Yup."

He glanced around. "Sometimes I wonder if all this is real, too, Dani."

She could feel his cock grow and press against her ass. "I know what you mean. It's like a dream, isn't it?"

He grinned and pinched her nipple. "An erotic dream."

"And I'm not ready to wake up," Danielle said, sliding lower until his hard cock breached her opening. "This place really is beautiful. I haven't been taking advantage of the facilities at all." She shimmied onto his cock, pushing it all the way up inside her.

"I know; you've only been taking advantage of me," Ethan teased, drawing small circles over her clit with the pad of his thumb.

She stroked his face, his neck, his chest, while rocking her hips back and forth, slowly, gently. Her soft sigh of pleasure filled the room. "I hate that I have to leave here in a week. This place is paradise."

His voice dropped to a whisper. "It's something else."

She closed her eyes and spent a long time rocking against him. He continued to touch her in a familiar way. His caress had satisfaction flowing through her body. She cupped her breasts, basking in the glow of Ethan's touch.

Minutes later, she opened her eyes and asked, "Have you been here long, Ethan?"

She watched his chest rise and fall in an erratic pattern. "Yeah, a few months. And this is the first time I've ever had a sea bath or enjoyed the facilities." He powered his hips upward, pushing a little harder against her.

"Really?" She moaned and turned her attention to the pleasure between her legs.

He nodded, and she could tell it was getting harder and harder for him to talk. God, she loved the easy, gentle way they were having sex. So soft, intimate, and tender, and every bit as powerful as when they were role-playing.

"Then we have one week to make up for that. Tomorrow we'll have a Vichy shower, and the day after we'll have a therapeutic rainforest scrub. The day after that we'll have a body massage and manicure. You can skip the manicure, but I'm definitely having that," she added.

His smile fell and the intense look that replaced it told her something was wrong. Something was definitely wrong.

Her stomach dipped. "What is it?"

He continued to look at her like there were going to be no tomorrows. Before he could speak, a knock came on the door.

"Your hour is up."

"Wow, already?" she asked. "I guess time flies when you're having fun." She angled her head. "Shall we finish this at my place? Or we could go to your place; it's closer."

He caught her hand. "The closer the better, because I have to tell you something."

FIVE

Danielle fell into step beside Ethan as they made their way to his cabana. Unfortunately, during their quick jaunt over the footpath, a small, localized rain shower had moved overhead, remnants of the previous night's storm, perhaps.

Despite the drizzle, she noticed that Ethan had slowed his long steps, allowing her to keep up with him. She also noticed the way he wrapped his arm around her in a protective manner, packaging her against his solid body when she began to shiver, the contact creating an instant air of intimacy.

The heat that radiated from him warmed her damp flesh. As his embrace pushed back the cold, it filled her entire being with want, with longing. The man was simply addictive.

She nestled into him. His earthy scent assailed her senses, and even though they'd just made love, she ached to lose herself in his arms, his kisses and his bed, once again.

When she tipped her head to meet his eyes, her blood pressure soared and her body hummed with anticipation. Danielle pushed her damp bangs from her forehead and blinked a drop from her lashes, wondering what he wanted to tell her.

By the time they stepped up to his door, the shower had passed. "Go inside and grab some towels. I need to put these tools away."

Danielle rushed to the bathroom and grabbed two towels. She dried her hair and began closing all the windows. As she pulled them shut, the breeze rustled a bunch of papers on the table, and a few sailed to the floor. She bent to pick them up. One paper in particular caught her attention. She scanned the words.

As her heart twisted, it occurred to her that this was what Ethan wanted to talk to her about. In less than twenty-four hours, he'd be leaving to go overseas. The one thing he always wanted; the one thing he desired most.

Her heart sank. Lauren was right. She should have kept this wild affair just about sex, because when it came right down to it, they lived completely different lives. So much for her desire to keep him around longer and see where this relationship would lead.

Unlike all the other guys she'd been with, Ethan had taken the time to discover her needs and pleasure her, but lessons learned long ago had taught her not to put herself out there. She drew a breath and berated her stupidity for doing just that, because once again she was going to find herself alone.

She rushed to replace the paper as he came inside. Danielle handed him a towel. Concealing her churning emotions, she straightened her spine and worked to sound casual, even though she felt rattled inside.

"I guess the magic elixir really did fulfill your deepest desires,

Ethan." Despite her best efforts, she knew her voice sounded tight.

His eyes moved over her face, perplexed. "What are you talking about, Dani? You know I don't believe in any magic elixir."

She nodded toward the paper and offered an apologetic face. "I didn't mean to read it. It just sort of happened." She shifted back and forth from foot to foot. She forced a smile, but it was as shaky as her breath. "Believe in the elixir or not, you just got exactly what you wanted."

As she stood there looking at him, everything in her wanted to ask him to stay with her. But she couldn't, and she wouldn't, not when this was the one thing he desired more than anything else. He deserved happiness and deserved to feel in control again.

"Congratulations. I'm happy for you, Ethan. Are you packed? Do you need any help?" She was rambling but couldn't seem to stop herself.

His smile fell from his face. He looked injured. "You are? No. No," he said, replying to her questions in sequence.

She rolled her shoulder. "Sure I'm happy. You told me it was your greatest desire. Now you get to go back to commanding fellow comrades. You must be thrilled."

She watched his throat work as he swallowed. He took one measured step toward her and scrubbed his hand over his chin like he was waging an internal battle.

"Not really," he replied soberly.

Looking lost, and a little forlorn, he stepped into her personal space and dragged her into his arms. His rich scent singed her senses and brought on a shudder.

They exchanged a long look, and then he drew a breath, as though centering himself. "Someone wise once told me that *there is no ambiguity in the truth.* So I'm going to lay it on the line and tell you the truth, Dani. Then it's your turn."

She nodded.

"You see, up until a few days ago, I never thought I'd feel like my old self again. But you changed all that for me. You gave me back my control, albeit in the bedroom. And when I lost that control again, it didn't seem so scary. Not when I had you in my arms. I always thought going back into battle and reclaiming my position was what I truly wanted and what I truly needed. Turns out I was wrong."

Danielle blinked up at him, hardly able to believe what she was hearing.

His eyes clouded, and she could feel his heart pounding in his chest. "I know you told me one night, but after spending so much time with you and making love with you all week, I know I want more." Emotions crept into his voice when he added, "We've been playing games all week, and now I want to play for keeps."

She swallowed, feeling the tension drain from her body. "You do?"

"Don't you see, Dani? It's not fellow comrades I want to command—it's you." His blue eyes glistened and his hands slid over her skin. "In the bedroom."

Her pulse leapt in her neck, heat bombarding her body. She met his probing gaze.

He gathered her against him and brushed a tender kiss over her mouth. Her throat clenched. God, being in his arms felt so right.

Her body responded to his touch and she became aware of the moisture between her legs.

"My destiny is in my hands, Dani."

She melted into him, her body aching to join with his. "I'm in your hands, Ethan," she whispered breathlessly.

He grinned. "Exactly." His hands slid to her ass, and she could feel his desire. Her nipples quivered in erotic delight. Her arms tangled around his neck, her fingers playing in his damp hair.

"Now, tell me. Is this just about fulfilling a fantasy for you, or do you want to play for keeps, too?" She watched the way he sucked in his breath and held it.

She took that window of opportunity to ease his worries and tell him exactly how she felt. "The truth is, I came here this afternoon debating whether to tell you how I felt, but the minute I looked at you I needed to feel you inside me again. I don't ever want to stop feeling you inside me, Ethan."

As he let out a burst of air and pushed back her bangs, she became aware of the passion rising in him. "Good. Then let's see where this crazy whirlwind relationship takes us."

Heart racing with excitement, she nodded eagerly and licked her lips. "There's nothing I'd like better," she said honestly. His mouth found hers for a deep, mind-numbing kiss. After a long moment, Danielle inched back. "You know, not only has the magic elixir fulfilled all my sexual desires; it has also fulfilled all my heart's desires."

Ethan threw his head back and laughed out loud. "You and that damn magic elixir."

She rolled her eyes. "Oh, he of such little faith." Grinning, she asked, "So where do we go from here?"

He touched her all over, like he couldn't get enough of her body. He nodded toward the lumber outside. "My destiny is working with my hands. I'd like to take up residence in Chicago and start my own carpentry business." He winked at her. "Maybe you could toss a bit of work my way."

She made a face and shivered when he slipped a hand between her legs. One simple touch made her delirious with pleasure. "Well, like I said before, I haven't seen your handiwork yet, so I'm not sure I can recommend you for any job," she teased playfully. Her libido was roaring to life.

His warrior features hardened to reflect the energy that filled the room. "Oh, I think you've seen my handiwork." With single-minded determination, he backed her up until the backs of her knees hit his bed. He pushed until she fell on it. His nostrils flared, his eyes glimmered with dark sensuality, and his gaze panned the length of her body as he made a slow pass over his bottom lip with his tongue.

Ethan grabbed his work apron and leather belt. Stepping behind her, he used them to secure her wrists to his bedposts. Her body started to shake, her cunt muscles trembling in anticipation.

Trembling with sexual need, she writhed against the mattress, ecstatic to submit to his control. "I wasn't referring to *this* handiwork, although I must say, you pass with flying colors." She could hear the need, the urgency in her own voice.

He stood beside her and brushed his knuckles over her hard nipples. He gave a low, rough laugh. "Oh, yeah?" he asked, his deep, sexy voice seducing all her senses.

"Yeah," she said, watching the front of his pants swell with need. Her body moistened from sexual fever and she gave a breathy moan.

He stroked her with expertise and then his hand trailed lower to slip under her dress. He pushed aside her panties and slipped a thick finger into her creamy core. She widened her legs for him.

With slow, torturous circles, his thumb worked her clit as his finger plunged deeper, slowly building her orgasm. Sparks shot through her body and heat blistered inside her, fragmenting her thoughts. Her breath hitched and she worked to think.

"Oh, yeah," she moaned. "I highly recommend you in this department."

He glared at her, his voice taking on a hard edge. "I highly recommend you in this department, who?" he bit out.

"I highly recommend you in this department, Master."

The Pleasure Pool

ONE

Ryan leaned across the pool table, positioned the tip of his wooden cue on the ball and took a shot, easily sinking the eight ball in the corner pocket. Fortunately, the bright artificial light overhead enabled him to see the table, even with his dark sunglasses on.

Six months previous, after an early morning surprise explosion had damaged his retinas and marred his skin, the glasses had become a permanent fixture on his face, hiding both his lacerations and his damaged eyesight. Now he wore the shades day and night, not that he went out much during the day, or was the wild social animal he used to be. Since he'd returned home from his overseas tour, he kept a low profile. The fewer people asking about his scars or prying into his personal life, the better.

He stood and glanced at Cody. "So, what do you think is taking Ethan so long? A man could die of thirst waiting for him."

"My guess is he's taken your stash of beer and made off with it," Cody said before grabbing the triangle and centering it on the table.

Ryan scoffed, adjusted his sunglasses and slapped his pool cue against his palm. "You'd think he'd know better," he said, grinning. "I can still track him down if I want to." Vision or no vision, Ryan's exceptional tracking skills and his memorization of the island's landscape meant Ethan didn't stand a chance.

Of course, both Ryan and Cody knew Ethan would never do anything of the kind. During their time together overseas and at the rehabilitation center, the guys had all bonded. The men were more than his friends and confidants. They were his family, his brothers. Men he trusted with his life.

Unlike the family he'd grown up in—an emotionally absent father plus a stepmother and two stepsisters who considered him a burden—and the longtime girlfriend who'd tossed him away faster than an armed grenade when he'd returned home injured, calling him damaged goods, these men all looked out for one another. Ryan knew he could count on his fellow comrades in the best and the worst of situations.

Cody's voice brought his attention back around to the game. "Ethan always was easily distracted," he said, gathering the balls from the pockets and sending them down the table. He shot Ryan a questioning look. "You think something shiny caught his attention?"

Ryan scoffed and gave a slow side-to-side shake of his head. "Yeah, something shiny, something sexy and something flirtatious."

One side of Cody's mouth turned up. "You saw that, too, did you?"

"Hell yeah. My eyesight might be damaged, but I'm not completely blind. Jesus, he was practically salivating over Danielle at dinner."

Cody positioned the balls, removed the triangle and grabbed his cue. "He needs a woman in his life. Maybe after a few good fucks he'll stop being such an angry son of a bitch." He paused and then added, "Hell, maybe that's what we all need."

Ryan couldn't deny that. It had been far too long since he'd held a woman in his arms, inhaled her sweet scent, felt her between his legs or sank into her tight heat. At the mere thought of getting laid, his mind raced to Lauren Sampson, the sweet yet sexy brunette who'd sat next to him at dinner. If he tried hard enough, he could still smell her fantasy-inspiring floral aroma. The scent was so goddamn erotic and stimulating, it nearly gave him a boner right then and there. Even her sultry voice had aroused him to the point of distraction.

He wondered what brought her to the exclusive resort. A woman as gorgeous as she was couldn't be here looking to fulfill a fantasy. She likely had countless men throwing themselves at her feet. The alternative was that she'd come here looking for therapeutic relaxation, an escape from the everyday. Yeah, that had to be it, he concluded. She had to be here looking for a little R & R.

As he leaned against his pool cue and watched Cody break the balls, Ryan took a moment to consider that further. If she was here looking for a fantasy vacation, he'd like to be the guy to give it to her. Sure, he could give her that wild ride, but he couldn't give her any more than that, because truthfully, he didn't have any more to give. Then again, what would a girl like her see in a guy like him, a guy who could barely *see* her in return?

Suddenly the words "damaged goods" echoed in his mind.

Cody gestured toward the table with a nod. "You want to go again?"

"Nah, I think I'll call it a night. I've got an early massage booked." Not to mention an afternoon appointment with his well-shaded hammock, his usual daytime hangout.

Cody nodded. "I'll catch up with you later, then," he said and turned his attention back to the pool table.

Ryan replaced his cue on the rack and made his way outside. As he left the air-conditioning behind, the warmth of the night washed over him and moistened his skin. In no time at all his clothes clung to his body like a second skin. Anxious to peel them off and jump into a cool shower, he carefully negotiated the stairs—but not carefully enough. On his last step his shins connected with the base of something concrete. He tripped and stumbled forward.

"Fuck," he bit out as he righted himself. He glanced at what appeared to be some sort of spiritual statue. Okay, that was new.

Once composed, he made his way to the footpath leading to his cabana. With the tall trees surrounding him, he paused to listen, amazed at how his other four senses had amplified after his injury.

The sounds of the night life closed around him, but there were no other footsteps to be heard. Small stones crunched beneath his feet as he followed the narrow path back to his place with ease. With a love of nature, and little else to do with all his spare time on the island, Ryan spent his evenings memorizing every footpath, every cave, and every nook and cranny at the resort.

When he reached his quarters, he tried the door. Shit. It was locked and Ethan had his key card. He knocked, but gut instincts told him Ethan wasn't inside. "Where the hell did he go?" he murmured to himself.

Ryan turned and made his way to the footpath, having decided to check Ethan's cabana. Concern had started to gnaw at his insides. It wasn't like Ethan to just blow them off.

"Out for an evening stroll?"

The voice came from behind him. Ryan stiffened and spun around. When his survival instincts kicked in, his hands automatically fisted. "Jesus. I didn't hear you come up behind me."

Malik lowered his voice to a calming level. "Are you out enjoying the warmth of the night, Ryan?"

Ryan tugged on his sticky T-shirt and pushed his hair from his forehead. "I'm locked out of my cabana. Have you seen Ethan? He has my key card."

"I saw him head up the mountain earlier this evening, toward the mood hut, I believe."

Ryan kept his face expressionless. "Did he seem . . ." He paused to find the right word, not wanting Malik to get the impression that something was amiss.

"Yes, he seemed fine; so did Danielle," Malik said, answering Ryan's question before he had a chance to ask it.

Ryan grinned, pleased as hell that it *was* something shiny that had distracted his friend.

"They seemed rather happy. I believe the elixir just might be working for the two of them."

The smile fell from Ryan's face. He didn't believe in the elixir any more than Ethan did. Ryan's strongest desire was to see perfectly again, and according to the team of doctors that had endlessly poked and prodded him, that wasn't about to happen, magic elixir or not.

As though reading his thoughts, Malik pressed his hands together and said, "You can see with more than just your eyes, my child."

His leg chose that moment to start aching. Ryan scoffed. "Tell that to my shins." Using the back of his hand, Ryan wiped a bead of moisture from his brow.

"The Pleasure Pool is a great spot to cool down," Malik said.

He had to admit, the idea of jumping into the refreshing pool of water did sound appealing, but he knew the chances of having it to himself were scarce.

Since Ethan's cabana wasn't too far from the Pacific waters, he said, "Maybe I'll head on over to the ocean for a dip and wait for Ethan to come back."

"Very well, then," Malik said with a nod. Before he left he added, "It's amazing what you can see with your eyes closed, Ryan."

With those cryptic words bouncing around inside his head, Ryan continued on his path. Strange thing was, he'd somehow gotten turned around in the dark and was now headed up the mountain toward the Pleasure Pool.

How the hell did that happen?

After their tour of Mr. Malik's temple, Lauren and Abby stepped out into the sultry night and watched Danielle disappear into the shadows.

Lauren arched a knowing brow. "I wonder where she is off to in such a hurry."

"Off to find her sea god, no doubt." Abby shook her head in amusement. "Damn, that girl works fast."

Thinking about all her own failed relationships, Lauren said, "Lucky girl."

Abby pulled a face. "More like lucky us. The chemistry between those two was explosive." She cut her hand through the air, gesturing toward the hillside. "I was worried they were going to blow like Mount Saint Helen's and take out the entire island."

Lauren chuckled. "Honestly, it's been far too long since Danielle has had a good, thorough fuck."

"Yeah, and Ethan looks like just the guy who could change all that." Abby slipped her arm inside Lauren's and squeezed. "I know I'm no sea god, but want to explore the island with me anyway?"

"Sure. Maybe we can take a dip in the Pleasure Pool and cool off." She wiggled her fingers and widened her eyes with optimism. "Hey, you never know, maybe our own Greek god will rise up out of the lagoon."

As they made their way to the path, Lauren thought more about Danielle and her fantasy man. Hopefully by now he'd be fulfilling all her secret desires. Out of nowhere, her libido stirred to life, urging her to find a man of her own and do the same.

Heck, since she'd pretty much given up on finding a guy who could look past her body and see her for who she really was, a man who didn't need to be looking at her nakedness to want and appreciate her, why shouldn't she indulge in a fantasy or two while on vacation? A smile touched her lips as she thought about the hot, enigmatic guy she'd like to play out a few of her secret desires with.

She took a moment to entertain her wayward thoughts. Dark, mussed hair, built like a damn linebacker—she was a Chicago Bears fan; everyone knew how much she loved linebackers—and as hot as hell, her fantasy man oozed sin and seduction. His rich alluring scent, a heady mixture of spice and masculinity, filled the air like a sultry invitation. He had an aura of mystery about him that she found a little dark, a little dangerous, and a whole lot sexy. He intrigued her, plain and simple. And even though she'd just met him, there was something almost animalistic about him that had captured her attention.

Too bad he seemed less than interested in her, barely sparing her a glance during dinner while he talked to the other men around the table. Then again, it was quite possible he could have been checking her out. It's not like she could tell where he was looking with those dark sunglasses cloaking his eyes.

She wondered if he was here for a fantasy-inspired vacation, or if he was an injured soldier. The way he'd kept to himself pretty much assured her that she'd never find out.

"I see you've both decided to take an evening stroll."

Startled, Lauren turned around to see Mr. Malik come up behind them. Noting how stealthy he was, she thought the man should wear a cowbell around his neck to announce his presence.

Mimicking his actions, Lauren nodded her head, returning his familiar greeting. "It's so warm out tonight, we thought we'd cool down in the Pleasure Pool."

Mr. Malik smiled and looked directly into Lauren's eyes. "It can be difficult to negotiate the dark jungle at night. You must be careful."

Lauren turned her head to glance into the mouth of the pitch-black path. There were likely scarier animals on the streets of Chicago than there were in there.

As though reading her mind he said, "My jungle is safe, and security is only a call away, but unless you know the landscape, it can be difficult to see."

"We'll make sure we keep our eyes wide open," Lauren said.

Mr. Malik qrew quiet for a moment, then added in a low voice, "Sometimes our eyes must be closed before we can really see, Lauren." With that he turned and made his way back to the temple. Lauren stood still and watched him go, her mind racing, sorting through his parting words.

Abby's voice drew her focus. "What do you think he meant by that?" she asked.

They began their ascent up the mountain. "Beats me. I don't understand half of what he's saying."

Abby chuckled. "He's sort of like a medicine man, isn't he? With more wisdom than we can even imagine."

"Then why doesn't he just speak in plain English? You know I'm not very good at puzzles."

Amusement danced in Abby's eyes. "There's no arguing that." She shook her head and added, "Maybe some things we're just supposed to figure out for ourselves."

As they moved deeper into the woods, the path narrowed and the natural foliage thickened. She glanced around, taking it all in, memorizing the landscape.

"Maybe we should have left a popcorn trail," Lauren murmured to her friend.

High overhead a canopy of leaves closed in over them, plunging them into darkness. Lauren listened to the strange night sounds, wondering whether venturing out into the wilderness after dark had been such a smart idea after all.

Abby's voice broke her concentration. "So, what do you make of the elixir? Do you think it really fulfills your deepest desires?"

No longer able to see Abby in the dark jungle, she turned toward her voice and let out a heavy sigh. "I don't know, Abby. My deepest desire is to find a guy who sees me and likes me for who I really am, one who can appreciate me for more than just my body. I've never met a man who wanted to have sex with the lights off, or even dimmed to create an erotic ambiance for my pleasure. Honestly, some day I would like for a man to talk into my eyes, not my breasts, and make love to *me*, not just my body."

Suddenly her ex-boyfriend's words came back to haunt her and she wondered whether he was right. Maybe she really was boring outside the bedroom, with nothing to offer a man but her body.

Abby squeezed her arm, offering comfort, and then rooted in her beach bag for her trusty pen flashlight. She flicked it on and pointed it forward. The narrow beam provided enough light for them to negotiate the path as they trekked onward, following the sound of rushing water. A short while later they stepped from the dark path into a moonlit clearing. Lauren took in the picturesque waterfall spilling over the smooth rocks. Cool mist reached the embankment and moistened their skin and clothes.

"This is absolutely gorgeous," Lauren said. She pulled her clothes off, keeping only her bra and panties on. After Abby followed suit, they climbed into the cool, silky water and slipped under the cascading stream.

"Mmm. So nice," Abby said. She moved backwards to let the ribbons of water pelt against her skin. After a moment of basking in the spray, she said, "Hey, did you know this is a magical lagoon and is supposed to attract love?"

Lauren nodded. "I read that in the brochure, but I've given up on love. I think I'll settle for a wild affair and live out a few of my fantasies instead. This island"—she paused to look around the jungle—"with its tall trees and thick foliage is the perfect setting, really."

Abby arched a manicured brow. "Oh, yeah? Perfect setting for what?"

"To play out one of my fantasies."

"Which is?"

Lauren hesitated and crinkled her nose. "It's silly. You don't want to hear it."

"Come on, tell me," Abby urged. The gleam in Abby's eyes turned wicked. Well, well, did Little Miss Abby have a few fantasies of her own? Lauren wondered.

Lauren glanced around the moonlit clearing and lowered her voice. "Well, since I've been in an orgasm drought, I figure I might as well use my feminine wiles and indulge in a little wild, animalistic sex. If men want me for my body, why shouldn't I just go with it, and take care of my sexual needs?" She pulled in a quick, excited breath as her mind raced. "Lord knows I could use a good fuck, too."

"And," Abby prodded, "who did you have in mind?"

She flashed her friend a playful smile. "I figure if I can't have my own sea god, maybe I could have a jungle lord."

"Jungle lord?"

"Yeah, someone wild, someone like Tarzan."

Someone like the man she'd met at dinner.

Heat bombarded her body and left her pussy quivering with yearning. She pressed her thighs together and shivered with need from just thinking about an untamed man of the jungle taking her under his care and giving her a good, thorough fuck after her six-month dry spell.

Abby let out a low whistle. "Wow, that's some fantasy, Lauren."

Lauren grinned. "I know. Wouldn't that be wild?"

Wild indeed.

Ryan hadn't meant to eavesdrop; he really hadn't. When he first heard voices coming from the Pleasure Pool, he'd turned, intent on leaving, but the sexy sound of Lauren's voice stopped him dead in his tracks. And when he heard the excitement, curiosity and lust in her tone, he'd nearly lost his ability to draw in air.

So she wanted to play a few jungle games, did she?

With her very own Tarzan.

He took a moment to run that scandalous scenario through his mind.

Late at night.

Shrouded in darkness.

Surrounded by foliage.

Identity camouflaged.

Oh, yeah!

Now, that was a fantasy he could easily fulfill.

He pulled his dark glasses off and squinted, catching the outline of Lauren's profile in the moonlight. Standing under the falls, she ran her fingers through her long hair. His mouth went dry as lust rose to the surface. His cock throbbed with an excitement he hadn't felt in a very long time as he envisioned himself lavishing her with his undivided attention.

The thought of stripping her naked and taking her like a carnal beast in the middle of the forest unearthed the primal animal in him.

From what he'd overheard, it appeared that she wasn't looking for anything that resembled a relationship, which suited him just fine, but that didn't mean they couldn't have a little fun together.

He began crafting a plan—a plan that would allow both of them to get what they wanted. As he plotted and tweaked the details, his heart beat in a mad cadence, eager to put his idea into motion.

TWO

Lauren was already a couple of days into her vacation, and instead of feeling relaxed and refreshed, she felt so restless, edgy and goddamn horny, she needed to take matters into her own hands. She kicked off her covers and cursed under her breath.

Hours earlier she'd fallen into a fitful sleep, throughout which sensually charged dreams intruded on her slumber, snapping her awake and leaving her hovering on the brink of an orgasm. Now, feeling needy and unfulfilled, her sex muscles were pulsing, demanding she do something about her current state of arousal.

Lauren slipped her hand between her legs, pulled open her blood-swollen lips and stroked her sopping-wet clit. As need drove her actions, her slow caresses became faster and more urgent. Her fingers picked up tempo, her breathing deepened and in no time at all her artful ministrations took her over the edge. A low moan crawled out of her throat as she rolled to her side and curled up, savoring each glorious, orgasmic pulse. After the tremors subsided, she blew a slow breath and stretched, noting with dismay that despite her efforts she still felt restless and needy . . . for a man's touch.

Damn, this magical island really was playing havoc with her libido. Not to mention Ryan Thomas. She was pretty sure the cock thrusting inside her during her erotic dream had belonged to him. Her body trembled and she drew a centering breath. She wouldn't have expected that a man she'd just met and had barely seen over the last couple of days could arouse such a fierce need in her.

God, that dream had felt so real. So raw, so wild and so damn delicious. Her skin flushed in remembrance and her body buzzed with pent-up need, aching to discover whether Ryan was as good in real life as he was in her dream.

It had to be his magnetic, animalistic lure that got under her skin and had her reacting like a wild, wanton woman. Either that or she really, really hadn't been fucked in a long time, and one glimpse of a hot, physically appealing hunk had awakened all her desires. Her mind raced as she wondered what it would be like to explore a rich, decadent affair with him.

With her body still burning from the inside out, Lauren let out a long-suffering sigh and wiped her damp brow. The air-conditioned cabana did little to help tamp down this kind of fever. Angling her head, she glanced at the clock and groaned out loud. Here she was, wide awake, and it was still hours before sunrise.

She decided she'd be better off getting out of bed and walking off her sexual frustration before she ended up with a throbbing headache. Lord knows, one throbbing body part was enough for the day.

She climbed from the bed, pulled on her shorts and tank top, slipped into her flip-flops and padded to her door. Before she stepped outside, she grabbed her favorite pink Chicago Bears ball cap and covered her long, untamed hair. She didn't expect to bump into anyone at this time of night, but still . . .

She made her way to the ocean, confident that a dip in the cool water would help douse the flames inside her. The light from the crescent moon overhead glistened on the spray and lit a pathway along the sandy shore as she walked. She dipped her toes into the Pacific and stood there soaking in the breathtaking scenery. Waves lapped at her feet and slapped against the rocks a few feet away from her. When she tipped her face to the moon, a gust of wind rolled in on a wave and blew her hat off her head.

She reached for it but was too late. It sailed away on the breeze and landed on one of the many footpaths leading up the mountain.

Lauren folded her arms and pursed her lips, debating her next move. She could wait until dawn to venture into the dark jungle, but by then her hat could be long gone. And, dammit, she loved that hat.

Gathering her bravado, she moved toward the jungle, wishing she had one of those cool flashlight pens like the one Abby always carried in her beach bag.

She squinted in an effort to see better, and then stepped into the mouth of the dimly lit path. She glanced around, but the canopy of leaves high overhead prohibited the moonbeams from breaking through. "Where the hell is it?" she cursed.

She took one cautious step farther on the path and glanced up when she caught the outline of someone blocking the walkway. Someone big.

Her heart picked up tempo as she struggled to see in the darkened jungle.

The shadows masking his identity made it impossible to discern his features. She could make out only his silhouette in the darkness. But his scent, his impressive size and his muscular physique told her that he was a man.

And she knew of only one man with a hard body like that.

Fighting a sudden surge of nervousness, she said, "Good evening," for lack of anything else, then added, "I lost my ball cap, and since it's my favorite hat I didn't want to wait until morning to look for it. I figure by then it will be long gone." She was rambling, she knew, but couldn't seem to stop herself.

He grunted something incoherent and advanced with purpose. His actions completely caught her off guard. In the next instant he was beside her, his hands on her hips. Taking her by surprise, he leaned forward, put his nose to her neck and inhaled. A low growl of longing crawled out of his throat. She fumbled backwards, her entire body stiffening.

He slipped one arm around her waist to anchor her to him, helping her gain her balance. "Easy," he whispered into her ear, his hot breath burning her skin.

Despite the way he'd purposely deepened his tone, that one simple word had given away his identity, confirming that it was indeed Ryan standing over her. She starched her spine and wondered what kind of game he was playing.

"What—"

He cut her off and spoke in whispered words. "Shh . . . Don't be afraid." His voice was soothing, coaxing and so damn hypnotic it pulled her under into a current of need and desire. His knuckles brushed over her cheek. "You're in safe hands." His deep tenor reverberated through her blood, and an unexpected curl of heat moved through her body. By small degrees her body relaxed. Ryan anchored her to him until skin touched skin. She became aware of his heat, and the passion rising in him.

He inhaled her scent again, like she was a female animal in heat, and growled. She couldn't deny that there was something very sensual and raw in his actions.

He leaned over her, and in a voice that was soft yet authoritative he said, "I can smell your desire, little one, and I'm going to take care of you."

She swallowed, hard, knowing he wasn't asking for permission, but instead telling her he was going to remedy her sexual longings. Every delicious one of them.

Holy hell!

She couldn't deny that she wanted this, wanted him, but she was also intelligent enough to know that he was purposely keeping his identity camouflaged. But why?

"I'm going to explore your entire body, and pleasure you like you've never been pleasured before. I'm going to make you come over and over again, and just when you think you can't take any-more, I'm going to fuck you until you come completely apart in my arms."

She trembled, but it wasn't from anxiety. Her knees wobbled with excitement, her pussy aching for this man's intimate touch. As her skin came alive, her breasts swelled and her nipples hardened in euphoric bliss. Suddenly, the air around them was charged with sexual electricity.

Filled with arousal, but not fear, she decided to play along, to see where this led them. She drew a fortifying breath and tilted her chin. "I'm not afraid," she murmured, glancing upward to see the outline of her ball cap on his head.

Her body stirred to life as he began circling her. He moved restlessly, like an animal marking its prey. She could feel the raw hunger emanating from him.

Walking slowly yet deliberately, he kept a tight berth and positioned his mouth so close to her flesh that she could feel the warmth of his breath on her neck. It burned through her skin and sizzled right down to her toes.

She stood watching him in speechless fascination. His primitive movements made her believe he was more animal than man. She couldn't fathom how much the thought excited her. As though attuned to her needs, he acted like he was about to launch himself on her and ravage her body, caveman style. With desire clouding her thoughts, her skin tightened and her pussy dripped in heated anticipation.

It suddenly occurred to her that Ryan had taken on the role of her very own jungle lord, her Tarzan. Her heart pounded with excitement. How did he know? Had he overheard her at the Pleasure Pool?

She took in his magnificent stature and inhaled, filling her lungs with his earthy aroma.

When Ryan grunted and brushed up against her, his primal

essence completely overwhelmed her—making it near impossible to move, to protest, if she had wanted to, but she was quite certain she didn't want to.

She narrowed her eyes and tried desperately to see his face, wishing like hell she'd had the foresight to grab a flashlight.

His hands, warm and strong, gripped her shoulders and pulled her from the beaten path. In a protective manner, one hand slid to hers and tugged, signaling his intent. Even though she knew she was acting out of character, primitive need propelled her forward. Abandoning any rational thought, she blindly followed, unsure how he could negotiate the dark forest when she couldn't see a thing. He either had excellent night vision or knew these woods like the backs of his hands.

They never spoke as he navigated them along a path less traveled. In a move that seemed to come naturally to him, he pulled her tight to his back, safeguarding her against the elements. His considerate actions told her this wild man had strength of character, and integrity. So different from the city animals she was used to.

She listened to the rustle of leaves as he cleared the branches from the trail. A moment later he stopped and turned to face her. His spicy, animalistic scent hit her like a powerful aphrodisiac.

His hands crushed through her hair as he grabbed her locks and pulled her head back, exposing the long column of her neck to him. A strange, primal, possessive growl ripped from his lungs. None too gently, he pulled her to him, his warm lips connecting with the hollow of her throat. He moved his mouth lower, trailing his tongue down her neck to the crevice between her breasts.

Taking a deep breath, he drew in her scent and licked her nipples through her T-shirt.

As he unleashed himself on her, her body spasmed with pleasure. Blistering heat exploded inside her, and she knew she wanted this as much as he did.

When she was no longer able to fight down her carnal cravings, she reached out to him, connecting her hand with a bare, rock-hard chest. Moaning her approval, she palmed his sinewy muscles. Her entire body quivered.

He stood to his full height and adjusted his footing, locking her legs between his, holding her in place. She could feel his cock pressing against her body. Almost dizzy with want, she tilted her chin upward, needing in some unfathomable way for him to claim her mouth the same way he was claiming her body.

When firm and hungry lips crashed down on hers, her senses exploded with an intensity that nearly drove her to her knees. Her legs wobbled and she locked them to keep herself upright. His soft tongue lashed out and tangled with hers, taking, demanding, never asking. Good God, never in her life had she experienced anything so wild or exciting.

When he broke the kiss, he left her breathless. She licked the moisture from her plump, kiss-swollen lips and savored the sweet taste his mouth left behind.

Seeking pleasure, she let her hands roam over his hard muscles. His flesh rippled beneath her touch. Her hands roamed lower to discover that he wore jeans. She opened the button and slipped one hand inside.

"Oh, God," she said when her palm connected with his hard

cock. "I want to see you," she murmured, stroking him once, then twice, brushing her thumb over the slit, dipping into the liquid arousal pearling on the tip.

He sucked in a tight breath and slipped his hand under her T-shirt, scattering her thoughts. She moaned and rubbed her pussy against him.

In one fluid movement, he tore her shirt off and tossed it aside. He pitched his voice low and growled into her ear, "Feel, don't think." With that he began to rock against her hand, his cock thickening with each stroke.

Deciding to abandon thought, she gave herself over to her desires and concentrated only on the erotic pleasures he was offering her.

He brushed his fingers over her flesh and palmed her curves. Her nipples quivered, demanding more. Her hand slipped from his pants when he dropped to his knees before her. Pressing his nose to her flesh, he inhaled deeply again. Her aroused scent saturated the air. The sweet aroma drove them both into a sexual frenzy. She wrapped her arms around his neck and pulled him to her.

Her jungle lord, her Tarzan, angled his head to position his mouth near her breasts. Flicking his tongue out, he circled her pale mounds, the blade of his tongue slowly approaching her engorged peaks.

"Take me," she murmured as she thrust her chest forward. That first sweet touch of tongue to nipple bombarded her body with lust. He blew a heated breath over her wet bud and then drew it into his mouth for a deeper, more thorough taste. His mouth closed around her extended nipple and bit down until she cried out in pain and pleasure. He changed tactics to give her a reprieve, kissing, licking and soothing her tight bud. She exhaled a shuddery breath and quivered in erotic delight. His hands continued to move over her soft contours while he began ravishing every speck of her needy body like a wild beast marking its mate.

Lust thickened her voice as heat burned through her veins. "Yes," she cried out, arching into his touch. "More." Hunger clawed at her insides and she became pliant in his arms. It was almost frightening the way she needed to feel him consume her.

With little finesse, he ripped her shorts from her hips, exposing her wet, naked pussy. He slid his hands around her body and cradled her backside. When he kneaded her tender flesh, she drove her pelvis against him and widened her stance in silent invitation. He growled his approval—his hands tracked the pattern of her curves, going lower to trail between her breasts, and over her flat stomach, coming to rest on her feminine mound. Deft fingers skimmed her folds and dipped into her wetness. Her pussy muscles began to undulate, begging to be stroked deeply where she needed it the most.

He opened her cunt lips and pressed a finger into her slick heat, pushing all the way inside her drenched pussy to stoke the fire inside her. As the rough pad of his thumb found her clit, a shiver wracked her body. Liquid heat rushed to the juncture between her legs. She grew dizzy at the scent of arousal in the air. He pressed another finger inside her and stroked her G-spot, instinctively knowing just how to touch her.

When a foreign noise crawled out of his throat, she sensed he was fighting down the primal beast inside him—a beast itching to plunge into her and stake its claim.

Her body convulsed as need consumed her and her liquid heat lubricated his hand. She felt wild, almost out of control, as he sank his fingers inside her.

Her heart beat in a mad rush as his feral, earthy scent closed around her, toying with her already overstimulated libido and playing havoc with her heightened senses. His burning mouth roamed her flesh as though he couldn't quite get enough. His heat branded each spot he touched on her body. The intensity between them was almost frightening to her.

He plunged deeper, stirring her desire. She moaned at the rippling approach of her orgasm. Erotic sensations traveled onward and upward through her body as his magical fingers drove in and out of her pussy, drawing out her orgasm. Fire licked over her thighs and before long the flames threatened to overtake her.

"Please . . . ," she begged him.

He pushed deep, stroking her, filling her with fiery need, until an explosion of color erupted before her eyes.

His deep growl sounded labored as his thumb applied the perfect amount of pressure to her clit. He sank another thick finger into her slick core, and the sensation turned her inside out.

Her body started shuddering as she came apart in his arms. He continued to feast on her, searing her clit with his tongue. Her sweet juices flowed into his waiting mouth. She gave herself over to her orgasm and bucked forward as his fingers and tongue took delight in her powerful release. Her nails dug into his shoulders when she tore at his flesh, but he didn't appear to mind the pain. In fact, the low guttural sounds rumbling in his throat seemed to indicate otherwise. She took deep, gulping breaths as her muscles tightened and clenched with each rippling wave of ecstasy.

After her tremors subsided, he climbed to his feet, never allowing his body to break contact with hers. She flicked her tongue over his lips, reveling in the taste of her own cream.

Restless to feel his cock in her mouth, to suck, lick and pleasure him in return, she shifted her stance and said boldly, "I want to taste you." Her voice wavered with husky desire.

Her Tarzan gripped her shoulders and pushed her to her knees. His eager fingers ripped his pants wide open, letting his huge cock fall into her hands. She inhaled his scent, then blew out a slow, unsteady breath.

Lauren moaned in delight and bent forward to draw him into her mouth. She worked her tongue over his substantial thickness and then widened her mouth to accommodate his girth, but there was no way she could take him all in. Her fingers slipped between his legs and cupped his balls. She squeezed them gently; he snarled. The savage sounds welling up inside him gained her attention and raised her passion to new heights.

She turned her focus back to his throbbing cock, sliding it in and out of her hungry mouth. She felt his balls tighten against his body and sensed he was struggling to hang on.

With a feathery light touch, she brushed her fingers over his balls, reaching past them to caress the skin between his sac and ass. Her fingers played around his puckered opening and his soft growl told her how much he liked it. Slowly, seductively, she eased her fingertip inside his sensitive cleft, urging him on.

As though that was all he could take, he whispered roughly, "Enough." His voice was raspy, strangled and unrecognizable. He gripped her hair and hauled her off him. She felt his untamed passion and his urgent, feral need to leave his mark, to claim her.

His breathing turned ragged. A fierceness overtook him—she felt it reverberate through her body. She listened to the rustling sound of him sheathing himself; then he backed her up against a tree and gripped one of her thighs, lifting her leg around him until it hugged his hip. The position opened her pussy to him. She pushed against him, offering him her body.

Groaning, he plunged into her heat. His mouth crashed down on hers, swallowing her erotic gasp. His rough, velvet tongue darted into her mouth. Pleasure forked through her. The feel of his cock jabbing her cunt aroused all her senses and reached so deep inside her, she thought she would die of pleasure.

Her pussy muscles gripped him and drew him in deeper. He pumped harder and faster until his balls slapped against her backside. He cradled her ass cheeks and pulled them open. One finger snaked around back and breached her cleft. He gave a low growl of satisfaction when she squeezed and wiggled his finger in deeper.

His cock pounded inside her while the width of his finger pushed open the tight walls of her ass. She tensed, then relaxed as his thick cock caressed her oversensitized G-spot, coaxing her next orgasm. She'd never felt anything so goddamn incredible. Her whole body moistened as she gave herself over to the sensations pulling at her. Her sex muscles clenched and vibrated as another rippling climax tore through her. She coiled her arms around his neck to hang on as she rode out every wonderful ripple of release, nurturing it and riding it out for as long as she could.

As her cunt squeezed him, he threw his head back, gave a loud Tarzan shout and erupted high inside her. His whole body shuddered with his powerful release.

Lauren squeezed her pussy muscles harder, holding him inside her, milking his climax, wanting to sustain the erotic, magical connection between them. At that moment she feared that she might never have such earth-shattering, untamed, fantasy sex again.

Panting loudly and trying desperately to catch his breath, Ryan held Lauren tightly against him. He took pleasure in the warmth and intimacy between them as he eased his cock out of her tight pussy.

As Lauren's hands raced over his naked body, Ryan thought about the way his body had reacted primally to her, even though it wasn't normally in his nature to do so. He'd never unleashed himself on another woman like he'd unleashed himself on her.

Single-minded determination to sink into her heat, to join them as one, had urged him on. Christ, he didn't have to pretend to be an animal; the second he felt her hot body next to his he'd become an animal. He winced and berated himself for his behavior. Delirious with pleasure and lost in the haze of lust, he had succumbed to baser instincts and he'd ravaged her like a feral beast in heat.

A soft moan from Lauren drew his focus and pulled him back toward her. Ryan pulled her tighter, brushing gentle lips over her cheek as he tried to shake the buzz from his head.

He couldn't deny that he'd enjoyed fucking her, and knew she'd enjoyed it too by her heated responses, but something in his gut kept gnawing at him. Sure, she wanted the Tarzan fantasy, but deep inside he suspected she deserved much more than a wild man mauling her.

"Hey," she murmured. He flinched at the touch of her soft, gentle hands on his face, wondering if she'd felt the scars beneath his eyes. He'd removed his glasses earlier, not wanting to wear anything recognizable, and had made sure to pitch his voice low when speaking to her. Her hands brushed over his lips and his jaw, then outlined the shape of his face. "I want to see you," she whispered into his mouth.

Goddammit, he wanted to see her, too. He wanted to see her face, her eyes and her body. He wanted to see her cheeks flush when she came for him. He wanted to open her soft folds and look at her gorgeous pussy. He wanted to watch her clit swell beneath his tongue. He wanted to rain gentle kisses over her flesh, every delicious inch of it, treating her the way a woman should be treated, instead of going at her like some fucking rutting animal.

He wanted a lot of things.

All things he knew he could never have anymore. He couldn't gamble with more than he was willing to risk. And he wasn't willing to risk her rejecting him because he was damaged goods.

She inched up on her toes. Her tongue made a slow pass over his bottom lip, tasting him. "Why don't we go back—"

Ryan pressed a finger to her lips and inched back. "Shh," he whispered, then gripped her hands and put them at her sides. Remembering he still had her ball cap on, he took it off and put it on her head.

She pushed it into his chest. "No, I want you to have it," she said with emotion thickening her voice. For some inexplicable reason, that small gesture touched him deeply. Perhaps it was because she'd told him how much the cap meant to her and she was willing to part with it, for him. Leaving him with a souvenir, something to keep the memories of their wild night together alive.

Needing to hold her a moment longer, Ryan dropped a soft kiss onto her mouth, greedily drawing her tongue in while he relished the sweet taste of her. As he captured her mouth in a kiss full of sensual promises, his hands raced over her body, trying to memorize every luscious curve, keeping it in the back of his mind to draw on later when he closed his eyes. Her soft, sexy moan triggered a ready reaction from his cock, but he quickly banked his desires.

Knowing dawn would soon be upon them, Ryan broke their heated embrace and searched the ground for their clothes. After they dressed, he guided her to the mouth of the path and turned her toward her cabana.

"Will I see you again?" she whispered. Her sultry voice bombarded him with a dozen sexual fantasies he ached to fulfill. Her hand connected with his face, and he felt a sudden flash of possessiveness. His whole body shook. Truthfully, he hadn't anticipated how deeply her intimate touch, or their sexy encounter, would affect him.

He hesitated for a moment, knowing he was unable to give her any more or pretend they had a future together. Stepping back from her, he said, "Only when you close your eyes."

THREE

auren took a quick shower, pulled on a new pair of walking shorts along with a lacy white tank top and hastily made her way to the ocean-view restaurant. She knew she was already fifteen minutes late to meet the girls for breakfast.

Although she'd gotten only a few hours' sleep after her sexy encounter with Ryan, she'd never felt more alive or more invigorated in her entire life.

She rushed into the restaurant and spotted Abby sitting by herself at the outdoor patio, engrossed in one of her sexy romance novels. A smile turned up Lauren's lips. Last night she'd felt like one of those heroines—a bold, sexually empowered woman who went after what she wanted.

Lauren crossed the wide expanse of floor to meet her friend. Trying for casual, yet feeling anything but, she smoothed her long curls and said, "Good morning. How's the book?"

"Great," Abby said, her face flushed. "I picked it up in the resort gift shop this morning."

Lauren glanced around. "Where's Danielle?"

"She called to say she can't make it. She's still off with her man, but she wants to meet us for a late lunch tomorrow." Abby narrowed her eyes, causing Lauren to squirm under her friend's scrutinizing gaze. "Forget about Danielle. I want to know what's going on with you," Abby announced.

Lauren offered Abby an innocent look, knowing after last night she was anything but.

Wild and untamed, yes.

Innocent, never.

"What?" Lauren asked, studying her menu.

Abby took a sip of coffee. "Don't 'what' me. Look at you."

Lauren glanced at Abby's pretty sundress and then glanced down at her own casual attire. "What, not appropriate for breakfast?"

Abby waved her finger at her. "You're glowing, Lauren, and I've seen you glow before, but never like this."

With a grin, Lauren dropped her menu and leaned in, deciding to entrust Abby with her secret. "That's because I've never had wild fantasy sex with my very own Tarzan before."

Abby's blue eyes widened. "Ohmigod, you're kidding me!"

Lauren shook her head. "If I didn't have the love bruises to prove it, I wouldn't have believed the experience myself. Trust me, it was so wild and perfect that for a while there, I was pretty sure it was all just an erotic dream."

Abby angled her head, glancing around the busy dining room. "Who is this Tarzan guy?"

"He never told me his name," she said truthfully. "Heck, I never even saw his face," she added to mess with her friend's mind. All she knew was that under the cover of darkness, her fantasy man appreciated *her* and pleasured *her* without having to ogle her body.

Abby's smile collapsed. She straightened in her chair and fixed Lauren with a look that clearly indicated her disbelief. "You have no idea who the guy was?"

"I have an idea, of course, but I haven't confirmed it one hundred percent yet," she said, smoothing her friend's ruffled feathers. "You see, last night I couldn't sleep so I went for a walk. Next thing I knew, I found myself in the jungle having wild animal sex."

Abby paled. "Are you insane?"

Lauren went to work on fixing her coffee, like having monkey sex with strangers was something she did every day. "I might very well be."

Concern grew in Abby's eyes. "Lauren—"

She knew it was reckless of her, but she believed Ryan was out to pleasure her, not harm her. She knew it the second he wrapped his arms around her.

"Relax, Abby. It's okay. I'm okay. I'm pretty sure I know who ravished me," she assured her friend. She couldn't have explained why he wanted to keep his identity a secret; she just understood that he did.

"You don't know what kind of crazies could roam the jungle at night. You could have been killed."

"Well, it sure felt like I'd died and gone to heaven." She gave her friend a wink and added, "A few times." With Abby still watching her in concern, she said, "You heard Mr. Malik; his jungle is safe, and security is only a call away."

"So this guy gave you the best sex of your life and he didn't even tell you his name."

Lauren shrugged. "For some reason he wanted to keep his identity a secret." She stirred sugar into her coffee and took a small sip. Her gaze surfed over the patrons dining nearby, and she wondered whether her fantasy man was in the restaurant. As she thought about Ryan, she wondered what else he hid behind those glasses. Maybe it was time to get to know him better, to explore his animal magnetism. "I think I need to do a bit of investigative research."

"You're the business manager of the decorating boutique, not a journalist. Remember what happened the last time you did a bit of investigative research."

Okay, so she ended up getting kicked off the school newspaper. Surely her skills had improved since then.

Turning serious, Abby asked, "Are you going to see him again?"

She let out a long sigh and remembered Ryan's parting words. "Only when I close my eyes."

Abby gave her a perplexed frown, then said, "I still think you're crazy."

She closed her hand over Abby's. "It wasn't like that. It was wild, yet safe, and he was carnal *and* protective. You had to be there to understand."

Averting her gaze, Abby looked out over the ocean, drifting into her own thoughts. When she brought her attention back around to Lauren, her eyes were alive with curiosity. In a low voice she said, "I can't imagine ever doing anything like that, Lauren."

Despite what she said, her friend seemed to have a glimmer of interest in her eyes.

Lauren glanced at the sexy couple posing on Abby's romance novel. "Why not? Wouldn't you like to experience deep passion like the heroine in your novel?"

Abby shrugged and held up her book. "Men like this don't really exist." She tucked her book away in her beach bag and grabbed the menu. "I'm starving. Let's eat."

Lauren wasn't deterred. "Tell me, Abby. Does Artie do it for you in bed?"

She hesitated before admitting, "Well, he can be a bit repressed." In his defense, she added, "But he's no different than any other man I've ever been with."

Lauren flashed a grin. "Well, he's a lot different than the man I was just with." After a pause she softened her voice and added, "Don't you want your nights filled with passion, Abby?"

"Men like that don't exist, Lauren."

Lauren glanced around the restaurant a second time. "Sure they do. Let me find one for you. Before you go back home and settle into your marriage with Artie, and have two point four kids— not that I think there is anything wrong with it if that's what you want—why don't you let the magic of this island take hold, live a little and have a wild affair."

Lauren glimpsed the fire in Abby's eyes before she blinked it away. "I don't know, Lauren."

So she was interested. . . .

Lauren gestured with a nod. "Come on, Abby, look at that guy over there."

Lauren watched Abby scan the room. Her gazed settled on Cody Lannon, the hot guy they'd met at dinner. Tall, with mussed light hair like he'd just crawled out of bed, and contrasting dark eyes—the guy was as sexy as hell. There was something about him that reminded Lauren of a caged animal.

"How about Cody?" Lauren asked, testing her friend. "He looks like he could get the job done."

Abby scoffed. "Not only is he distant and cool; he represses his emotions, Lauren. He's no different from any other guy I've ever met. Face it; wild, passionate men exist only in fiction."

"You're wrong, Abby. Think about it. What happens when a caged animal is let free? It goes wild. Maybe, through your erotic touch, you're just the girl to help him unearth those buried emotions. Then you'll see that wild, passionate men exist in real life, too."

Abby arched one manicured brow. "You think?"

Lauren watched Abby's responses. "Just think: not only would you get what you want; you'd be helping him in the process."

Abby laughed. "Yeah, I'm a regular philanthropist, Lauren."

"Wouldn't you want that guy to strip you naked and run his tongue all over your body?"

Abby's eyes glimmered with dark sensuality. A ruddy hue colored her cheeks. Gone was her hesitation; in its place was intrigue. Her telltale actions urged Lauren on. "Wouldn't you want him to unleash all that pent-up energy on you, until you climaxed all over him?"

"More than anything," Abby whispered under her breath.

"Then you might need a couple of these." Lauren grabbed a

handful of condoms from her purse and dropped them into Abby's beach bag.

As moisture gathered between Lauren's thighs, her whole body quaked in remembrance of her Tarzan's erotic touch. With heat coloring her skin from head to toe, a shudder overtook her. She clamped her legs together, having momentarily forgotten where she was. "Wouldn't you want some guy to talk dirty to you, telling you all the delicious things he's going to do to your body? Close your eyes, Abby, and let your imagination run wild."

Lauren let her own eyes drift shut, and a low moan of longing crawled out of her throat. She gripped the table and began gently tossing her head from side to side. "Hot, passionate, fuck-you-up-against-a-tree sex. Oh, yeah; now, that's what every girl needs, at least once."

What the fuck was she doing?

With her back to him, Ryan couldn't see her face, but he could hear her, and what he was hearing was giving him a goddamn boner. Lauren was making sexy bedroom noises, like she was reenacting last night's encounter with him.

Fuck, he knew he shouldn't have followed her into the restaurant. Not only was her nearness making him breathless; her scent was obliterating any control he had left.

After his morning massage, he'd planned to head back to his cabana to sleep the day away, but the second he glimpsed the silhouette of Lauren rushing into the restaurant ahead of him, his plan had changed.

He followed her inside, made his way to the outdoor patio,

and chose a table in the corner, where he hoped to go unnoticed. When he caught the scent of her provocative aroma, and her bold, sexy words reached his ears, he damn near erupted on the spot. As her scent called out to him, his lust clawed to the surface, urging him to get up, gather her into his arms and answer that call. All night long.

Ryan worked to tamp down his lust, but his dick betrayed him, refusing to cooperate. The woman oozed a sensuality that stimulated his body as well as his mind, and he wanted her like he'd never wanted another.

So much for going unnoticed. Any second now the table was about to levitate from his hard-on, and that was really going to raise all kinds of unwanted attention.

Christ, he ached to taste her, smell her and run his tongue over her sweet pussy again until she creamed in his mouth. He wanted to feel her hot little body writhe beneath him as he drove his cock in and out of her tight cunt. He wanted her to call out his name. He wanted her to want him.

Ryan, the man.

Not Ryan, the Tarzan man.

That last thought caught him completely off guard.

His nostrils flared. His fingers fisted. A low groan of frustration welled up in his throat.

Okay, he needed to get the fuck out of there and gain control over his body before he acted on his urges; otherwise, he was going to haul her off to the nearest corner and fuck her. And a girl like Lauren deserved more than a quick fuck.

To give his cock a moment to retreat before he made his exit, he took a moment and let his mind drift, thinking about the woman he'd ravished in the woods. Why would a woman as sweet and gorgeous as Lauren be here on this island looking for a man to fulfill her fantasy? Had no man ever satisfied her before, or looked below the surface to see what she really wanted? From last night's encounter alone, he knew she was warm and compassionate, passionate and daring, adventurous and uninhibited.

Surely she wanted, even expected, more from a man?

As her voice seeped under his skin, it suddenly occurred to him that he wanted to be that man. He wanted to be the guy to peel away the layers and get to know the real Lauren. After the intimacies they'd shared the night before, something in his gut told him she just might be different from his ex—someone who wouldn't see him as damaged goods and bolt the first chance she got.

Just then Malik stepped up to his table, pulling him back to the present. "Did you find what you were looking for last night, Ryan?"

If he was talking about a crazy night with an amazing woman, then the answer was yes. Ryan shifted, notably uncomfortable, wondering whether Malik knew what he'd been up to. He certainly wouldn't want to put Lauren in an awkward situation.

Before he had a chance to answer, Malik said, "I take it you managed to get into your cabana."

Relieved, Ryan said, "Yeah, I got a new key card from security."

After a long pause, Malik said, "It's nice to finally see you out during daylight hours. Perhaps you've decided to join us on the sailing excursion?"

No matter how many times he asked, Ryan's answer would always be the same. "I think I'll pass. I have better things to do." Plans that involved a hammock and memories of the previous evening.

"That's unfortunate, Ryan. I thought the other guests would benefit from your knowledge of the jungle and learn from your tracking skills during their exploration of Pearl Island. I'm sure you could teach them many things."

Jesus, he was sick and tired of Malik trying to get him to be a tour guide and teach guests about the woods. "I don't track anymore."

Malik twisted sideways. "Lauren, Abby, good morning."

Shit. Ryan adjusted his glasses. He wasn't prepared to see Lauren just yet.

Lauren turned around. "Good morning," she said. "I didn't see you two there."

"I was just asking Ryan if he'd be joining us on our cruise and exploration. But he said he had better things to do."

Ryan listened to her shift in her chair and could feel her scrutinizing gaze on him.

"You both plan on attending, don't you?" Malik asked.

Lauren's friend Abby spoke up. "Count me out. Lauren is the adventurous one, not me. I have a book to finish, and then I think I'll just explore this island instead."

"Abby, perhaps you'd enjoy our water activities instead. We have snorkeling lessons later this afternoon."

"Oooh, sounds like something I just might try," Abby replied, sounding excited.

Seemingly pleased with Abby's enthusiasm, Malik turned his focus to Lauren. "Lauren, perhaps you can help me convince Ryan to come along to Pearl Island. I thought he'd make a great guide and could share his knowledge of the jungle with us."

Ryan watched Lauren push her hair off her shoulder and lean forward. His mind raced to last night and how he'd tugged that long, silky hair of hers to expose her creamy neck.

Her voice pulled him back. "Honestly, Ryan, I would love for you to come. You see, I like adventure, but coming from the city, I get lost easily. So trust me, I can use all the guidance I can get." She gave a soft chuckle and continued, "I can find my way around any department store, especially the shoe department, but put me in the woods and I'm done for." After a short pause she sat up straighter in her chair and added, "Do you know your way around the woods, Ryan?"

She was testing him, he suspected. He rolled one shoulder. "No."

Malik piped in. "Don't be modest, Ryan. Few men have your exceptional tracking skills."

"Had," he bit out. "Past tense."

"Had?" Lauren asked. He could hear the curiosity in her voice.

"Yeah, had," he said, figuring she might as well know the truth. He watched her carefully under the bright light of the sun, gauging her reactions. "Ever since the explosion damaged my eyesight, I don't do much tracking anymore."

"I see," she said, sinking back into her chair, disappointment apparent in her voice. As he read her body language, he scoffed inwardly, hating that for one second he'd allowed himself to think she might have been different from his ex-girlfriend.

With that sobering reality, he stood quickly, sending his chair sailing backwards. "If you'll excuse me, I have to go." He hastily made his way from the restaurant. It was time to put Lauren out of his mind once and for all. They'd had one night of wild sex, nothing more.

Which made him wonder why he'd taken a left on the footpath instead of a right and now found himself headed toward the sailboat.

FOUR

As Lauren watched him go, she couldn't help but feel disappointed that he wouldn't join them on the sailing excursion. Maybe he really did have better things to do. Or maybe he thought she'd be boring in the light of day.

When she thought about his damaged eyesight, she had a moment of doubt. How could a visually impaired man negotiate the jungle with such ease, the way her Tarzan had? But surely she couldn't have been mistaken about her lover's identity.

After she finished her breakfast with Abby, the two of them took a stroll around the resort, and then Lauren made her way back to her cabana to fill a beach bag. She tossed in a swimsuit, lotion, bug spray, a change of clothes, bottled water, walking shoes, and a granola bar in case she got lost. She might be a city girl, but she was going to be a prepared city girl. Then she made her way to the wharf. She glanced around, her gaze surfing over the boat, aptly named *The Cascade*, and then perusing the intimate crowd that had gathered for the excursion. She recognized a few familiar faces from the restaurant.

Their tour guide stepped onto the wharf and summoned their attention. "Welcome, everyone. I'm Ben, your captain for the day." Lauren turned her attention to him, taking in his sun-kissed blond hair, surfer-boy tan and easy demeanor. "Before we set sail and explore Pearl Island, I'd like to take a moment to go over the rules." Lauren could imagine that with his playful, bad-boy grin he had women swooning at his feet. Granted he was cute, but she preferred her men tall, dark and handsome. Cliché or no, that's what appealed to her.

"Rule number one is to have fun," Ben said. When chuckles originated in the crowd, he took on a serious tone and added, "Rule number two is to never venture anywhere on Pearl Island alone. We have a buddy system here, no less than two people. So if you would all take a moment to buddy up, we'll be set to go."

Turning her attention away from Ben, she lifted her hand to block the sun. She glanced around in search of a companion when she noticed Mr. Egotistical—muscles flexed—coming her way. His walk, his facial expression and his arrogant attitude told her exactly what the stud was interested in. And it wasn't her personality.

He hooked his thumbs on his swimsuit, letting it ride down low on his hips, as if that would entice her. She resisted the urge to retch.

"Hey, dollface, how would you like to be my *buddy?*"

Lauren had met lots of cocky, pretentious men in her life— heck, she'd dated a million of them—but this wolf made those guys look like puppies.

She stood before him, watching his slow perusal of her body. Okay, that was enough. It was time to shut this guy down. She tilted her chin and held her hands up. "I—"

"There you are, sweetheart. Sorry I took so long."

Just then Ryan came up beside her, gathered her into his arms and pressed her to him. She swallowed, noting with equal measures of curiosity and intrigue that there was nothing impersonal in the way he was touching her.

He brushed a wayward strand of hair from her face. The intimacy of his gesture caught her off guard. His arm tightened around her waist and he held her the same way her Tarzan had last night. His touch eased any doubts she had and confirmed what she already knew.

Ryan and Tarzan were one and the same.

When she let her arm slip around him in return, the sizzle between them was instant and all consuming. She looked at his sensuous mouth and ached to feel it on her body again.

She shook her head to clear it and placed her palm on his cheek. "There you are. I was wondering if you were going to make it," she said, playing along.

Putting on a good show, he positioned his mouth near her ear and spoke in whispered words. "I wouldn't miss it for the world, sweetheart."

Mr. Egotistical murmured a few unsavory expletives and stormed off.

Once he was out of earshot, Lauren dropped her hand, inched back and smiled. "Thank you."

He grinned. "My pleasure. The guy was an asshole."

She made a face. "That's not the first name that came to my mind. You're being generous." She took note of the way his palm lingered on the small of her back. Her body warmed all over as the heat from his fingers spread under her skin. A wave of desire and need whipped through her blood. The rush of sexual energy hit her so hard that she nearly lost her balance. She dusted her hands off, needing to lighten things up before she lost all composure.

"I was just about to take care of him," she said.

Amusement laced his voice. "I know. I just thought it would be fun to mess with him."

Oh, it was fun. Fun, sexy and arousing.

She rolled her eyes. "I was just about to toss him over the wharf, but I suspected, with his bloated ego, he'd likely float anyway."

A rich rumble of laughter sounded in Ryan's throat and bombarded her body with erotic sensations. A shiver tingled down the length of her body, pausing at each erogenous zone along the way.

With Ryan up close and personal, she allowed herself a moment to admire his roguish good looks and wondered whether he ever took those dark glasses off.

She arched an inquisitive brow, her pulse kicking up a notch. "Have you decided to come along after all?"

His face tightened warily. "No."

"Too bad. I really need a buddy for the excursion. Plus I'd like to check out these tracking skills you have."

"Had," he reminded her.

"I'm sure it's like riding a bicycle."

He adjusted his dark glasses. "I can't see well enough to track anymore, Lauren."

"I'll tell you what. You come along and I'll be your eyes."

A look she didn't understand crossed his face. "Yeah?"

"Sure." She glanced around. It appeared everyone else had already buddied up. "Either that or I'll be stuck with our new friend over there." With a nod she gestured toward Mr. Ego. "I'd hate to find myself alone in the jungle with him." She mock shivered.

He dipped his head. "I thought you said you could take care of him."

He was playing with her, she knew, but the truth was, she liked it. She liked him. A lot.

"Oh, I can." She stopped to flex her girly biceps. "But it was so much more fun watching you mess with him. Plus, if I get lost in the woods, I'd really like to have someone with enough knowledge to get me back to shore. Remember, I'm a city girl."

He offered her a lopsided smile and shook his head. "More likely you'll be getting me back to shore."

Goddammit, he was cute when he grinned at her like that. She batted her lashes playfully but wasn't sure whether he could see her or not. "I think between the two of us, we'll manage."

When he lowered his tone, a delicious warmth spread across her skin. "You're very persuasive, Lauren."

"One of my many skills." She tucked her hand into the crook of his arm, giving him little choice in the matter. "Shall we?"

Together they made their way onto the sailboat and took their seats. When Ben proceeded to give a history lesson on Pearl Island, she leaned in to Ryan and spoke in whispered words. "You know, Ryan, I've never sailed before." Then, in an even lower voice she said, "I've only been here a couple of days and already I've done a few things I've never done before." She watched him, looking for a reaction. When none came, she tilted her face back, letting the sun warm her skin as she gazed up at the deep blue sky. "Now, this is the life." When the wind caught the sail and jolted her forward, her eyes sprang open and her stomach lurched.

As though sensitive to her discomfort, Ryan grabbed her and quickly engaged her in conversation, an attempt, she knew, to keep her mind off the choppy waters. She appreciated the gesture immensely.

"I hear Pearl Island received its name from pirates who used to bury their loot there," he said.

When the boat turned, she sagged against him. Being so close to him was playing havoc with all her senses, not to mention her hormones.

"Really. Has anyone ever found anything?" she asked, intrigued.

"Nope, but maybe we'll be the first."

She relaxed into the conversation. "Yeah, especially with your knowledge of the woods and your tracking skills."

His mouth slanted. "I could probably track a pirate, but I can't track a buried treasure."

Enjoying their easy banter and interested in learning more about him, she asked, "So, tell me, have you always had great tracking skills?"

"They're learned, but I will tell you, I kicked ass at hide-and-seek when I was a kid."

Lauren laughed. "You sound like my older brothers. I could never hide from them. Somehow they always had an edge on me.

Then again, other times they let me hide for hours, knowing full well where I was."

He gave a soft laugh. "You sound like you were close." She heard an ache of longing in his voice.

"If you consider daily noogies and wedgies close, then yeah." She gestured with her head. "Since you did such a good job with stud boy over there, maybe I'll have to bring you home with me so you can put them in their place too." She winked. "Payback is such a bitch."

After they shared a chuckle, Ryan said, "It sounds like the perfect family, Lauren."

She nodded, getting the sense that he longed for the same thing. "Yeah, I love those two boneheads despite all the hell they put me through." After a moment she asked, "Do you have any brothers and sisters?"

His posture noticeably tensed as he answered her. "Two stepsisters. Both much older than me. We weren't what you'd call a well-adjusted family."

In an attempt to ease his discomfort, she said, "I'm not sure you could call daily noogies well adjusted, either, Ryan." When he laughed, she relaxed against him. They both fell into a comfortable quiet as they stared out over the sunlit ocean.

"This place is an oasis," she whispered. Before she knew it, the boat came to a stop and the anchor was set.

Ryan nudged her. "Come on, we have to take the zodiac to the shore."

"Zodiac?"

He brought his hands close together. "Think smaller, rougher waves."

She made a face. "Great."

He reached out and squeezed her hand. "Don't worry. I won't let anything happen to you."

Fortunately, the boat ride to shore was uneventful. They shared the zodiac with Kayla and Blake, a couple who had recently found love at the resort and believed the magic elixir had everything to do with it.

Once they reached the sandy beach, Lauren slipped off her sandals and squeezed the warm white sand between her toes. After luxuriating in the warmth, she pulled on her walking shoes and grabbed her bug spray. She coated every inch of her body, then turned the can on Ryan. Once he was sufficiently covered, she tossed the can back into her bag and threw the bag over her shoulder.

Ryan coughed and waved away the fumes. "You really are a city girl, aren't you?"

She angled her chin and grinned. "Hey, play nice or I'll rub my honey granola bar all over you. Then we'll see who's laughing after our excursion."

When he threw his head back and laughed out loud, her insides turned to mush. She grabbed his hand and glanced around at the gorgeous foliage in search of a distraction. She inhaled, pulling the sweet scent of the landscape into her lungs. Birds took flight as the other guests moved through the jungle, invading their habitat. She wondered what kind of wildlife lived on the uninhabited island, wishing she'd paid more attention to Ben's discussion.

"Come on, there's a walking path just up ahead." She tugged on his hand.

As they negotiated the footpath, Lauren turned to Ryan. Desire stirred inside her as she gazed at him. "Ryan, you never did tell me where you were from."

His lips quirked. "That's because you didn't ask."

"Are you always such a smart-ass?"

"It's a gift," he teased.

She feigned exasperation. "Okay, I'm asking."

"Well, before I joined the forces I lived in Ohio."

"Will you be going back there after you leave here?"

"I'm not interested in going back."

Lauren swatted at a bug, noting how warm and sultry the midday air had become. "Why not?"

He shrugged, brushed a bead of moisture from his forehead and avoided answering her.

"So, who is she?"

When he offered her one of his sexy lopsided grins, she nearly creamed in her panties. "Perceptive, aren't you?" he asked.

She took a moment to gloat. "Very. I once thought about a career as an investigate journalist." She crinkled her nose and added, "But that didn't work out so well for me."

He angled his head. "No? Too bad. I bet you would have been good at it. You're very . . . nosy . . . I mean, inquisitive."

She swatted him. "Hey."

Ryan moved a branch to clear the path. His actions reminded her of their Tarzan encounter. God, she still couldn't believe that she'd had wild monkey sex with him last night. Nor could she understand what kind of game he was playing, or why he came to her under the cover of darkness. She could ask him, of course, but if he was so intent on keeping his identity a secret, he'd likely deny it, or if by some small chance it really wasn't him, he'd think she was crazy. Or a cheap slut. Which could very well be the case.

"Seriously, I'd rather work at the boutique than as an investigator."

As they ventured farther into the jungle, the tall trees obscured the sunshine and darkened the walkway. She noticed how Ryan's steps slowed, becoming a little more cautious. She abandoned his hand, slid her arm through his, and pulled him to her.

"Boutique?" he asked. "Tell me more."

"My friends and I own an interior-decorating business. Danielle and Abby are the brilliant designers, and I'm the accountant, taking care of all business matters."

He shivered.

"What?"

"You're an accountant. . . ."

"And?" she urged.

He grinned. "And . . . I don't find you the least bit boring."

She chuckled lightly. "No? Really? Not even a little?"

He laughed. "Fishing, Lauren?"

"Hell yeah."

"Okay, I find you interesting, exciting, funny, adventurous and intelligent." When he stopped she blinked up at him. "Shall I go on?" he asked.

She crinkled her nose in thought and then said, "No, that's good for now." She laughed as her insides fluttered with joy.

He didn't find her the least bit boring.

She brought the conversation back around to him. "Tell me more about this girl back in Ohio."

With a bemused expression on his face, he said, "Perceptive and relentless."

"That's me."

"It just didn't work out for us."

An uneasy feeling closed in on her. "Are you still pining after her?"

"Hell no."

O-kay, so that big wave of relief really took her by surprise. "So we hate her, then?"

Ryan laughed. "I don't hate her. She had to do what she had to do."

"And what exactly was it she had to do?"

Ryan shook his head before giving her a wicked smile. "Like I said, nosy—"

"Inquisitive," she corrected, loving how easy he was to be with, how much she enjoyed his playful side.

"Right, inquisitive." He grew quiet for a moment and then said, "When I came home injured, she left me. Said I was damaged goods." Lauren watched him carefully, sensing he was sharing something very private with her.

"Well, you might not hate her, but I do." Lauren stopped to pull a water bottle from her bag. She took a slug and offered Ryan a drink.

"Thanks." He took a long swallow and handed it back to her. As they continued forward, Ryan asked, "What brought you to this island, Lauren?" She heard real interest in his voice. "Did you come here because of the magic elixir?"

"I don't put much faith in it, but if it works, then great, especially where Abby is concerned. Danielle and I are hoping that after some time away from her soon-to-be-fiancé, Abby will see that marrying him isn't her deepest desire. We're hoping she'll indulge in a wild affair and come to understand that not all men are emotionally reserved."

His voice turned serious. "Do you believe all men are like that?"

"No. But I do believe that the men I attract only want me for my body. Honestly, if the elixir really does work, my desire is to find a man who appreciates me for me, without needing to see my body. A man who looks at me, and talks to me, not my breasts." She tipped her head and glanced at his dark glasses, the angle of his head letting her know he was looking into her eyes. "Sort of like you're doing right now. Then again, I guess you can't really see my body."

"I can see your body."

His sexy tone caught her off guard, and then suddenly, the air around them changed.

"Oh." She swallowed. "How much can you see, Ryan?"

"Some days, enough. Other days, not enough." The sensuality in his voice felt like an intimate caress.

"Today? How much can you see today?"

His powerful muscles bunched as he closed the space between them. He dipped his head and she quivered in response. He caught hold of her hand and the world around her faded. With his mouth close to hers he said in a husky tone, "Not enough."

Just then the couple they'd chatted with on the boat stepped into the path, breaking the magical moment. Ryan inched back.

"Hey, you two; we're having a bonfire down at the beach. Come join us." Kayla hooked her arm through Lauren's and tugged.

A few minutes later, they all hunkered down onto the sandy shore with the rest of the group. With Ryan so close to her, Lauren had a hard time concentrating on conversation. Everything about him played havoc with her libido as well as her emotions.

Lauren spent the next few hours watching him as they sat around the fire. She watched the way he moved, the way he talked and the sexy way he angled his head and cast a glance her way when he felt her eyes on him. She especially loved the way the sea breeze ruffled his mussed hair when he looked out over the horizon.

Hours later, after the marshmallows had been eaten and group conversation had dwindled, Lauren turned to Ryan and picked up their conversation where they had left off. She appreciated how they could talk about everything and nothing. She kept her voice close to a whisper, ensuring that their conversation remained private. "So, tell me, what's your deepest desire, Ryan? If the magic elixir was true, what would be the one thing you'd want?"

He rolled one shoulder. "Naturally, I'd like to be able to see again and go back to my old job."

Lauren grew quiet for a moment and then asked, "What will you do when you leave here?"

"I don't know. If I'm not in the field anymore, what good am I? My skills have no value anymore."

Just then she yawned.

Ryan laughed. "Am I boring you?"

He was anything but boring. She couldn't believe how much she enjoyed his company. She loved being with him, just talking, as they got to know each other better. The other men she knew certainly weren't interested in engaging her in conversation.

"No, remember I'm a city girl and I sit at a desk all day. I guess I'm just not used to so much sunshine and exercise."

He nodded. "It seems like everyone is packing up. We should, too."

"Yeah, I think I'll be calling it an early night tonight. Especially after last night."

"Last night?"

"I didn't get a whole lot of sleep." She studied him, giving him time to confess that he was her mysterious lover.

"Traveling does that to me for days on end, too."

Upset that he continued to hold his secret close, she stretched out her fatigued limbs. "I'm so tired, I could sleep through a hurricane." She glanced up at the sky, noting the dark clouds moving in on the horizon. A low rumble sounded in the distance.

When Ryan smiled at her, she drew a breath, deciding then and there that Ryan Thomas was the perfect package. A man who gave her the best sex of her life during the night and treated her like a woman during the day.

Now, if only he'd admit that Ryan and Tarzan were one and the same . . .

FIVE

Okay, so maybe she couldn't sleep through a hurricane, after all. Shivering, Lauren pulled the covers up to her neck and listened to the gale-force winds pound against her small cabana. The clock beside her flickered with the threat of a power outage.

Damn, this was kind of scary. She wondered whether Danielle and Abby were just as afraid. Deciding to go check on her friends, she climbed from her bed and pulled on a pair of jogging pants and a matching gray jacket. After slipping into her running shoes, she crept to her door. When she pulled it open, lightning crackled overhead and she nearly jumped out of her skin.

She glanced back at her clock and noticed it had powered down. When she turned back to her door, she came face-to-face with Ryan. He stood outside in the pouring rain, wearing a yellow slicker with the hood pulled over his head.

He reached out and covered her hands with his. "Lauren, are you okay?" She heard genuine concern in his voice.

Despite the chill in the air, everything inside her warmed when she looked at him. She pulled him inside, out of the pelting rain.

"I was just on my way to check on Danielle and Abby. Some storm, huh?"

"Yeah, power is going down all over the resort. I came to check up on you."

Her heart skipped a beat at his thoughtfulness. "I'm okay." It was a half-truth. Normally she wasn't afraid of storms, but normally she wasn't on a secluded island in the middle of nowhere surrounded by huge trees, either.

"Everyone is headed up to the lodge. The generator is going and they've built a fire in the stone fireplace. I believe there are even marshmallows and hot chocolate."

Her stomach rumbled, and not in a good way, at the thought of more marshmallows. "Sounds cozy."

"Do you have a raincoat?"

She'd come to the island prepared for two weeks of sunshine. "I never thought to bring one."

"Here, we'll share mine."

He opened his huge coat. When he hauled her inside, she melted against him. Okay, that was it. That sweet gesture could easily cause her to fall in love with him.

As he ushered her outside, his body protecting her from the elements, she asked, "What about my friends?"

"I'll walk you to their cabins so you can check up on them."

Lauren tried Danielle's cabin first and found Danielle and Ethan inside with tangerine-scented candles lighting up the room.

The ambiance inside the cabin seemed very warm despite the fierce storm outside. Danielle had assured her that they were quite happy to wait out the bad weather in her cabana. Lauren suspected her friend was in very good hands and moved on to Abby's cabana. When a search of Abby's room showed it to be empty, she worried her lower lip.

"Let's check the lodge," she said.

They hastily made their way to the lodge. Ryan opened the door and guided her inside. Lauren glanced around, letting her gaze surf over the crowd, but Abby was nowhere to be found. She frowned in concern. "Do you think she's okay?"

"I think," Ryan said, a grin pulling at his face, "that my buddy Cody is taking good care of her."

"Really?" Lauren asked, both surprised and delighted. Had Abby taken her advice and let the magic of the island take hold of her? She sure as hell hoped so.

When Ryan peeled a wet strand of hair from her cheek, desire twisted inside her.

"Something tells me Abby is just fine. After we returned from Pearl Island, I saw her and Cody together. Trust me, you can count on Cody. He won't let anything happen to her. But if you're still worried—"

She cut him off and brushed her hands against his without conscious thought. She entwined her fingers through his. "Ryan, if you say she's okay, then I know she's okay."

She watched something in his expression change, soften, and in that instant everything inside her reached out for him. She shivered with longing.

As though mistaking her reaction, Ryan bent close, so close she could feel his warm breath on her face, and rubbed her arms, creating heat with friction. With a tender expression, he said, "Let's get you something warm to drink; you're shivering." The sexy cadence of his voice covered her like a soft blanket.

She looked at his mouth, aching to feel his lips on her body. Blood pounded through her veins as desire jolted her. She drew air, in an effort to compose herself. "You grab us a seat by the fire, and I'll get the drinks."

A moment later she snuggled in next to Ryan, ignoring everyone else in the room. As the storm raged outside, soft firelight cast shadows on the stone walls. The warmth and ambience drew her into a cocoon of need and desire. The Asian décor set the mood for romance and relaxation. Reclining against him, she sipped her hot chocolate and fell into an easy conversation. Every now and then Ryan touched her, his hand brushing her arm or legs, making intimate contact.

She took pleasure in his features and noted that his skin had darkened after a day in the sun with her. Now that he was tanned, he definitely fit the cliché of tall, dark and handsome.

She touched his cheek to draw his attention to her. "There is something I've been wanting to ask you."

Ryan offered her a smile. "Ask away."

"Why do you wear those glasses at night?"

At first silence met her words; then he said, "I'm more comfortable with them on."

What was it he didn't want her to see?

"What color are your eyes?"

He pulled his glasses down his nose a tiny bit and peeked out over the top. "Blue."

She drew a shaky breath and moistened her lips. They were blue all right, but not just any run-of-the-mill blue—they were the most amazing shade of blue she'd ever seen.

With concerted effort, she spoke calmly, "Your eyes are gorgeous, Ryan."

She detected a glimmer of vulnerability in the depths of his baby blues before he adjusted his glasses, pushing them back in place.

"So are yours." He lifted his steaming mug. "They're like warm chocolate."

That took her by surprise: She didn't fully understand the extent of his damage. "I wasn't sure if you could discern color."

"Just a bit, and only in the right light."

Suddenly, Lauren yawned. Fatigue was overtaking her.

His soft chuckle seeped under her skin. "There I go boring you again," he teased. "Come here."

He put his arms around her and pulled her close. She inhaled his warm scent and gave a soft sigh. "Why don't you try to get some sleep," he suggested.

She let her eyes drift shut, enjoying his comforting touch as they took shelter from the storm outside. She didn't sleep; she just stayed there, realizing how dangerously close she was to falling for him. She couldn't deny that she was feeling something for him. How could she not? They talked and laughed, and they shared intimacies that she'd never shared with another, and for the first time she felt that a man saw her for who she really was.

After a long time, Ryan whispered into her ear. "Lauren, the storm is settling. Let's get you back to your cabana. You're exhausted." He stood and eased her from the sofa. When he yawned, she knew he was dead tired, too.

The sun began its ascent as he walked her back to her cabana. She noted how he moved with such confidence, such ease, so different from the way he walked on Pearl Island.

She squeezed his hand, and giving him an opening, she said, "For a guy who can't track anymore or see very well, you sure have no trouble getting around this resort."

"I've been here a while and have learned the landscape." Then suddenly, as if he'd given too much away, he changed the subject. "What are your plans for tomorrow? Any big adventures?"

"I'm meeting the girls for a late lunch, and then I have a massage booked. After that I thought I'd do a little skydiving," she teased. "Want to join me?"

He laughed. "I'm afraid you're on your own. Tomorrow I have a date with my hammock. I've been neglecting her lately, and I have a lot of catching up to do."

She chuckled and turned to him when they reached her door. Her laughter died off when he brushed the pad of his thumb over her bottom lip. Her pulse quickened, and she moistened her lips.

Ryan leaned in, dropped a soft kiss onto her mouth and said, "Get some sleep." The first touch of his lips to hers sent her heart racing. As he turned to leave, she pressed her fingers to her mouth and knew something better than she knew her own name. She was falling in love with Ryan.

* * *

Ryan couldn't sleep, not with Lauren preoccupying his thoughts. He'd gotten up at midday and met with Cody for a game of pool. They talked for a while, and Ryan noticed that Cody seemed distracted and was acting completely out of character, especially when Cody brought up the subject of Abby Benton, asking what Ryan knew about her. Except for her impending engagement, Ryan knew very little.

After the game, Ryan took to the jungle. He spent the rest of the daylight hours walking and thinking, sorting through matters.

He'd come to one final conclusion. He was crazy about Lauren. So goddamn crazy about her, she had *him* acting out of character, too. Shit, could that be Cody's problem as well? All Ryan knew was that if he didn't feel her in his arms again soon, he was certain he was going to go mad with need. He ached to hold her, to kiss her, to have her crawl inside him so he could keep her forever.

Lauren was bright, real and down to earth. He couldn't ever remember having such a wonderful time with anyone. During their time together, they'd opened up to each other and talked, really talked. For the first time in a long time he'd let his guard down with someone.

Surely he'd read her body language wrong at the restaurant the previous morning. During their afternoon excursion and over a mug of hot chocolate he'd gotten to know her better, and she'd shown real interest in him, despite his injury.

Darkness closed in on him as he made his way along the footpath. With the ground still soaked from last night's heavy rainfall, he moved with caution, not wanting to slip on the wet jungle floor.

A shriek up ahead caught his attention. Moving quickly, he rushed along the path and spotted Lauren climbing to her feet. He couldn't see her face in the dark but instinctively knew it was her. The minute he saw her, he knew he had to have her again immediately. His body instantly became aware of her proximity. He needed to feel her in his arms, between his legs. He needed to feel her warm body next to his, to make love to her the way she deserved.

When he'd decided to be her fantasy lover come to life, he had no idea how she would affect him. His interest in her now went much deeper than just a wild night of Tarzan sex. He was completely unprepared for the emotions she brought out in him. What the hell did he expect, really? Lauren was one hell of a fun-loving, adventurous, giving woman.

"I was looking for you," she whispered, her voice dark with desire.

Awareness flared through him as he weighed her words carefully. Here she was, alone in the dark.

In the jungle.

Late at night.

He knew exactly whom she was looking for.

Her Tarzan.

He couldn't deny that he felt a quick stab of jealousy. He was falling hard for Lauren, yet she still wanted sex from her fantasy man.

Pushing his jealousy aside, he removed his glasses. He ached to pleasure her the way she deserved to be pleasured, to give her exactly what she wanted.

As he listened to her work to get the mud from her clothes, everything inside him softened. His protective instincts came out in full force.

He walked up to her, slipped his arms around her waist and pitched his voice low, the same way he had the last time he'd ravished her in the jungle. "Come with me," he whispered. Ryan guided her along the path until they reached one of the many huts strategically scattered throughout the island. He grabbed a few blankets, a torch and a couple of bottles of water.

He felt her shiver with excitement. "Where are you taking me?" she asked. Her voice sounded eager.

Continuing with his role, he grunted and ushered her into one of the dark caves that he'd discovered during his explorations.

Once they were inside, he spread a blanket and lowered her onto it. He walked outside and lit the torch, providing them with enough light to create a cozy ambiance in the cave, but not enough for her to discern his features.

"Where are you?" she asked. He could hear her moving around in the dark, reaching for him. "I need you." Her voice was so achingly gentle that everything inside him softened.

"Shh," he whispered and settled down next to her. "It's okay. I'm here."

He touched her face, his fingers outlining her jaw. When he felt the remnants of mud, he grabbed one of his water bottles and poured a generous amount onto the corner of a blanket. Crowding her, he dabbed her with the makeshift washcloth and cleaned her face.

When he heard her small gasp, and her hands connected with his arms, his voice came out sounding unstable. "Are you hurt?"

"No," she murmured seductively. Her breathing grew a little erratic. "I've never felt better in my life."

As he cleaned the mud from her skin, he felt her body move under his touch in a telltale show of her needs. Waves of pleasure thickened his cock, and he fought the desperate need to plunge deep inside her tight sheath. If he wanted to give her what they both craved, he needed to gain control of himself first. His heart pounded so hard in his chest, he feared it would burst through his rib cage. He gave a lusty groan and clenched his jaw.

He felt her hands caress his face, then slip around his neck. Sexual heat flooded him as she pulled him to her. Groaning, he put his lips over hers, pillaging her with his mouth. He drank in her sweetness, yet still couldn't quench his thirst. A deluge of passion overcame him. Every nerve in his body came alive. He deepened the kiss while his hands roamed over her skin and caressed every angle, every lush curve.

Lauren thrust her pelvis forward to indicate her needs. Her hands intertwined in his hair. "Please, I need you inside me. I need you to fuck me," she whispered, giving a small, impatient whimper. He felt the rush of her warm breath over his cheeks.

Ryan sucked in air, hungering for her in ways that almost frightened him. He had every intention of fucking her, but first he wanted to introduce himself to her body, slowly this time, so he could savor every inch of her, and treat her the way a woman deserved to be treated.

Despite the raw desire searing his insides, and the lust settling deep in his groin, he forced himself to slow down.

"Easy, baby, easy," he murmured.

He brushed his lips over hers, trailing kisses over her jaw, and then buried his mouth in the deep hollow of her throat, where he could taste her skin and inhale her feminine aroma.

The heat of her body scorched him, flooding his senses with need. He stroked her neck and could feel the elevated thud of her pulse. She moved against him, and her sexy moan echoed in the dark cave, closing around them. Needing to have her completely naked, Ryan gripped her shirt and pulled it off. He touched her skin and was pleased to discover that she wore no bra.

His mouth trailed lower until he reached her full, delicious breasts. With intimate possession, he circled her nipples with his tongue. She tasted so goddamn sweet, it was all he could do not to ravish her and fuck her senseless.

He spent a long time savoring her breasts, treating each to a luxurious tongue bath until she moaned in delight.

"That's so good," she murmured breathlessly, as though lost in the sensations. His fingers began a slow journey up her thighs, coming perilously close to her sex. He could feel the heat radiating from her pussy. It called out to him in ways that made him mad with pleasure.

He slipped a finger inside the leg of her shorts, feeling the dampness of her panties. A jolt of lust ripped through him and nearly shut down his brain when she bucked against him. He loved how wet and wild he made her.

She writhed, undulating against his hand, her aroused scent saturating the cave. He listened to her shaky breath.

Tightness settled in his chest. "What do you want, baby?" he asked. "Just tell me and I'll give it to you."

"I want your finger inside me. Please . . ."

Ryan tugged aside her panties and gently brushed the pad of his thumb over her swollen, passion-drenched clit. Oh, fuck . . .

"Is this what you want?" he whispered roughly. When he breached her opening, she began trembling from head to toe. God, he loved how responsive she was.

She wiggled her lush backside, and the sudden need to plunge into her, to claim her, overcame him.

"More," she begged shamelessly. Lust and impatience colored her voice, making it barely recognizable as she whimpered for release. He could almost feel the heat whipping through her blood. "I need more. I need it harder and deeper."

He inched back and listened to the hiss of her zipper as he removed first her shorts and then her panties. He gripped her legs and spread them wide open. He climbed between her thighs and idly stroked her cunt with the pad of his thumb. She was so hot when she opened up for him like that.

As he took in the outline of the woman lying beneath him, everything in him ached for her, and he knew no matter how many times they made love, it would never be enough to satisfy him. His cock pushed against his zipper, clamoring for attention, reminding him that he was still completely overdressed.

His voice dropped to a whisper. "I want to fuck you with my tongue first. I want you to come in my mouth so I taste your cream."

"Yesss . . ." she murmured and offered herself up to him. Her fingers moved to his chest, where he felt her tug at his shirt.

"I want to touch you, too," she purred, the sound low and sultry as her eager hand trailed lower. "I want to feel your cock."

Fuck, he loved how she wanted him, how eager she was to please him in return. He took a deep breath as a barrage of emotions caught him off guard.

When her palm closed over the bulge in his pants, he caught her hand and positioned it beside her. Right now he wanted this to be all about Lauren, about giving her everything she'd ever wanted, everything she'd ever needed. He wanted to show her how desirable she was, inside and out, and show her how a woman as amazing as she was should be treated.

"Don't think; just feel," he reminded her, inching open her damp lips with gentle fingers. He felt her small tremors and knew she was close. Leaning forward, he brushed his tongue over her cunt. That first sweet taste nearly sent him spiraling out of control. "Fuck, you taste amazing." With that he delved in deeper, licking, sucking and pushing his tongue inside her until her entire body quaked with passion.

Her fingers raked through his hair and held him to her pussy. "God, yes," she bit out. "Don't stop. Don't ever stop."

With no intention of ever stopping, he scraped his thumb over her clit and pushed one finger up inside her, where he luxuriated in her tight heat. His cock jumped with anticipation; so goddamn anxious was he to sink into her cunt it nearly broke through his zipper. He pumped in and out of her and continued to brush expertly over her G-spot.

Her breathing changed, became deeper, but he wasn't ready to bring her over just yet.

He wasn't nearly done feasting on her hot pussy. When he eased back, she nearly sobbed.

In a haze of lust, she cried out, "No, don't . . . please." There was a frantic edge to her voice. Her hand went to her pussy to finish herself off, but he pulled it away. He'd be the one bringing her to orgasm tonight.

"Up on your knees," he commanded. He put his palm on her stomach and felt her shiver with excitement. "And spread your legs for me. Wide."

Once she'd taken her position, he slid between her thighs and gripped her hips. "This way I won't lose a drop of your cream."

"Oh, my God," she whimpered.

He widened her slick lips with his tongue and pulled on her until she straddled his mouth. Her swollen clit brushed against his upper lip as it screamed for his attention. Like a cat tasting its cream, he lapped at her pussy and said, "Fuck my mouth, baby, and come for me. Let me taste you."

Her sharp intake of air pleased the hell out of him. She began moving, riding his mouth hard, driving her pelvis back and forth against his face while making sexy noises, the kind that drove him into a frenzy of need. As he inhaled her rich, sensual scent, he tongued her tight opening and then turned his attention to her lush clit. He kissed her hungrily and lashed at her pussy with his tongue. A shudder ripped through him as he savored the exotic taste between her legs.

He could feel small ripples start at her core and begin to take over her body. He slowed his pace and applied more pressure to her clit, instinctively knowing what she needed to orgasm. As he kept up his gentle assault, stirring the fire inside her, she arched her back and drove her pussy against his face. He could feel her clit throbbing against his mouth. He spanned her waist with his hands and held her against him, pulling her oversensitive clit into his mouth. When he dragged it between his teeth, a tremor wracked her body.

That's a girl.

Her skin tightened over his mouth, and a moment later he felt her splinter into a million pieces. Her breathing turned ragged and her body quivered in delight.

"I'm—" was all she managed to get out as she creamed into his mouth, her liquid heat drenching his face. She took deep, gulping breaths as he drove her beyond the brink of sanity. Their moans of pleasure blended as the air in the cave grew thick with the scent of their lovemaking.

Using gentle strokes, he brushed her cunt with his tongue, drinking her creamy nectar while she rode every delicious wave of ecstasy.

When her body stopped vibrating, she slid down his chest and collapsed on top of him. Her lips found his just as her warm fingers brushed his hair from his face.

"That was perfect," she whispered into his mouth. Her hands roamed over his jaw. With a soft, gentle touch she explored the angles of his face. "So damn perfect . . ."

As she nestled against him, he wondered if she could feel the pounding of his heart. Wondered if she knew it was pounding for her. "You're perfect," he said, pulling her lips to his. She shimmied lower as he kissed her, until his cock brushed against her wet opening.

She put her mouth close to his ear and whispered, "I need you inside me." Her breath whispered over his skin, and the urgency and need in her voice amped up his desire for her. He wound his arms around her and held her close, their moist bodies sealing together. She wiggled, teasing his dick between her lips. Her soft moan gave way to a lusty groan. She slid down farther, settling her sweet ass on his legs, and grabbed for her shorts. A moment later he felt her sheath his cock. Goddamn, he loved a woman who came prepared.

She shimmied forward until his dick nudged her damp folds. "You know how I like it," she whispered.

"Yeah, baby, I know how you like it." Fueled by his need to fuck her, his body began trembling intensely. Dragging in a huge breath, he gripped her hips, pulled her onto his shaft and then sank all the way inside her. With a little cry, she straightened her back, gripped his hands and moved them to her breasts. A rumble of pleasure sounded from the depths of her throat as he kneaded her tender flesh.

His body convulsed as his cock pushed open the walls of her cunt. Her heat scorched him. Jesus . . .

"I want you so much, baby," he whispered into the dark as he indulged in her body, her pussy doing delicious things to his cock.

"I . . . want . . . you . . . too." Her words came out broken, choppy. He loved the way she wanted him, the way her beautiful body reacted to his.

"Show me," he whispered, stroking her lust-swollen nipples. "Show me how much you want me, sweetheart."

With need consuming them both, Lauren adjusted her body and

began riding him, impaling herself on his rock-hard cock. Her erotic whimper made him crazy with lust. He slipped one hand between their bodies and massaged her sensitive cleft. She pitched forward, letting him know without words how much she loved his touch.

He was delirious with pleasure, and the room began to spin. He stroked deep, fully aware that he was seeking more than just her heat.

"Your cock is so perfect," she murmured, while tossing her head from side to side. "I love how you fill me."

His whole world shifted as her liquid desire dripped over his cock. When he felt her soft wet quakes massage his shaft, his body nearly went up in a burst of flames. A thin sheen of perspiration covered his skin. His body rippled with pleasure, and a low growl ripped from his throat.

She leaned forward and gripped his shoulders hard enough that her nails bit into his skin. Her hair fell forward and brushed over his skin like an intimate caress.

"Oh, God, yes, Ryan."

He hovered on the brink of an orgasm, so lost in a haze of lust, he couldn't make out her words, couldn't comprehend what she was saying. All he could do was focus on the intense pleasure between his legs as she lifted her hips up and down, driving his cock in and out of her tight cunt, ravishing him with dark passion.

Muscles trembling, he powered upward and drove inside her. He buried himself so deep, he'd never find his way out. But he didn't want to find his way out. He wanted to lose himself in her heat forever.

Her muscles clenched around his cock. Yesss . . .

"Harder," she bit out as her orgasm approached.

Together they established a rhythm, each giving and taking in tandem. He swallowed and pumped faster, joining her in release.

"That's so good," she whimpered, coming all over his cock. Her moan of joy echoed in his head and filled him with satisfaction.

Ryan closed his eyes to give himself over to his orgasm. He arched his hips forward and released inside her.

After a moment she rolled beside him and snuggled in close. With exquisite gentleness, her hands trailed over his body, palming his muscles. There was something deeply intimate in the way she was touching him.

"I love how you feel inside me." The emotion in her voice generated a sense of possession inside him. "We're so good together."

"Come here," he murmured, impressed that he managed to form a sentence, and pulled her to him. His mouth settled on top of hers.

They traded warm kisses for a long time, until exhaustion overtook them both. Ryan knew dawn would soon be upon them. Despite wanting to hold her longer, he knew he needed to walk her back to the mouth of the cave before sunlight hit and she discovered his identity. Tomorrow, when he was thinking more clearly, he'd talk to her, tell her who he was and how he felt about her. Right now he just wanted to bask in the afterglow of their beautiful lovemaking and enjoy this magical moment.

"I need to walk you back," he murmured.

Lauren snuggled in tighter. "Soon."

He closed his eyes in surrender and contentment, letting his emotions rule his actions. Something that felt like love whipped through his veins, and he knew, with each passing second, that he was falling harder and harder for her.

SIX

Ribbons of early morning light drifted in through the mouth of the cave and covered their bodies in a warm golden glow. Lauren rose on one elbow to watch Ryan sleep, enjoying the soft noises he was making and the slow rise and fall of his chest.

As she gazed at his hard, naked body, she quivered in delight. Heat moved through her bloodstream as she remembered every delicious minute of last night's—all-night—lovemaking marathon. Over the course of the evening, she'd experienced an intimacy with Ryan unlike anything she'd ever experienced with a man. Through his gentle touch he'd proven to her over and over again that he cared about her as a person, not an object. He'd found her interesting and exciting in the light of day, and in the dark of night had made sweet love to her. To *her*. Lauren the woman, not Lauren the hot body.

Even with impaired vision, he could see her for who she really was and had a talent for knowing exactly what she needed.

Lauren remembered her advice to Danielle over a late lunch the day before that she should just go have fun with her fantasy man, have a good fuck and get him out of her system once and for all. But despite her advice, she couldn't ignore the churning emotions inside her. She was head over heels in love with Ryan. And she wanted a lot more than just wild Tarzan sex from him.

Her attention glided over his face. Her heart swelled as she reached out and brushed her fingertip lightly over the scars beneath his eyes. Now she understood his fears, his vulnerabilities and why he'd always kept his dark glasses on.

The words "damaged goods" ran through her mind, and it occurred to her just how much his ex had hurt him, how deeply her words had cut. She knew firsthand how cruel words could create doubt and damage. But Ryan had helped her dispel her innermost fears. Her fingers fisted as her heart ached for him, and his deeply ingrained scars.

She knew last night when she'd run into him that he'd immediately fallen into his Tarzan role. Since he was so intent on keeping his identity a secret, she went along with the role-playing. Even though she didn't fully understand it, she respected his need for privacy. When she'd called out his name in the midst of an orgasm, she suspected he was too far gone to grasp the meaning.

She ached to wake him, kiss him and spend the afternoon making love inside the cave, but she was also smart enough to know he wasn't ready for that. Deep in her gut she knew he wasn't quite ready for her to reveal that she had discovered his identity.

She pulled a blanket up to cover his naked body as she went in search of her clothes. After dressing, she quietly left the cave. She needed time to think. Time to figure out how she could show him what he meant to her, and that his injuries didn't mean he was damaged goods. She liked him for who he was on the inside.

As she negotiated the damp footpath, a movement up ahead caught her attention. She glanced up to see Mr. Malik coming her way.

"Good morning, my child."

"Good morning," she said, feeling suddenly sheepish. Did he know she'd spent the night in a cave making sweet love to the man she was absolutely crazy about?

"Where are you off to in such a hurry?"

"I . . . uh . . . was just heading back to my cabana."

"You look . . ." He paused and then said, "Flushed."

She fanned her face. "Yes, it must be this tropical air."

"The Pleasure Pool is a great place to cool down. It's very private this time of the morning, as well."

She nodded, silently agreeing it was the perfect spot to spend some time alone, where she could think about how to get Ryan to come out of the dark, overcome his insecurities and see that she liked him for who he was. "It sounds perfect."

Mr. Malik loosened two red sashes on his robe and handed them to her. "I think these might come in handy." With that he turned away from her, but before he left he commented, "We can see with more than just our eyes."

Lauren stood there staring at the pretty red sashes dangling from her fingertips, when understanding dawned.

Oh, yeah, she knew exactly how to open Ryan's eyes and get him to see. By blindfolding him.

*   *   *

Jesus H. Christ. She was gone.

Ryan felt a quick flash of panic as he rubbed his eyes and ran through the events of the previous night. He hadn't meant to sleep through the night, hadn't meant for the two of them to wake up together and for her to discover his true identity like this. Not like this . . .

His stomach plummeted. He'd only wanted to close his eyes briefly, only wanted to hold her a bit longer before he walked her back to the mouth of the cave. He'd figured tomorrow he'd find a way to tell her who he really was.

Lauren had gone to bed with her Tarzan and had woken up with Ryan. Was she angry that he'd kept his identity a secret? Or had she seen his scars and bolted, realizing how physically damaged he was?

His mind raced, sorting through the recent turn of events. Goddammit, he knew she wasn't like that. She was sweet, caring and compassionate, everything he'd ever wanted in a woman.

So was he going to just let her walk away?

Hell no!

The surge of warmth and love that filled him pushed back old insecurities and fears. He needed to find her, to tell her how he felt.

He wanted to talk to her, to explain why he'd ravished her in the dark and kept his identity a secret. He wanted to tell her about his fears and insecurities, and tell her what she meant to him. He never was one to go down without a fight, and he wasn't about to now. Because unlike other women in his life, Lauren was worth fighting for.

He stood, dressed quickly and stepped out into the sunshine. No matter where she was on the island, he'd find her. Deciding to put his tracking skills to use again, he set out to hunt her down. He'd tear the whole damn resort apart until he found her, if that's what it took.

When a search of her cabana turned up empty, he began to stalk around the resort, watching and listening for any signs of her.

"Is everything okay, Ryan?"

He turned around to come face-to-face with Malik. "Yes, everything is fine," he said, keeping his personal matters, well, personal.

"You look like you're about to tear the resort upside down."

"I'm looking for something."

"Something or someone?" When Ryan didn't answer, Malik said, "It's nice to see you put your tracking skills to good use again. You see, Ryan, just because you're not in the field anymore doesn't mean your abilities have no value."

Okay, so maybe he did still have some value, but right now that wasn't the most important thing on his mind. Finding Lauren was.

"I believe what you are seeking is at the Pleasure Pool."

Heart beating in a mad cadence, Ryan said, "I don't have time for your cryptic words right now."

"Check the Pleasure Pool, Ryan, and you'll *see* everything in a new light."

Ryan quickly made his way to the Pleasure Pool. When he spotted Lauren's silhouette under the falls, his heart began to race. He slowed his steps, unsure of her mood, fully expecting her to be angry for his deceit.

When she spotted him, she swam to the side of the pool and climbed out. "Good morning," she said in a low murmur.

He gathered her hands in his and read her body language, only to discover there wasn't a trace of anger to be found there. He took a deep breath and said, "Lauren, about last night—"

"Shh," she whispered.

"I need to tell you something," he insisted.

Undaunted, she brushed against him, touching him with intimate recognition, and rushed on, "First I need to show you something." She tugged on his hand. "Come with me."

"Where?"

"Into the water."

Ryan peeled off his T-shirt, kicked off his shoes and climbed into the Pleasure Pool with her. He followed her to the waterfall. She turned to face him once they were standing waist deep in the water. When he felt her remove his glasses, he flinched.

"It's okay," she assured him.

The bright sunshine overhead provided him with sufficient light to see her eyes. What he saw there filled him with happiness. Her expression was one of longing and affection. A melee of emotions and sensations ripped through him.

She put something silky against his face. "What are you doing, babe?" he asked.

"I'm tying scarves over our eyes." There was something deeply sensual in the way she touched him. "You see, Ryan, someone wise once told me that sometimes we can see with more than just our eyes."

"Yeah, he basically said the same thing to me."

"So let's close our eyes together, and *see* each other."

As her soft voice caressed him all over, Lauren grabbed his hands and put them on her face. When she did, something potent passed between them. "Now, tell me what you see." The softness in her tone pulled him under like a coastal wave. Desire and need thrummed through his veins as he took a moment to process and digest the importance of what they were doing.

His heart skipped a beat as he ran his fingertips over her contours and enjoyed the soft texture of her skin. He felt her body tremble beneath his intimate touch. He inhaled her feminine scent, cradled her face between his hands and said, "I see a woman who is strong, adventurous, kind and giving. A woman who trusts when no trust has been warranted. I see that what I want now and forever is right in front of my eyes. All I had to do was open them and *see* . . ." He hauled her to him and dropped a soft kiss on her mouth. Enclosing her in the circle of his arms, he asked, "What do you see, Lauren?"

Lauren let her fingers roam over his jaw, his lips, his nose and the scars beneath his eyes before saying, "I see a man who is afraid to put himself out there. So afraid of rejection that he only comes out at night." When he tightened at her blunt words, she continued, "For the first time in my life, I see a man who sees me for who I really am. I see a man I am falling for. A man I will fight for." His heart twisted at the sound of her voice growing soft with desire.

A wave of love moved through his bloodstream, and he felt a new closeness between them, one that went well beyond sex. "Why did you leave this morning, Lauren?" he questioned in a soft tone.

"I knew you weren't ready, Ryan. You weren't ready to see or to be seen."

He circled his arms around her waist and anchored her body to his. They remained pressed up against each other for a long moment. "You're right. I guess I wasn't." He drew a shaky breath as his mouth found hers. "Lauren, I'm ready to see now."

With her vision cloaked by the sash, Lauren slid her arms around Ryan's neck and held him tightly. As his hands roamed her body in aroused eagerness, she soaked in his heat and kissed him with all the love inside her.

Suddenly, Mr. Malik's words of wisdom came back to her. *Sometimes our eyes must be closed before we can really see.* It occurred to her that her deepest desires had been fulfilled on the island. It had taken a near-blind man to finally see and appreciate her for who she really was.

With skilled fingers, Ryan unhooked her bikini top and tossed it aside. Her nipples quivered with excitement. The air around them became charged as her body trembled. He growled deep in his throat, splashed water on her breasts and made a slow pass with his tongue that made her wild with pleasure. She tilted her head back and moaned.

Shivers of need whipped through her blood and tingled her toes. She raced her hands over him, feeling and *seeing* his every hard contour. Eager fingers dipped below the water and found his cock. Her furtive brush against his rock-hard erection filled her with primal hunger.

"Mmm, so nice," she whispered. "I think I'd like to have that inside me."

He gave a low, throaty chuckle. "Your wish is my command," Ryan said, his sexy cadence bombarding her with lust. Skilled fingers skated over her bare skin, going lower and lower until he found her bikini bottoms. With one quick tug, he tore them from her hips and then leaned forward to swallow her surprised gasp.

"Oh, my," she said when he broke the kiss. His muscles rippled as he backed her up. Ryan felt around the embankment with his hands, and then he gripped her hips to lift her before setting her down gently on a flat rock. Her heart hammered as he urged her thighs apart and insinuated himself in between. The position gave him clear access to her pussy.

As her body beckoned his touch, he slipped his tongue inside her mouth so the soft blade could tangle and mate with hers. His kiss, his touch and the intimacy of their actions nearly stopped her heart.

"You are so beautiful, Lauren." His tone was imbued with love.

She heard a rustle of clothes and then could feel his cock near her entrance. When his thumb brushed over her clit, and one thick finger slipped inside her warm, wet heat, preparing her, a violent shudder overtook her. Breath rushed from her lungs in a whoosh as the sweet torment took her to the edge of sanity.

"*Jesus*," she whispered, arching into his touch, demanding what she wanted without saying anything more. He kept his finger inside her for a long time, pleasuring her in the most delicious ways. Her cunt began rippling and tightening, crying out for his cock.

"You're on fire, baby."

With effort she spoke. "I need your cock inside me."

Ryan braced shaky arms on either side of her, dusted soft kisses over her face and then put his mouth close to her ear. "Condom?" His warm breath tickled her neck.

She slipped her hands between their bodies and grasped his erection. It jumped eagerly in her palm. A moan escaped from his lips and reverberated right through her.

"We don't need one," she said.

"Oh, God, Lauren, are you sure?" Emotion thickened his voice and his body shivered.

Aching to join them as one, she widened her legs and shimmied closer, showing him just how sure she was.

He brushed her hair from her face, and she could feel a rush of tenderness overcome him. His voice hitched. "Lauren——"

His concerned words died away when she fed his cock into her pussy. "It's just you and me, Ryan, with nothing in between us ever again. No glasses, no fears, no secrets."

Moaning in acquiescence, he growled and plunged deep inside her.

"Yes," she cried out, angling her body for deeper thrusts. Lauren wrapped her arms around him, holding him tight as she grew slicker with each delicious stroke.

Her body began pulsing, throbbing, trembling and burning as he stroked her. His fast, steady thrusts and the depth of his penetration took her to the brink in record time. Fire licked over her thighs and she could feel her body suffuse with color.

She began panting, melting in his arms as he pumped into her. She slid her fingers through his hair. "Oh, God, Ryan . . ."

"I love when you call my name, baby," he whispered into her mouth. His breath scorched her.

Her body responded to his soft, sexy words with a hot flow of release. Her muscles clenched in euphoric bliss, and pleasure like she'd never before experienced swamped her. A low whimper filled the silent air.

He growled and buried his face in her neck. "I can feel your cream all over my cock."

"I want to feel you come inside me, Ryan. I want to feel you splash up inside me."

When she squeezed her pussy, he immediately stilled. Then his muscles bunched, his cock thickened and he threw his head back and growled. *"Lauren . . ."*

"Yesss . . . ," she whispered, savoring every delicious pulse of his cock. "You feel so good."

When their lips met, deep contentment settled in her bones. She inhaled the sweet scent of their lovemaking in the air. Ryan remained inside her for a long time, until his cock grew flaccid and slipped out.

After a moment, Lauren pulled her blindfold off and gave a low, contented sigh. Teasing, she said, "I guess the magic elixir really did work. We both got what we wished for."

He chuckled and removed his own sash. "I don't think the elixir is magic. I think love is magic."

When she glanced into his beautiful blue eyes, it triggered a craving deep inside her. Her body quaked as she acknowledged the love and intimacy between them. "I think you're right."

Ryan slipped his arm around her waist and pulled her under the waterfall. The cool water caressed their heated skin.

She palmed his face, glanced into his gorgeous eyes and wondered what was next for them. "Have you decided what you're going to do when your time here is up, Ryan?"

"Yeah, I've been giving it some thought. You know the old saying. Those who can't—teach."

She laughed and dropped a soft kiss onto his mouth. "Oh, but you can, Ryan. You proved that to me over and over already."

Ryan smiled and dropped his hands to the small of her back. "I think I know why Malik has been trying to get me to go on excursions and share my knowledge of the woods. I think it's his way of telling me it's time I go back and train soldiers. I have a lot of knowledge that I should share."

"I think Mr. Malik is one very wise man." She frowned and said, "I guess that's going to take you all over the world, then?"

"No, I want to be close to you. I want to meet your family. And soon, Lauren, if you're in agreement, I want to start my own family. It's something I've always wanted. I didn't think I had any more to give, but I realize I have a lot to give; it just took the right woman to show me that."

She nodded, hardly able to believe what she was hearing, so happy was she to realize that the man of her fantasies was also the man of her dreams. Overwhelmed by his tender words and gentle touch, she looked into his eyes and saw gentleness there, seeing the inner man, a man he'd kept so well hidden behind his dark glasses.

Aware of how much he loved hearing her say his name, she put her mouth close to his and whispered, "Ryan . . . ," before they shared a long, passionate kiss.

Ryan inched back. "Now, about these brothers of yours. Tell me again all the rotten things they did to you."

She laughed. "You're going to love them."

"I know I will because anyone you love is worth me loving, too," he said. "I can't wait to go back to Chicago with you to meet them."

She gave him a playful smile. "Just because we're going back to civilization doesn't mean we can't play a little Tarzan and Jane every now and then, does it?"

With that he let out a low Tarzan rumble and gathered her into his arms. "Hell, no," he growled and crashed his lips to hers. "Now that you've unleashed the beast in me, you have no idea what you're in for."

She sank into his touch and whispered, "I can't wait to find out."

The Sunset Sauna

ONE

"Oh. My. God," Abby whispered under her breath as lust prowled a lazy path through her body.

Panting from excitement, Abby dropped the spicy novel that had been singeing her fingertips—among other body parts—and glanced around the beach cove just outside her cabana. Not that she expected to see or hear anyone in her private nook, but still . . .

With her heart beating wildly, she jumped from her chaise longue, and began pacing. Needing something, anything, to get her mind off her libido, as well as the erotic scene that she'd just read, she concentrated on the hot sand between her toes.

But she'd rather have a hot man between her legs . . .

Holy hell, she'd never read about exhibitionism and voyeurism before and had to admit, it damn well excited her. She wiped a bead of sweat from her forehead and worked to regulate her breathing. Her throbbing pussy continued to clamor for a hard cock, despite her desperate battle to focus her attention elsewhere. Goddamn, she was so riled up, she was ready to take matters into her own hands.

In an effort to take her mind off her needs, she stalked back to her lounge chair and grabbed her binoculars. After adjusting the black strap around her neck, she scanned the horizon.

"Oh, hell . . . ," Abby murmured to herself as the binoculars slipped from her fingers. No matter how hard she tried, she just couldn't get away from it.

Sex, sex and more sex.

Were the gods testing her, trying her last nerve?

If so, they were winning.

Curiosity and need getting the better of her, she sank back down on her chair, readjusted her binoculars and stole another peek at the guy licking his girlfriend's pussy on the bow of their boat. Goddamn, it was the hottest thing she'd ever seen.

As her sex throbbed for that kind of attention, her palms itched, aching to take the edge off, using any means possible, even if it meant taking matters into her own hands . . . *and fingers.*

Abby let her gaze surf over the cove. Flanked by tall, lush mountains, the Pacific water lapped against the sandy shore a few feet away from her chair. All was quiet and private, just as Mr. Malik had promised. This beach area was hers and hers alone. A secluded spot to sunbathe, read, swim or even delve into a little masturbation if she wanted to.

She was pretty damn sure she wanted to.

She might be a good girl with a mapped-out future, but that certainly didn't mean she didn't have needs. Needs that had been neglected for far too long.

Unable to fight the inevitable any longer, she ran her hands over her breasts, taking the time to tease her engorged nipples before moving lower to her new bikini bottoms. Pulling on the small yellow band, she slipped her fingers inside and brushed the pad of her thumb over her wet pussy.

"Mmm," she moaned under her breath as desire resonated through her. No longer able to ignore her cravings, she spasmed with need, realizing it had been far too long since she'd taken personal care of her desires. Far too long, indeed.

Warmth spread over her skin as raw desire seared her insides. Heck, she'd had no idea that she had such voyeuristic tendencies until she'd read that spicy novel and caught that couple having sex.

Returning her focus to her swollen clit, she caressed it lightly, stoking the fire inside her as the sun beat down on her libidinous body. "Oh, damn . . . ," she murmured. The scent of her arousal impregnated the air and mingled with the provocative aroma of sand and surf. The combination raised her passion to new heights.

Abby rolled her tongue around her suddenly dry mouth, her thoughts taking her in a tantalizing direction. Completely caught up in pleasuring herself, she lifted her hips from the chaise to push two long fingers inside her hot cunt. She pumped in and out as her palm applied the perfect amount of pressure to her engorged clit. She sucked in a tight breath. Her sex muscles began clenching around her fingers; her blood began boiling with the approach of an impending orgasm. Quaking, she bit down on her bottom lip and moaned without censor as she drew out her release.

As her orgasm approached, air rushed from her lungs in a loud whoosh. Her muscles clenched so hard, she thought she would black out from pleasure. A shiver wracked her body. Instinctively, she clamped her legs together and squeezed as she tumbled into climax.

She worked her fingers over her clit faster, riding out every delicious ripple, prolonging the ecstasy for as long as she could.

When the last orgasmic pulse subsided, she dropped her hands to her sides and collapsed in a flushed heap. After a few moments, she blinked her eyes back into focus and gave a needy sigh. She still didn't feel completely satisfied. Her fingers had managed to get the job done, but she had to be honest with herself and admit that they paled in comparison to the real thing.

Remembering where she was, Abby shook the fog from her lust-filled brain and looked out over the glistening water. She decided to take a quick swim before she went on her island exploration. Since Lauren had already ventured off earlier, hoping for another wild Tarzan encounter in the jungle, and Danielle was making the most of her vacation with her sea god, Abby would set out alone. Not that she minded. She was happy that her friends had found what they were looking for—what they secretly desired—while on vacation.

She, on the other hand, already had everything she desired. Since the magic elixir was wasted on her, she spent her time in paradise relaxing, enjoying the spa treatments, reading and thinking about her upcoming engagement to hardworking stock broker Artie Drummond.

Don't you want your nights filled with passion?

Lauren's question kept coming back to haunt her. Honestly, Abby had never slipped between the sheets with a passionate man.

She could only dream about sex with a man who wasn't afraid to unleash himself on her, show his emotions, let his needs and hunger rule him during lovemaking and give himself over to his primal desires. Completely. Thoroughly.

Unapologetically.

Her whole body shook just thinking about it. Surely guys like that existed only in her romance novels. Because she'd yet to stumble across such a man.

Pushing those thoughts to the far recesses of her mind, she climbed from her chair and took a dip in the water. Off in the distance she noticed a band of dark clouds. Could a storm be moving in? She hoped it held off until after her island exploration and her late afternoon snorkeling lesson, which, she had to admit, she was really looking forward to.

Once she was sufficiently cooled, she gathered her belongings and glanced around. She suddenly felt like she was being watched. Strangely enough, a small thrill raced down her spine at the sensation.

Jeez, she really was a wild woman at heart; either that or this seductive island atmosphere was doing the strangest things to her libido, fueling it in the most interesting ways, and urging her to explore her budding fetishes. Abby hadn't even realized she had interesting sexual fetishes she might want to explore until this vacation opened her eyes.

Holding a hand up to shade her eyes from the sun, she scanned the mountaintops for movement, but her gaze met with only large trees, natural foliage and a few local birds that had just taken flight and now hovered over the cliff like a heavy rain cloud.

Deciding it was nothing more than her passion-starved libido playing tricks on her, and her lack of male-induced orgasms, she made the short trek back to her cabana. Once inside she consulted her agenda book. Being on vacation didn't mean she couldn't organize her activities. The only thing she had scheduled for today was the snorkeling lesson. Tomorrow she had a hot-stone massage booked in the morning, a late lunch with the girls, and then, later in the evening, a sea-salt scrub.

After pulling on a pair of shorts, a tank top and her walking shoes, she stuffed a towel and bathing suit into her beach bag, took one last, wistful look at her novel and then stepped outside. It was time to explore this beautiful magical island, and forget about ever falling into the arms of a wild, passionate man like the one from her erotic book.

Cody lowered his scope and brushed his palm over his chin, scratching the day-old growth shadowing his jaw as his body turned mutinous.

He drew a deep breath yet still couldn't manage to fill his lungs. As a military-trained sniper, he'd witnessed a lot of grizzly shit through his scope, but the one thing he'd never sighted was a sexy woman pleasuring herself.

That was definitely a first, but sweet Jesus, he sure as hell hoped it wasn't the last time. Because he'd never been so fucking turned on in his entire life.

He hadn't meant to spy; he really hadn't. But how the hell could he possibly tear his gaze away from that erotic show once he had spotted her? He was male, after all.

The truth was, he'd been watching Abby for days, ever since he met her at dinner. He wasn't sure why, but there was something about her that held his attention.

Abby Benton, with legs longer than an eternity in hell, gorgeous, passion-drenched blue eyes and lush curves, reminded him that despite everything he'd been through over the last year, he was still a red-blooded American.

With physical needs.

His cock twitched as his mind revisited the way her hands had dipped under her yellow bikini bottoms and the sensuous way her hips had come off the chair as she pushed her fingers inside her pussy. The erotic vision triggered a craving deep inside him, prompting his dick into action.

Fuck . . .

Biting down on his bottom lip, Cody broke into a sweat and stifled a moan of sexual frustration. His muscles ached—throbbed, actually—and the compulsion to climb down from that mountain and satisfy Abby Benton the way a wicked woman like her deserved to be satisfied sang through his veins, shepherding lust and heat to his coldest corners.

His powerful scope had allowed him to see the lack of fulfillment in her eyes after she'd brought herself to climax. He suspected that fingers alone could never really satisfy a hot little number like her. What she needed was a rock-hard cock inside her before she could attain true sexual fulfillment.

And wouldn't you know it. He just happened to have one.

A slow tremor moved down his spine, stirring his hormones along that southern path before settling low in his groin. His thoughts careened in an erotic direction as he continued to take pleasure in his covert mission. He watched her wade into the warm Pacific water and reveled in the way her damp tanned skin glistened under the midday sun. His whole body tightened and beckoned her touch.

Her sexy solo act reminded him that even though he'd sealed off his emotions long ago, burying them deep inside and shutting himself off from others after his overseas tour, there was still one part of him that hadn't turned to ice.

One very big, very hard part, to be more accurate.

Cody's skin prickled in warning and his stomach churned, a good indication that his solitude was about to be interrupted. A moment later he heard a rustling noise a few feet away. Composing himself, he ignored the incessant ache between his legs and twisted around, preparing for a confrontation. As far as Cody was concerned, it'd be a cold day in hell before he—the predator—became the prey. No one caught Cody Lannon off guard. No one.

Cody watched Malik step out from behind a foxtail palm tree and close the gap between them. How the man always managed to find Cody hidden in the thick foliage, Cody would never know.

"Good afternoon, my child." Malik narrowed his gaze and scrutinized him.

Cody pinched the bridge of his nose. "Good afternoon," he replied, without bothering to keep the annoyance from his voice.

Malik held his hands out and touched Cody's shoulder. "Still so cold." He mocked shivered. "So cold."

Fuck, he hated when Malik put him under the microscope, dissecting him like a damn lab rat. Ignoring that blatant, albeit accurate observation, Cody turned his attention back to the water. When he spotted a boat off in the distance, he focused his scope and murmured under his breath, "Well, I'll be damned."

It appeared that something shiny, sexy and flirtatious had caught his buddy Ryan's attention.

Speaking of something shiny . . .

With renewed concentration, he focused his lens on Abby again and watched her gather her belongings and make her way back to her cabana.

"What is it?" Malik asked him. The sound of branches crunching beneath his feet startled a few local birds.

After watching the red-throated lorikeets take flight only to hover over the cliff like an Apache helicopter, Cody shot Malik a glance and said casually, "I just saw Ryan on the excursion." He shrugged and added, "I never thought I'd see the day."

Malik pressed his hands together so that the sleeves on his robe dangled near his knees. "Yes, well, maybe the elixir has finally opened his eyes."

Cody clenched his fists when anger began to take hold of him. Jesus, if he heard about the elixir one more time he was going to drown the man in it. And no court in the land would ever hold that against him.

Truthfully, his deepest desire was to be left alone, and Malik continued to make damn sure that never happened. From sneaking up on him to constantly hounding him to go on the snorkeling and scuba-diving excursions, Malik ensured he never had a moment's peace. Just because he could spot what others couldn't didn't mean he wanted to go under the sea and look at fucking tropical fish.

He hated fish, tropical or otherwise. And he hated snorkeling and scuba diving, goddammit.

Determined to regain his solitude, Cody shifted, offering Malik his back, his body language telltale.

"Would you like to walk with me?" Malik asked, despite Cody's silent message to the contrary.

With his voice deceptively patient, he said, "No, I just want to be left alone."

"Are you sure that's what you really want, Cody?"

"Yes. It's my deepest desire," he replied flatly, twisting back around to face Malik. "Since that isn't happening, I guess the elixir isn't working for me."

"Very well, then."

A creature of habit, Cody turned his attention back to his scope and scanned the horizon.

"What are you looking for?" Malik asked.

"Nothing," Cody murmured.

Malik made a strange noise and said, "Remember, Cody. You can't find what you're not looking for."

Cody scoffed. Okay, what the fuck was that supposed to mean?

TWO

When Abby stepped into the mouth of the path, she glanced up and spotted Mr. Malik coming her way. Smiling, she adjusted her beach bag higher on her shoulder and nodded her head in greeting.

"I see I'm not the only one out for an afternoon exploration," she said, stopping to chat with him.

Mr. Malik smiled. "Abby, I was just on my way to pay you a visit."

"You were?"

"Yes, a call came in for you at the main office."

Her eyes widened. "Really?" Besides Artie, she couldn't imagine anyone calling her here. Not that Artie had called.

"I believe it had something to do with a Mr. Drummond."

She stiffened, her heart leapt and her mind raced. She hoped everything was okay back home.

In response to her tense body language, Mr. Malik said, "Everything is fine."

Her smile restored, she took a moment to think about Artie. Perhaps he'd simply called to say hello, to say he missed her and that he couldn't wait to hold her in his arms again. But why would he call the main office and not her cabana?

Mr. Malik's voice filtered through her thoughts. "His receptionist called to inform you that Mr. Drummond will be out of town for the next few days."

Her smile faltered. "Oh, I see," she said. Once again his receptionist was giving her news that Artie should have given her himself. "Did she say whether Artie wanted me to call back? Did he leave a number?"

"I'm afraid she didn't say. Perhaps it would be best for you to call her back."

With disappointment settling in her stomach, Abby schooled her face and nodded. She glanced past his shoulder, focusing on the many winding paths up ahead. "Perhaps it would," she murmured halfheartedly.

"Is everything okay, Abby?"

She forced a quick smile and turned her attention to Mr. Malik. "How could it not be? I'm about to explore this beautiful island and I have everything my heart desires."

Just maybe not everything her libido desired . . .

Mr. Malik stepped to the side to clear the way for her to continue past him. "Then, by all means, get on with your exploration. I've taken up enough of your time."

Abby glanced up ahead, taking in the maze of paths, wishing she had a map to consult. She'd hate to lose her way. "Where does this path lead?"

Mr. Malik narrowed his eyes. "Maybe sometimes we have to venture off the beaten path before we can find what we're really looking for." With that he walked away, leaving her with nothing more than her thoughts and his cryptic words to sort through.

Abby began her ascent up the mountain and took a moment to think about why having plans and a mapped-out future were so important to her. Perhaps it was because her parents had preached goal-setting to her and her older sister their entire lives, only to sit back in disappointment and watch their oldest daughter veer off her life's plan. And now her sister was pregnant, without a professional career and living with an artist who could barely support them. But despite all that, she had to admit, her sister did seem happy.

Now Abby was the only "good girl" in the family, as her mother still called her. But maybe she was growing tired of always playing by the rules. Maybe during her time away she wanted to veer off the path just once, to see what happened.

With those thoughts spurring her on, Abby deliberately took two steps to her left, pushed through the thick foliage and stepped over the root-choked weeds that veiled the jungle floor. A variety of birds inhabiting the area took flight as she disturbed them. She trekked onward, noticing just how beautiful she found the untouched, overgrown surroundings.

The higher she climbed, the heavier the air felt around her. When she reached the top, she made her way toward the edge. It was a slow process, but the second she reached the cliff she knew it had been worth it.

The foliage thinned to reveal the blue skyline. Smiling as she took in the island in all its seductive splendor, she stood there staring down at the water, realizing that she was overlooking her private cove. A movement out of the corner of her eye caught her focus. Startled, she stiffened and turned sideways.

"Oh," she said, her hand flying to her chest, her smile dissolving. "I didn't realize there was anyone else out here," she added in alarm at seeing Cody Lannon stationed at the top of the mountain, like some predator, or a caged animal ready to pounce. He sat perched on the edge of the cliff, dressed in military-issue fatigues and boots, with some sort of scope in his hands. She faltered backwards when his intense gaze locked on hers.

In the blink of an eye he was standing in front of her. His large hands spanned her waist, and he quickly anchored her body to his to keep her from falling backwards.

"Careful . . ."

She tilted her head back to look at him. Dark eyes met hers, and in that instant she felt like she'd just been sucker punched. There was something very sexy about a broad-shouldered, rock-hard man in military fatigues, she decided. Shock waves rocketed through her body, and the spark from his dark eyes was all that was needed to ignite her blood and dampen her panties.

When it finally occurred to her that she'd stopped breathing, she sucked in a tight breath, filling her oxygen-starved lungs with the moisture-laden air.

Taking full advantage of their up-close-and-personal stance, she let her gaze sweep over him for a long inspection of his fine body, firm, square jaw, sun-kissed hair and dark, intense eyes. She took in his watchful gaze, noting his body's primal reactions to her presence. There was a restless energy about him that swirled around them. It raced over her flesh and exploded on her senses.

His face might have remained expressionless, icy even, but his eyes bore into hers with a gaze so intense and probing, it was all Abby could do to keep herself upright. Ripples of sensual pleasure started at her core and traveled onward and outward.

Her entire body trembled. Almost violently.

Aware of the way he was affecting her libido, and needing to gain control over her hormones, she stepped back and reclaimed her personal space.

Lord, it was one thing to fantasize about the hero in her spicy novel, but to fantasize about this hot, enigmatic man while he stood before her, in the flesh, was another thing entirely. She berated her wayward thoughts and focused her attention.

"I'm Abby Benton," she said, holding her hand out in greeting in case he didn't remember her.

After he glanced at her outstretched hand, guarded eyes met hers. "I remember." Like any well-disciplined soldier, he closed his hand over hers for a firm shake, and she wondered whether he even knew he was idly stroking the soft pad of his thumb over her wrist.

Sensing she was encroaching upon his solitude, she glanced past his shoulder to the sandy beach below. She tried for casual. "I didn't mean to disturb you." Her voice sounded tight, even to herself.

He grunted something incoherent and took a distancing step back. Hard, corded muscles shifted as his arms fell to his sides. It was all she could do not to stare.

Curious to know what he'd been looking at, what he'd been *watching*, she angled her chin and focused on his scope.

"What are you doing up here?" she asked him.

"Bird-watching."

Even though his words said one thing, the dark look in his eyes suggested otherwise. She shot him a dubious glance. "Bird-watching, huh?"

"Yeah." He widened his stance, folded his arms and arched a challenging brow. "Bird-watching."

Her glance raced over his fatigues. "You don't seem like the bird-watching type to me," she said. Her words implied that he was some kind of Peeping Tom.

His mouth lifted in a mocking half smile. His expression was coy but sexy. "As opposed to all your other bird-watching friends?"

Okay, he had her there. She wanted to test him, to see whether he'd been peeking in anyone's window or invading anyone's privacy, so she asked, "Have you spotted anything unusual? Anything rare? Anything that *piqued* your interest?" She stretched out that one word, hoping he'd catch her double meaning.

A quick grin momentarily softened his warrior features, and she suspected he knew full well what she was referring to.

"Just a few red-throated lorikeets and a couple of fruit doves," he responded.

She arched a brow, impressed. "Oh, so you do know your birds. Mind if I have a look?"

She caught his hesitation, sensing a desire for solitude. "I'll just take a quick look and then be on my way."

He reluctantly conceded. "Fine."

Seeking shade under a palm tree, Abby sat on the ground, dropped her beach bag beside her, and crossed her legs, tucking them under her thighs. Crispy, sun-burnt grass and twigs crunched beneath her. Cody moved with stealth and precision in beside her and helped her position his scope.

"Like this," he said. His warm breath fanned her face and fragmented her thoughts.

His close proximity made her feel weird and jittery, and it took all her effort not to moan in frank appreciation when his rich, manly scent closed around her.

"You sure have a long range of sight with this thing." She shot him a sidelong glance. "Perhaps the guests should be warned to keep their curtains closed." She scanned the sandy shore below until she reached a chaise longue—the same chaise longue she'd masturbated on less than an hour before.

Had Cody been stationed here then?

Watching her?

An unexpected burst of lust whipped through her veins. Moisture dampened her panties and the nerve endings in her clit screamed for attention. Oh, boy!

Under her breath, she added, "Or reserve their intimate indiscretions for behind closed doors."

"Well, that depends." His voice was low, maybe even a little harsh.

"On what?"

"If they like to be . . . *watched* or not." One brow arched as though he was fully aware of her budding fetishes.

Abby gulped air. This guy was far too perceptive.

She admitted it was possible she had pleasured herself on the beach deliberately, hoping someone would catch her . . . *watch her.*

Maybe that did excite the hell out of her.

She cleared her throat and shot him a questioning glance. "And obviously you like to watch," she managed to choke out.

"It comes with the profession, Abby. Watching, waiting, calculating . . ."

Her body broke out in a sweat at the sensual way his voice had softened when he said her name. "You must be a very patient man."

"Whatever it takes and no matter how long it takes to get the job done."

Her gaze raced over his face, wondering whether he was still talking about his job, or something else entirely . . .

She looked through the scope again in search of a distraction and smiled when she spotted Lauren on board *The Cascade,* Ryan seated next to her. Was it possible that Ryan was Lauren's Tarzan man?

Abby decided to redirect the conversation. "You watch over everyone like you're some sort of guardian angel." Abby noted the way his eyes froze over, his body going cold. She studied his body language a moment longer. Oh, yeah, she mused. This guy was repressed, all right. Certainly no different from any other guy she knew. She recalled her conversation with Lauren, and the way her friend had encouraged her to have an affair with Cody. She suspected he could get the job done sexually, but as far as unleashing himself on her, driving them both into a frenzy of need and passion, she had her doubts.

"Sniper," he corrected her. His expression turned dark. His

hands fisted, and the anguish in his gaze turned her blood to ice. She shivered.

As she considered his combative stance, and sorted through matters, understanding quickly dawned. "I see," she said. She was intelligent enough to know that such a job would undoubtedly require cold calculation.

Was this why she sensed an iciness inside him?

Why he was so guarded?

Needing in some inexplicable way to make a connection, to help ease his anxiety, she put a placating hand on his leg. He flinched at the feel of her palm on his thigh.

Despite his obvious discomfort, Abby kept her hand there, offering her warmth and sympathy. "I'm sure your job must be a very difficult one."

He made a face; surprise registered in his eyes.

"What?" she asked, unable to understand his reactions.

"Nothing, really. You just caught me off guard for a second there. Most people think it's a pretty cool job, and the first thing they want to know is how many kills I've made."

"I don't see anything cool about it." Narrowing her eyes, her glance swept over him again. "Were you injured?"

By small degrees his body tightened and his jaw clenched. There was something sad in the depths of his eyes. "No."

His behavior contradicted his words, and he didn't fool her for a second. He might not be injured on the outside, but she could only guess that it would require him to build a wall of defense around his heart to survive in the field. Abby knew there was a form of protection in closing off one's emotions.

"Then why are you here if you're not injured?" Abby inquired with one raised eyebrow.

He shook his head at her, but his smile seemed genuine. "You don't pull any punches, do you?"

The spark of warmth and passion she glimpsed underneath his cool exterior caught her by surprise. It disappeared as quickly as it had appeared. But there was no mistaking what she'd seen. Her pulse leapt in her throat. Her breath quickened and her entire body buzzed to life.

Was it possible that Lauren was right? That passionate men did exist in real life? That if she unearthed Cody's buried emotions through her erotic touch, he'd go wild on her, like the hero in her spicy novel?

Even though she had the distinct impression she was playing with fire, her entire body shook and she suddenly wanted . . . no, *needed*, to find out.

Something in Abby's gaze changed, darkened when her eyes met his. As Cody took in her lingering glance, he wasn't prepared for the passion he saw brewing beneath the surface or the way that it reached out to him and stirred his emotions. The change in her mood occurred so swiftly that it completely caught him off guard and left him feeling a little shaky.

Abby pulled her gaze away and returned her focus to his scope. He studied her profile as she scanned the cove below. With bright-eyed enthusiasm, she shot him a glance and said, "The view from up here is spectacular."

Trying for nonchalant, and feeling anything but, he mumbled, "You think?"

"Yeah, it's gorgeous." She gave him a strange look. "Haven't you noticed?"

"Not really." Truthfully, he hadn't noticed a lot of things since he'd come back. Things like the sunset, the sunrise or even nature in all its beauty. Nor had he participated in any of his favorite activities, like deep-sea diving, hiking and snorkeling, yeah, even snorkeling—things, as a true outdoorsman, he used to take great pleasure in, despite what he'd told Malik.

But the one thing he was noticing now was Abby's arousing scent and how it was seeping under his skin. The exotic aroma was awaking his senses and raising his internal temperature.

She moved restlessly against him, leaning into him, crowding him, her silky blond hair brushing against his cheek in the most tantalizing ways. She pointed one slim finger and he followed the direction.

"Look at the palm trees over there," she said. Her voice was an arousing combination of sweet and sultry.

"I'm looking," he murmured into her ear, merely seeing a clump of trees fringing the water.

"Look at how they are bent forward, the provocative way the leaves are kissing the water. Dipping in and out, in and out . . ." Abby handed him the scope. "See for yourself."

He looked through the scope, but the way her leg pressed against his was highly distracting. It definitely affected his concentration. When he turned back to her, they exchanged a long, lingering look, one that left a peculiar feeling in his gut.

He rolled one shoulder. "I guess I never noticed that before."

"Look at the water, Cody," she whispered, her low, husky voice playing havoc with his libido. "Can you see the different colors based on the depth and sandbars below? Look at how the warm blues and greens flow from one to another so sensually. It's like my decorator's palette. The colors are merging, blending, becoming one . . ." The soft tone of her voice caught his attention. He watched, transfixed, as her vibrant blue eyes grew wide, enchanted with the view.

"I guess I never thought of it as sensual before."

She gave a breathy, intimate laugh and said, "Maybe I see the seductive allure in nature and everything around me because I'm an interior decorator."

"Maybe," he responded. "Or maybe we're just not looking for the same things."

You can't find what you're not looking for.

Pushing the medicine man's cryptic words aside, he scanned the horizon. "What else do you see, Abby?" He handed the scope back to her. Perhaps it was the sniper in him that found, in some odd way, her enthusiasm and eye for detail interesting.

Or perhaps it was the man . . .

When her hand touched his, he trembled in reaction. "Look at the cluster of smooth rocks out there and the way they keep breaking through the surf as the tide shifts. They kind of remind me of a turtle poking its head in and out of its shell. Just watch the motion for a minute," she urged. As they studied the waves, Abby moistened her lips and once again murmured, "In and out, in and out." Her voice sounded deep and sensual, throwing him completely off balance.

Cody adjusted his pants, his thoughts careening off track. If she was trying to get a rise out of him, she'd succeeded.

Her voice dropped to a whisper. "Doesn't it remind you of a turtle, Cody?"

Not even for a minute.

"Yeah, I guess." As he took in her mischievous look, it occurred to him that not only was Abby deliberately toying with him; she was having one hell of a good time doing it.

She flashed him a grin. "Let's walk to the other side and look out over the beach," she said, her voice hinting at something far more intimate. "Maybe something over there will pique our interest." Her eagerness made it damn near impossible to decline.

As sensual awareness arced between them, he couldn't deny that she'd *piqued* his interest—in more ways than one.

Cody pitched his voice low. "Now look who wants to do the *watching . . .*"

Undaunted, she pushed to her feet and gave a low, throaty chuckle. "Coming?" She made that one word sound deeply suggestive.

Cody grabbed his scope and stood. Instincts kicking in, he stepped in front of Abby, preparing to lead the way. "Follow me. This cliff can be difficult to negotiate."

When she caught hold of his hand, and her warmth seeped under his skin, his body responded eagerly. Lust and need rose to the surface, and his cock thickened inside his fatigues. He bit back a moan, and it was all he could do to keep himself from bending her over right then and there and driving his cock into her so deep and hard that neither one of them would walk away unscathed.

A shiver ripped through him, and he groaned.

"Are you okay?" Abby asked.

"Fine," he bit out with much more force than necessary. He turned and shot her a glance. The sexy, playful gleam in her eyes evoked a myriad of sinful thoughts.

So she wanted to play with him, did she?

The carnal image of Abby sprawled out before him, completely at his mercy, while he took care of their sexual needs, rushed through his mind.

Then play they would . . .

THREE

Abby was shadowing Cody, which put her in perfect position to race her eyes over his body and take pleasure in the graceful, stealthy way he moved. She also enjoyed the way his combat fatigues hugged his tight buns with each forward step. Her thoughts raced to Artie, and she felt a twinge of guilt for flirting with this trained warrior.

But the reasons for her actions were twofold. One—she wanted to see what happened when she ventured off the path, and two—she needed to prove to herself that passionate men did not exist outside of romance novels.

"Watch your step," Cody said, his voice interrupting her wanderings.

Abby ducked under the branch Cody was holding up for her. "Thanks." She studied the path before her, deciding she'd better pay closer attention to her surroundings and less attention to Cody's hot body before she put an eye out. Although something told her even though he was distant and reserved, Cody had deeply ingrained protective instincts and wouldn't let anything happen to her.

A short while later they reached the other side of the cliff, coming up on the north side of the mountain.

"Let's rest here," Cody suggested.

Abby stepped to the edge, shaded the sun from her eyes and perused the breathtaking mile-long stretch of beach below them. People were sprawled across towels on the pristine white sand, sunbathing under the tropical rays, while others frolicked in the warm water. Secluded at the far side of the beach were tables near the seashore where guests could enjoy a luxurious hot-stone massage.

She gestured to the massage tables with a nod. "I have one of those booked for tomorrow morning. Have you ever tried it?"

He shook his head. "It's not my thing."

She angled her body and admired him. "What is your thing, Cody?"

He dipped his head and met her glance. A muscle in his jaw flexed, and his dark, intense gaze nearly knocked her off balance. "Like I said, *watching* . . ."

A shudder ripped down her spine. With shaky hands she grabbed the scope from him. Part of her couldn't believe she was playing such a dangerous game with him, but another part of her desperately ached to discover if this was it, or if life had something else to offer.

"Then, let's watch," she said.

Abby took a seat near the cliff and positioned the scope the way Cody had shown her. As she scanned the beach and surf, secretly watching others, desire moved into her stomach. It occurred to her that not only was she an exhibitionist; she really was a regular old Peeping Tom, too.

"It feels so naughty watching all these people without them knowing," she whispered quietly, even though no one else could hear her. "So scandalous."

"It is naughty and scandalous, Abby. But damn exciting, too. Don't you think?" Cody shifted beside her, stretched his long legs out in front of him and rested his back against a tree. His nearness made her breathless. Without waiting for an answer, he continued, "Now, tell me what you see."

When he spoke, his soft, sexy tone seeped under her skin, his deep masculine tenor playing some mysterious alchemy with her libido. She redirected her thoughts, focused the scope and surveyed the landscape. A moment later she zeroed in on a couple sunbathing near the shore.

Trying to keep her voice light, she said, "Well, I see a guy and a girl sharing a huge beach towel. They're both positioned on their sides facing each other; their bodies are close but not touching. She's in a cute red bikini, and he's in a pair of blue, knee-length swim trunks."

As she watched them, pleasure resonated through her and her body lubricated. The intimacy in their posture made her feel restless and reminded her that she was a woman with many unfulfilled needs.

"What else?" Cody asked.

She turned her attention to the rolling waves and continued her narrative. "I see a girl swimming out to a guy on a blow-up lounge chair. It looks like she's trying to sneak up on him." She took a moment to wonder whether they were lovers, and then went back to her observations. "I see guests on the massage table relaxing, and a few people jogging along the surf."

"On the rocks, Abby. What do you see on the rocks?"

Eyes alive with curiosity, she made a quick brush over the rocky shore, going just beyond the beach area.

"I see . . ." Her words fell off and she gasped, shivers of pleasure racing down her spine. "Holy. Shit," she murmured, sucking in a tight breath.

Cody leaned into her, pressing close. "What is it?" he asked, but something in her gut told her that this guy, this trained sniper, already knew the answer to that question. "Tell me what you see," he commanded in a soft voice that whispered over her nape like a lover's caress, turning her on in a way she'd never been turned on before. Her pulse leapt in her throat, and the moisture between her thighs hadn't gone unnoticed.

She tilted her head back to look at him. She tried to give him her full attention, but her thoughts were preoccupied with the sexy show below.

"I . . . uh . . . I see a couple," she whispered with effort, her arousal evident in her dark tone.

His eyes glided over her mouth. He had a bemused expression on his face. "A couple, huh? What are they doing?"

She turned back to the scope; warm and wicked sensations wrapped around her. "I think they're having sex."

"You think?"

She swallowed. "Yeah, I think."

"So you don't know for certain?"

Flustered, she just shook her head.

Cody's tone turned raspy before all the humor disappeared from his voice. "Then, why don't you tell me exactly what they're doing, Abby, and I'll give you my best educated guess."

Equal measures of excitement and nervousness flared inside her when she realized just how much that thrilled her. "Well, right now it looks like he's kissing her."

"Are they standing?"

"No, she's lying on a flat rock, and he's on top of her."

"Is he dressed?"

"He's in a bathing suit, but with his body covering hers, I can't tell what she's wearing. But they both look wet."

He cleared his throat. "I bet they do."

Abby squirmed. "I mean they look wet, like they've been swimming."

"I know what you mean, Abby," he whispered, the heat in his tone boiling her blood.

Sexual awareness flared through her, and she could feel her skin grow hot, tight, and needy. "She's saying something to him, but I can't make it out."

"What do you think she's saying?"

She darted him a quick glance, instantly aware of the voyeur game they were playing. As Cody's gaze brushed over her face, he tossed her a devilish, challenging grin. Had Cody known she'd been playing with him earlier and was now turning the tables, regaining control over the situation as he tapped into her fetishes and played his own sexy game with her?

"What?" she asked, having forgotten the question, but needing desperately to play along to see where it led them.

Desire flickered across his face as the air around them crackled with sexual tension. His dark eyes narrowed. "What do you think she's saying, Abby? Do you think she's talking dirty to him?"

"I'm not sure."

Giving her no reprieve, he asked, "If it were you, what would you be saying?"

Oh. My. God.

Her breasts grew heavy, achy, needy for a man's touch. Liquid desire pooled between her thighs. Although she'd never talked dirty to a man before, she had to admit, the idea excited the hell out of her. Since she'd come too far to back down now, she drew a fortifying breath, gathered her courage and said, "I'd probably ask him to remove my wet bathing suit."

Remove her bathing suit.

Kiss every inch of her body.

Tease his cock between her legs.

And fuck her with wild abandon until he reduced her to a quivering mass of contentment.

The low groan crawling out of Cody's throat bombarded her body with lust. "Then what?" he asked, encouraging her to go on. Jesus, what was it about Cody's voice that aroused her to the point of distraction and made her feel so brazen?

In a low, seductive tone she continued without censor, "Then I'd guide his mouth to my breast," she said, hardly able to believe her bold words. She tightened her hand on the scope and fought the natural inclination to rub her nipples. She briefly closed her eyes against the flood of heat.

"Is that what he's doing?" The sound of Cody's voice brought her attention back around to the couple. When she didn't answer right away, Cody instructed her, "Tell me everything, Abby. Otherwise I won't be able to give you my best educated guess."

Goddamn, that excited her. Abby moistened her lips. Complying with his instructions, she said, "He's now removing her bikini top." She lowered her tone. "Do you want to watch, Cody?"

He angled his head and looked pointedly at her, as though reading her every secret desire. "No, I want you to watch and tell me what he's doing, Abby. Tell me what *you* see."

Her pussy muscles clenched. A heated tremor made her quake. "He's climbing back over her, and she's parting her legs in invitation."

"Show me."

She turned, ready to hand Cody the scope, but when their gazes collided, he stopped her. "No," he said as his voice dropped an octave and his eyes clouded with desire. "Show me how she's widening her legs. Only then will I understand if it's meant to be sexual . . ."

Her entire body came alive with carnal desire. Abby shimmied backwards, pressed her back against the tree and widened her legs. "Like this," she said, her heart racing from exhilaration.

"Very sexy," he murmured. He signaled toward the scope with a nod. His mouth curved. "Now what?"

She turned her attention back to the scope. "He's running his hands over her legs, widening them even more." Her low, erotic whimper lingered in the air.

When she felt Cody's hand on her bare leg, mimicking the action, it was all she could do not to gyrate her hips forward to position his fingers where she really needed them most. As though sensitive to her wants and needs, he ran his hands over her thighs with aroused eagerness. Her chest heaved as his intimate caress went right through her.

"He's . . . he's saying something to her, but I can't make it out." As her breathing grew labored, it became more and more apparent just how turned on she was. It took great effort to speak while the sexy show seduced her senses. "What do you think he's saying, Cody? What would you say?" she asked without masking her enthusiasm, eager to hear him talk dirty to her.

She listened to Cody swallow, secretly thrilled that this voyeur game was turning him on as much as it was her.

"I'd tell her how desirable she is, what her beautiful body does to me, and all the ways I want to pleasure her, using my fingers, my tongue and my cock."

His response stunned her. Okay, that had to be the sexiest thing she'd ever heard in her entire life. She exhaled a shallow breath and quivered, wishing it was her on those rocks—with Cody. No man had ever talked so deliciously naughtily to her before. And she found it exciting.

A shiver skipped down her spine as heat ambushed her pussy. She turned her attention back to the scope and started tracking the man's every movement, not wanting to miss a thing. "He's kissing her stomach and moving lower," she murmured, fully aware of the way Cody's earthy scent was curling her toes, making her delirious with pleasure.

Cody leaned forward and inched her top up to expose her skin. Warm lips touched her flesh. His mouth felt so deliciously hot against her stomach.

"He's . . . he's removing her bikini bottoms."

She listened to the hiss of her zipper, then lifted her hips when Cody nudged her. "Like this?" he asked.

Barely able to formulate a response, Abby just nodded. Cody proceeded to ease her shorts from her hips and discard them, leaving her half dressed and fully aroused. Dear God, the heat arcing between them was tremendous. Any minute now she expected the trees behind them to go up in flames.

He ran his fingers over her flesh. Everywhere he touched he left a trail of fire. His blatant masculinity had her juices flowing like a waterfall. Leaning forward, he inhaled her aroused scent and made a slow pass over his bottom lip with his tongue that only fueled her hunger.

"Do you think he's going to lick her pussy?" he asked.

Oh, God, she hoped so!

When she concentrated on the man's actions, her body convulsed. Her voice wobbled. "Oh, Jesus."

"What is it, Abby?"

She took a deep, labored breath. With her voice full of want, she said, "He's parting her with his tongue."

"Like this?" he asked, dipping his head between her legs, pulling open her pink lips, and invading her with his warm tongue. That first sweet touch had her sex muscles spasming, screaming for release. "Mmm," he moaned, delving in deeper.

"Yesss," she moaned. "Just like that."

When the soft blade of his tongue found her clit for a slow exploration, her hips came off the ground and she dropped the scope, entirely lost in his touch.

"Keep watching, baby," he whispered, his warm breath scorching her thighs. "I need to know what he's doing."

Her shaky hands gripped the scope, refocusing on the couple while Cody pressed his lips hungrily into her sweetness and deepened the kiss. The dual assault turned her inside out, taking her to the edge long before she was ready—long before she wanted this sexy interlude to end.

"I wonder if she tastes like peaches, too."

"*Cody* . . . ," she murmured, surprised to find her voice functioning. "Oh, God, Cody. He's putting his fingers inside her."

A low chuckle rumbled in his throat as he inserted a finger into her slick core and stilled his movements. "Like this, baby?" She heard the raw ache of lust in his voice.

She sucked in a tight breath. Her nipples tightened with arousal. "Yeah, just like that," she cried out. She began moving, pressing against him, seeking what her body craved, encouraging him to finger fuck her.

He didn't.

The sweet torture made her throb. Her heart hammered and a whimper escaped her lips. "Please . . . ," she begged shamelessly.

"You have to tell me what he's doing, sweetheart."

Quickly catching on, she swallowed hard and said, "He's moving his fingers in and out of her. In and out. In and out."

Without preamble, he began to stroke her. She purred in erotic delight.

"Does that feel good, baby?"

"So good," she cried out.

"Now, tell me how he's finger fucking her. Slow, like this?" he said, pumping in and out of her gently while his thumb stroked her clit. "Or quickly, like this?" he asked, picking up the pace. She heard desire in his voice, and it excited her to know how much this turned him on, too.

Her blood pressure soared and pleasure forked through her as he swirled his fingers inside her. Deft fingers circled her G-spot with precision and pushed her to the precipice so very, very quickly. Lord, the man had a talent for knowing exactly how she liked it.

As he coaxed an orgasm from her, his movements were slow, methodical, controlled, and even though it felt damn incredible, she sensed his restraint, aware of the way he was leashing the wild animal lingering beneath the surface.

"Cody, please," she said, not wanting him to hold anything back.

With hunger consuming her, she grew slicker with each delicious stroke. But it wasn't enough. She wanted him to unleash himself on her. She wanted him to ram his cock inside her and ride her feverishly. She wanted him to drive into her, hard and fast, pushing them both beyond anything they'd ever known. She wanted him to render her senseless.

When he slipped another finger inside for a deliciously snug fit, the erotic sensations pulled all her concentration. Her pussy muscles clenched around his thick fingers. She could feel the pressure building inside her, coming to a peak.

Cody brushed his tongue over her engorged clit. "You're so slick, baby. Does watching him lick her hot little pussy make you this way?"

As soon as those naughty words left his mouth, her body pulsed and throbbed with the hot flow of release.

She dropped the scope so she could rake her fingers through Cody's hair, holding his face to her cunt while her body moved restlessly beneath his mouth. "Yes," she whispered wanting to cry out in ecstasy. "Fuck me with your tongue, Cody."

Her muscles tightened and contracted; then her sweet cream spilled into Cody's mouth. He gave a low, lusty groan and lapped at her pussy with slow, easy strokes. She stared at him with fascinated excitement, watching his every movement. He remained between her legs for a long time, drinking her cream. His soft moans of pleasure were doing delightful things to her pussy.

"Cody, that was so . . . so . . ." She struggled to find the right word.

Cody soothed his thumb over her kiss-swollen clit and glanced up at her. In that brief moment, she saw depth, empathy and emotional turmoil before he quickly blinked it away.

Her breath caught. *"Cody . . ."* she murmured, her heart tightening in her chest, her pulse racing. Emotions gathered in a knot in her throat. Swallowing, Abby touched her hand to his cheek, desperately needing an intimate connection to him. When his dark, soulful eyes met hers, she felt a strange warmth rush through her blood.

For a brief moment, silence stretched between them. Then Cody spoke with a light tone, even though she suspected it took great effort. "Like I said, Abby, naughty, scandalous but so damn exciting."

After her tremors subsided, Cody climbed out from between her legs and moved in beside her. She glanced at the massive bulge in his pants, everything in her craving to pleasure him, and needing almost desperately to break through his protective shield.

Formulating a plan, Abby picked up the scope and looked through it.

"Cody," she said, striving for normalcy.

"Yeah, baby."

"She's taking his cock into her mouth." She felt Cody's body tighten as he shot her a scalding look. "See for yourself," she said, handing him the scope in an effort to push him past his comfort zone and encourage him to lose his control. It hadn't taken her long to figure out that there was so much more to this man, so much repressed passion, buried deep inside, where he kept it carefully guarded. She felt it with every fiber of her being. She pressed her hand over the bulge in his pants, squeezing his erect dick.

His eyes flared hot when they met hers. *"Abby."*

She crawled between his legs and brushed her mouth over his pants, taking pleasure in his size and thickness. When she tugged on his waistband, Cody eagerly lifted his hips for her. She quickly removed his fatigues and turned her attention to his beautiful cock. Yummy. Her pussy quivered in delight.

"Beautiful," she whispered as she stared at him, deciding then and there that it was the most beautiful cock she'd ever set eyes—or mouth—on. She brushed her fingers over his length and watched him throb beneath her touch. "Tell me what she's doing, Cody."

She heard him pull in a tight breath. "She's sucking his cock, baby. Taking it deep into her mouth."

"Like this?" she asked, bending forward to draw him into her mouth.

"Oh, fuck . . . ," he bit out, pushing against her. "Yeah, just like that."

She worked her mouth over his dick, taking it as deeply as she could, swirling her tongue over his swollen head until juices pearled on the tip. One hand moved to his sac and cupped his balls for a slow, gentle massage.

She inched back and glanced up at him. "Keep watching, Cody. If I'm not doing it right, let me know."

"Oh, baby, you're doing it right." His voice sounded strangled, labored. Desire danced in his eyes. "So damn right . . . ," he groaned.

"Make sure you tell me everything she's doing, so I can give you my best educated guess on the situation." Abby turned her attention back to his cock and licked the tangy juices from his slit.

"Jesus . . . ," he murmured. "She's rubbing her hot pussy on his leg. Sliding back and forth, back and forth, wetting his thigh with her cream." He growled deep. "Christ, that is such a turn-on."

Never taking her mouth from his cock, Abby straddled his leg, brushing her drenched cunt over him, back and forth. As she stimulated her oversensitized clit, she settled into a nice, steady rhythm.

"Yeah, baby, just like that." She could hear the pleasure and raw desire in his voice. "That's so good."

The feel of his cock pulsing and thickening told her that he was only a few strokes away from fulfillment. "That's it, Cody. Come for me," she murmured. "Let me taste you."

As though desperate for release, he rushed out, "She's picking up the tempo now, running her hands up and down his shaft, her mouth following the motion. Oh, fuck, I think the guy's coming . . ."

Abby followed suit, taking him deep into her mouth and moaning with excitement as Cody's orgasm approached. She listened to the sound of the scope hitting the ground. A second later Cody gripped her head and tugged.

"I'm going to come, babe."

She eased her mouth off and shot him a quick glance. "Did he come in her mouth?"

"Oh, Jesus . . ."

That was enough of an answer for her. She cupped his sac tighter and sucked him in deep, until his head hit the back of her throat. He began rocking with the motion, groaning and grabbing fistfuls of her hair. When she felt that first sweet clench of fulfillment, she circled his bulbous head with her tongue.

She inched back to speak to him. "I want you to come in my mouth, too, Cody."

Then he began trembling and panting as he fed his cock back into her mouth. "Fuck . . . ," he moaned and bucked against her. A moment later he splashed hot seed into the back of her throat.

After she drank every delicious drop, she glanced up at him and smiled. It thrilled her to see him looking all ruffled yet contented. She gave a happy sigh, thinking how much she liked the way he looked right now. Thinking how much she'd like to make him look like that every single day.

"So what's your conclusion, Cody?"

"My what?" he asked, his chest rising and falling with his heavy breathing.

God, she loved the way she frazzled him. "Your conclusion. Your best educated guess. Were you able to tell if they were having sex or not?" As Cody sat there watching her, satisfaction written all over his handsome face, she suspected at this particular moment that a reply was simply beyond him. Abby angled her head, licked her moist lips, and teased, "Or do we need to watch some more?"

FOUR

oly. Fuck.

Those were the only two words Cody's brain could formulate under the present circumstances. Nothing more. Nothing less. Jesus, that had to be the most exciting, mind-boggling thing he'd ever done, with the most exciting, mind-boggling woman he'd ever met.

As he watched Abby lick the moisture from her plump lips, sunlight glistened on her silky blond hair and shimmered in her baby blues. When he reached out to brush a strand from her cheek, tucking it behind her ear, she offered him a dazzling smile.

His heart skipped a beat, and everything in him reacted to the warmth in her gaze and the contented expression on her glowing face.

"That was amazing," she whispered to him.

It rattled him how her soft voice penetrated his protective layer and the way her eyes mirrored her every emotion. His insides clenched. What was it about her that spawned such peculiar reactions in him?

"Come here." Feeling a little shaky, he dragged her to him and quickly reminded himself that this was nothing more than one afternoon of hot sex and physical pleasure. It couldn't go beyond that. So why did he get the uneasy feeling that she had no intention of leaving it uncomplicated?

As she climbed out from between his legs to nestle in beside him, and dropped a soft kiss onto his mouth, his body tightened in response. Warm lips brushed over his, shaking him right down to his core, making him feel edgy and out of control. And if there was one rule he lived by, it was to always maintain control.

"It really was great, Cody." She cupped his cheek and met his gaze unflinchingly. "But next time I don't want you to hold back," she said, as though peering into his deepest corners and reading his innermost thoughts.

Chaos erupted inside him as emotions he wasn't prepared for threatened to crack the icy barrier protecting his heart. Even though this game had started out with his domination, this sweet, sexy woman continued to throw him off guard, and suddenly he was feeling more like prey than predator.

As the reality of the situation inched its way back into his brain, every instinct in his body told him to bolt. It occurred to him just how close he'd come to losing his control with her, and it was that control that got him through the rough times, and kept the demons at bay.

Jesus, he needed to get the hell out of there. Fast. He needed to escape and find solitude. He retreated physically, inching away from her as he commanded himself to get control of his emotions and put as much distance between them as he could. He could tell by the look in her eyes that she felt his retreat, both physically and emotionally. Good. Because he really needed her to understand that this was a onetime affair, one afternoon only. They'd played a game, and now she could go home with a few sexy memories.

"Abby . . ."

She glanced at her watch and cut him off. "Oh, shoot, look at the time. If I don't hurry I'll be late for my snorkeling lesson." Wide eyes questioned him. Her sensuous mouth curved. "Do you want to join me?"

He shook his head quickly. "No."

When she pursed her lips, clearly disappointed, he felt like a goddamn son of a bitch, but there was no fucking way he was going to cross that emotional line, where pain ruled. He needed to push her away. It was the right thing to do.

The only safe thing to do.

When she moved out of the circle of his arms to gather her clothes, he couldn't deny that he immediately missed her warmth, which gave credence to his logic to keep his distance.

"Let me help you," he said, shuffling to his feet, happy for the distraction.

Cody helped her gather her clothes and then sank back onto the ground as she dressed. He tried to focus on anything and everything except Abby and the way she made him feel. The truth was, he was angry. Angry with himself for the way she got under his skin, and angry that she so easily could.

Once she was fully dressed, Abby stood near the cliff's edge and glanced at the horizon, with her lush ass staring him in the face. He had to admit, she made one hell of a breathtaking view.

Her mere presence drew his attention, despite his best efforts to focus elsewhere. As he watched her take one last look at the horizon, he became hyperaware of how he wanted her again. He fought down the overwhelming urge to grab her, peel her clothes from her beautiful body, sink his cock all the way up inside her and unleash himself on her.

She turned and aimed a longing glance at him. Her smile was slow and inviting. "Tell me something, Cody."

"What's that?"

"Did you know that couple would be there, on the rocks, having sex?"

"Yup," he said, not bothering to deny it.

"So you *are* a voyeur?"

"I don't normally watch people have sex, if that's what you're wondering. I've never sat through their whole show before."

She angled her head. "No? Then why did you come here with me if you didn't want to watch?"

He pitched his voice low. "For you, Abby. You wanted to play. So we played," he said, letting her know that he was privy to her most intimate thoughts—her budding fetishes.

He watched her chest heave with excitement, her face glowing with sexual awareness. "You really are a wild man at heart, aren't you?" When he didn't answer, she arched a curious brow and went on, "So you've never sat through a whole sexy show before?"

As his gaze brushed over her body, sexual tension hung heavy in the air. "Not *their* sexy show, anyway."

He saw a glimmer of understanding as awareness dawned on her, and then heat flooded her cheeks. "I see," she said, her eyes dimming with desire as they raced over his body. His cock brushed against his inner thigh, reminding him he was still sitting there half naked.

Abby turned back around on the cliff, her elevated position once again affording him a view of her fabulous ass. A thin sheen of perspiration broke out on his skin and he wondered if she felt the sexual tension rising in him.

"It looks like everyone is getting ready for the lesson. I guess I should go."

Cody glanced at the dark sky, where heavy black clouds lingered in the distance. "Be careful, Abby."

She spun back around to face him. Her brow furrowed. "Why?"

"It looks like a storm is moving in. The surf and current can be tricky when the wind picks up."

Her eyes gleamed, her face softened and her body relaxed. "I'm not worried."

"No? Why not?"

She shot him a suggestive look while the gleam in her eyes turned wicked. "Because I know you'll be *watching* . . ."

He gave a curt shake of his head. His voice was gruff when he told her, "You're wrong, Abby. I won't be here."

With that she picked up her beach bag, turned, shook her hot little ass at him and then disappeared into the dense jungle. Once again he was left alone with nothing more than his scope and the surrounding wildlife. But this time he had one hell of a big-ass boner to contend with.

Cody spent a long time sitting there, taming down his ever

determined erection. When he finally got his dick somewhat under control, he took that opportunity to pull himself back together. After he hastily dressed, he picked up his scope and prepared to leave. He had every intention of going back to his cabana, putting Abby out of his mind once and for all and taking a long nap. But, despite his best interests, he took cover under a large palm tree and allowed himself one last look through the lens. He caught Abby in his crosshairs as she came from the changing room, dropped her beach bag onto the sand and joined the lesson.

Who the hell was he kidding? He had no intention of leaving his perch, not when Abby was about to go underwater with a storm approaching. It gave him some measure of comfort to know that the instructors were trained for every type of emergency, but Cody still felt the need to watch over her. And watch over her he would, goddammit.

She stood there with her hands on her hips, seducing him from afar with her gorgeous body and playful grin. She looked so fucking sexy standing there that it took every ounce of strength he could muster to keep all his blood from rushing south. She really was one hell of a cock tease. Every few minutes she would cast a glance his way and gift him with an amused smile, knowing he was there watching, waiting, calculating his next move, despite what he had told her.

He spent a long moment studying her, thinking about how good she'd felt in his arms, how delectable she'd tasted between her legs, how her sweet peach taste exploded on his tongue, and how she had the prettiest pussy he'd ever had the pleasure of licking. His body quaked with the onslaught of memories.

When a shudder overtook him, he turned his attention to the dark, ominous clouds overhead. Once again his skin prickled in warning. He didn't like the look of those storm clouds. Not one little bit.

As soon as the land lesson was over, Abby pulled on her mask, snorkel and fins and made her way to the water. Fortunately it was easy to spot her with that bright yellow bikini on. His trained eyes scanned the ocean, catching and holding her in his crosshairs once again. He watched her wade out until she was submerged to her waist, take one last glance toward him and then dip below the choppy surface.

Cody spent a long time tracking her motion. Minutes slipped into hours, and before he knew it, he was stifling a yawn. Exhaustion pulled at him, a reminder that he'd been up since the crack of dawn. He dropped the scope for a moment when his vision started blurring, pinched the bridge of his nose and blinked his eyes back into focus.

After clearing his vision, he returned his attention to the water only to spot Abby far from shore, bobbing up and down in the water, waving her arms in distress.

Shit . . .

Leaping into action, he negotiated his way to the foot of the mountain at breakneck speed. When he landed on the beach, the lifeguard was reaching for a rescue board, signaling the other guards to the emergency.

Cody grabbed the board. "I got it." With that he ran into the surf and swam out to Abby.

Keeping himself calm, he pulled her shivering body into his arms. "I got you, sweetheart."

A relieved rush of air exploded from her lungs. "Thank God, Cody."

"Hold on to me tightly while I get you to safety." Tucking her under his arm, he swam to the shore. Once they reached the sand, he removed her gear and laid her out for a closer inspection. His gaze raked over her in concern. Just then the skies opened up with a vengeance. He leaned over her and used his body to shield her from the cold rain. He'd never felt such a strong surge of emotion as when her big blue eyes blinked up at him. He brushed a fat raindrop from her lashes and let out a breath he hadn't realized he was holding.

"Jesus, Abby, you scared me." Cody shook his head, disgusted with himself. He should have gone with her when she'd asked.

Her smile eased his tension. "Danielle has her sea god, Lauren has her jungle lord and I have my very own guardian angel."

He angled his head and studied her. Had he imagined it, or did he detect a devilish gleam in her eyes? Even though he'd just rescued her, he suddenly had the feeling that she was rescuing him.

He arched an inquisitive brow. "What makes me think you orchestrated this whole rescue?"

She shot him an innocent glance and, he assumed purely for effect, coughed. She feigned hurt and levered herself up on her elbows. "I have no idea why you'd think that."

"How did you know I'd be watching, Abby?"

She touched him with intimate recognition; her hands roamed over him like she couldn't get enough. "Because you're my guardian angel."

His gaze shifted to take in her hard nipples, and then he settled his focus back on her face. "Did you ever stop to think that maybe I'm really just the devil in disguise?"

Smoldering eyes met his. Her gaze was warm and seductive, tempting him at every turn.

But why?

What more did she want from him?

He'd made it clear that he'd given her all he had to give. Why was she pushing him? Tempting him? Taunting him?

She touched his fatigues, curling the fabric through her fingers. His body began vibrating with need.

"Maybe we should go somewhere where we can shed this disguise and I can give you my best educated guess on the matter," she murmured, sending a direct hit when his defenses were weak.

As the cold rain pelted down on them, thunder rumbled in the distance and lightning zigzagged a ragged pattern across the dark sky. When she began shivering, Cody gathered her, along with her belongings, into his arms to offer her his warmth. Despite everything in him urging otherwise, he gave in to his primal needs and desires.

"Let's go get you warmed up," he said.

With determined strides, and blood pulsing hot, he carried her up the beach, toward the lodge, no longer able to rein in his lust.

"Where are we going?" she asked breathlessly.

"To the sauna. To get you warm." He neglected to tell her that he planned on fucking her senseless once he got her there.

Full, round breasts pressed into his chest, and he could feel her body quake. He watched her swallow. "But I am warm, Cody. In fact, I'm hot." She snaked her arms around his neck, her fingers tangling in his damp hair.

Her sultry smile combined with her soft, seductive voice completely unglued him. He groaned and quickened his steps, hurrying along one of the footpaths. With the instinctive knowledge that he was walking a dangerous road, he carried her into one of the private saunas.

Once they were inside, he set her on her feet and sprayed water on the hot rocks to create steam. As the humidity rose, the warm, aromatic scent of cedar drenched the room. Cody turned his full attention to Abby. The soft sconce lighting allowed him to take in the warmth in her eyes, her sensual smile and her beautiful, voluptuous contours. Christ, he really had no idea the sauna could be so seductive. His guts twisted and his cock throbbed to the point of pain.

"Does it hurt?" she asked.

"Does what hurt?"

When her glance strayed to his cock, he threw his head back and groaned out loud. "Abby, I swear you're going to be the death of me."

She moved toward him so he could see the moisture pebbling on her flesh, begging to be licked clean. She dragged her finger down his chest until she reached the bulge in his pants. "I was just thinking if it hurt, then maybe I could kiss it better." The way she was looking at him nearly stopped his heart. Despite everything urging him to run the other way, he couldn't.

He wanted this. And never before had he ever wanted anything this much. He needed her in a way that scared the shit out of him.

Cody dragged her into his embrace. When she became pliable

in his arms, his lips found hers for the first time. They kissed long and deep. Even though he'd been between her legs, licking her most private parts, this kiss felt far more intimate than anything he'd ever known.

Their tongues joined and tangled. She moaned, drew his tongue deeper into her mouth and sucked like she couldn't get enough. He echoed the sentiments. Everything about the way their mouths came together turned him inside out. Cody began pillaging her mouth with his tongue until tremors rippled across her skin.

He slipped his arms around her back. With a slight shift, he drove his hard cock into her in a thrust that allowed his thickness to indent her abdomen. The action would tell her in no uncertain terms what she did to him. She thrust her pelvis forward, urging him on.

He brushed her wet hair back and began trembling. He broke the kiss before it obliterated all his control. He inched back and said, "You are so beautiful, Abby." He took a breath and filled his lungs with her sweet, feminine scent. His hands skimmed her curves. "Your body makes me so fucking wild. I want to kiss every inch of your skin. I want to spread your pussy with my tongue and drink your sweetness. I want to put my fingers and cock deep inside you and make you come for me, again and again. I want to pleasure you like you've never been pleasured before."

She moaned in acquiescence, her body spasming with need.

"Will you come for me, Abby? Will you do that for me?" Beneath her wet bikini top he could feel her nipples tighten with arousal.

"Again and again," she murmured, impatience lacing her voice.

She offered herself to him so openly, so honestly, that a rush of tenderness overcame him and nearly knocked him off his feet.

"Cody," she murmured. Her gaze was dark, full of urgent need.

"Yeah, babe?"

Shifting her stance, she widened her legs and rubbed up against him. Bold, aggressive eyes met his. "I want you to remove my bathing suit and kiss every inch of my body," she demanded. "Then I want you to tease your cock between my legs and fuck me with wild abandon until you reduce me to a quivering mass of contentment."

Seeing her so aroused, and knowing he was right there along with her, prompted him into immediate action. "My pleasure," he said, desperately needing to get her naked and writhing beneath him before he lost all ability to think rationally.

Cody slipped his hands behind her back and untied her top. The thin scrap of material fell to the floor, forgotten. He drew a sharp breath when his gaze settled on her supple breasts. His body registered every delicious detail. He dropped to his knees and shimmied close to her. He gripped the bands of her bikini.

"Wiggle for me, Abby."

As she wiggled her hips, he pulled her wet bathing suit down to her ankles. Hunger consumed him at the sight of her standing completely naked, her blond curls damp from her cream. Her body called out to him in seductive ways, ways that made him wild. He brushed her inner thighs with the backs of his hands, feeling her wetness, thrilled that he'd made her this way.

He moved his mouth to her breasts, taking one beautiful nip-

ple between his lips. Abby arched her back and plowed her fingers
through his hair. He brushed his tongue over her breast, teasing
her swollen nub. She let out a wild cry and pressed harder against
him. Growling in delight, Cody turned his attention to her other
breast. He brushed his lips over her nipple and tweaked it between
his fingers.

He moved one hand between her thighs and felt her creamy desire. He pushed a finger into her warm, wet pussy. She was so goddamn slick he nearly lost it then and there. As pleasure swamped him,
he cursed under his breath and exhaled a slow, controlled breath.

He slid his finger in and out of her and watched the way her
eyes rolled in ecstasy. "Does that feel good, Abby?" he breathed
into her mouth. He pushed another finger inside for a snug fit.
"Do you like it when I fuck you with my fingers?" Her purr resonated through him and her clenching muscles answered his question. Needing to taste her, he buried his face in her cunt, ravishing
her with his tongue until she came in his mouth.

"Ohmigod," she whimpered as her body quivered all over.

"Mmm," he moaned, lapping up every delicious drop of her
liquid desire.

Breathing hard, he stood and pulled her to him. His mouth
found hers for a deep, wet kiss, and she moaned when she tasted
her creamy essence on his tongue. She sagged against his body, and
Cody pushed her damp bangs from her forehead. Hot and sweaty
from the steamy heat, their bodies melted together as one.

She ripped at his shirt; her hands drove him wild as they raced
over his body. Lost in the sensual haze, he stepped back and tore
his clothes off, desperate to answer the pull in his groin.

"Jesus Christ, Abby. I don't have any protection."

He was in dire need here, in the middle of a goddamn crisis, and didn't have any condoms.

"My beach bag. Hurry."

Thank God.

Cody quickly rooted through her bag until he found a condom. He wasted no time sheathing himself and gathered her into his arms for a heated kiss. Then, taking her by surprise, he spun her around and bent her over the bench, pressing her breasts into the cedar slats. At first she gasped at his roughness, and then she tipped her ass up, offering herself to him.

"Please fuck me, Cody." He heard the raw ache of lust in her voice.

A low growl of longing rose from his throat. Unable to help himself, or slow himself down, he widened her sex lips and plunged into her, so hard and so deep that he drove her into the cedar slats. Then suddenly, as her heat closed around him, he stood stock still, afraid to move, afraid to breathe, afraid of losing it.

He sucked in a sharp breath at the thought of what might happen next. Oh, Jesus, what the hell had he gotten himself into?

"Abby," he whispered. He was so damn close to losing himself in her.

Thunder overhead shook the walls and caused the lights to flicker. As the weather raged outside, inside Cody was facing his own storm. He closed his eyes in distress, calculating his next move.

Abby's sweet cunt tightened around his dick, tormenting him to new heights. She glanced at him over her shoulder and angled her body. Her hips began moving, pushing him in and out. In and out. Christ, she was so hot, so tight, so slick.

So damn perfect.

Their sweet union felt more emotional than physical, and the sudden swell of emotions terrified the hell out of him. Truthfully, he needed this to end, almost as much as he needed it to go on.

"Cody," she murmured, as though reading his distress. The warmth in her eyes never failed to affect him. "I want you to let go," she encouraged. As her words sank in, the longing to do just that ripped a hole in the shield around his heart. "And make wild, passionate love to me," she urged.

Her open display of emotions stirred things up inside him, unlocking the door that kept him safe. Feelings long ago restrained swam to the surface, and he suddenly found himself ruled by emotions. A deep passion that he had absolutely no control over raged through him.

Ravenous and completely out of control, he unleashed himself on her, unlocking the caged animal, driving his cock into her, slamming her body against the cedar bench, crushing her beneath him.

"That's it, Cody." When he gripped her hips, she reached behind herself to close her hands over his. "Just like that," she whimpered.

Through her erotic touch, every emotion he'd ever stifled came rushing to the surface—pain, pleasure, joy and sorrow. But in some strange way, there was a freedom in opening up to her.

He pumped harder and faster. He'd slow down in a minute. In just one minute. Then he'd gather his control and make it good for her. He knew he was being a selfish prick, taking more than he should, but at the moment he couldn't seem to help himself.

"Cody." Her erotic whimper made him throb. "More. Harder," she demanded, the pleasure in her voice fueling his need.

They both began trembling and panting, breathing raggedly. He rode her impossibly harder, slamming into her, giving her everything he had to give. Her muscles contracted and her slick juices poured over his shaft as she came all over him, again and again. Her tremor reverberated through his blood, and the explosion of his senses pushed him over the precipice.

As her cunt tightened and clenched around his cock, he climaxed so hard, he nearly lost consciousness. "Holy fuck," he bit out, shock waves rocketing through his body.

After the tremors subsided, he remained inside her, their bodies joined as one, still unable to move.

"Oh. My. God," she murmured, breaking the quiet. "Cody. Oh. My. God . . ." It seemed that was all she could say.

Cody laughed. It was a strange reaction, he knew, but nonetheless, he laughed. He laughed long and hard, until Abby joined in. The two of them laughed together, sharing in something private, something special.

When the laughter finally subsided, he pulled his cock out, removed the condom and dropped to the bench. He pulled her to him and kissed her deeply, passionately.

"You're amazing, Abby." As he gathered her into his embrace, it occurred to him that for the first time in a long time he felt contentment, even peace.

When her eyes met his, her sweet voice roused him from his

wanderings. "Well, my best educated guess is that you really are the devil in disguise," she teased.

Cody chuckled, a calmness settling over him. "I think you just bring that out in me, sweetheart."

When the lights flickered again, he ran a soothing hand over her flesh. Suddenly the power shut down, plunging them into darkness. Abby snuggled in closer. "Don't be afraid, Abby."

"I'm not afraid."

Somehow the way she trusted him readily and completely really got to him, leaving her mark on his soul. He fumbled around in the dark, in search of their clothes. "We'd better get out of here."

He heard a rustle, and then Abby flicked on a pen flashlight.

He grinned. "You're always ready for every crisis, aren't you?"

"I'm a planner. What can I say?" He heard the amusement in her voice.

Once they were both dressed, they slipped from the sauna and made their way outside. Bodies touching, shielding each other from the elements, they trekked back to Abby's cabana. Cody couldn't deny there was a new intimacy between them. Nor could he deny that opening himself up to her had helped calm the demons, contrary to what he'd believed. He knew he still had a long way to go, but at least this was a start. . . .

He glanced at her. When she smiled, it warmed his soul. Curious to know more about her, he asked, "Why are you here, Abby? What brought you to this resort?"

"My friends talked me into coming. They wanted to live out their deepest desires."

"I take it you're referring to the magic elixir."

"Yeah."

"So, do you have any deep desires you'd like fulfilled?" he asked.

"I never used to think so. In fact, I thought the elixir was wasted on me."

He sensed she was holding something back, which seemed out of character for her. He was about to ask when she cut him off and asked a question of her own.

"Do you have any deep desires, Cody?"

"To get off this island and be left alone," he said, quick with his usual response.

"Is that why you spend your time on the mountain, all by yourself, with only your scope?"

"Yeah, I guess."

"What are you looking for when you're up there?"

"Solitude."

You can't find what you're not looking for.

As he decrypted Malik's words, it occurred to him that maybe he wasn't looking for solitude at all. Maybe he was merely hiding from the real world, and maybe his deepest desire was to feel love, laughter and happiness again. And he couldn't find it because he wasn't looking for it.

And maybe it took the right woman to show him that.

A jolt of lightning flashed up ahead, startling them both. He tightened his hold on Abby. "We'd better make a run for it."

She gave a breathy, intimate laugh that stroked him from head to toe. "That's not so easy to do with rubbery legs, Cody."

He clasped her hand. "Come on. I won't let you fall." Together they hustled down the footpath. Less than two minutes later they burst into Abby's cabana, laughing like silly schoolkids.

"Let's get undressed and get under the covers," Abby said, peeling her clothes off like they got naked in front of each other every day.

When they were both under the covers, they snuggled close, talking quietly and touching each other intimately. As the storm raged outside, their lips connected once again, and before he knew it they were making love long into the night, slowly, sensuously, passionately, savoring every soft touch, every delectable kiss, every sweet climax.

After a quick nap, they made love again and talked until the wee hours of the morning, until the storm died down and the sun was on the horizon. They talked about his job, her job, the past, the present and everything but their futures, because at the moment, he had no idea what his held.

As the sun burst through the lace curtains, Cody rolled to his side to watch her sleep. A bone-deep warmth coursed through him. She looked very peaceful, angelic and so content. He grinned. Maybe he really had reduced her to a quivering mass of contentment. He dropped a soft kiss onto her mouth and slipped from her bed, not wanting to disturb her sleep.

"Cody," she whispered, her soft voice surprising him.

"Yeah, baby? What is it?"

"Will I see you later?"

"I'll see you."

"Yeah, why?" she asked, sounding drowsy, her eyes barely open.

"Because I'll be watching . . ."

FIVE

bby woke to birds chirping and bright sunshine streaming through the lace curtains in her room. She stretched out her tired limbs while her thoughts rushed to Cody and all the wonderful, amazing, passionate things they'd done the night before. Every muscle in her body clenched at the memory.

She turned to her side and spotted her agenda book. Lord, she might be a planner, but she certainly hadn't planned on the feelings Cody aroused in her.

She knew they'd connected on a deep level, and truthfully, thanks to her taking a chance and veering off her path for once, she'd experienced intimacy and passion with him unlike anything she'd ever experienced before.

So now what? Did she go back and marry Artie now that she knew life had more to offer and that passionate men really did exist—it just took the right woman to bring it out in them? But did that mean she was the right woman for Cody? Or that he'd even want more?

Confused, and no longer content with her well-mapped-out future, Abby climbed from her bed and made her way to the shower. Even though sleep pulled at her, she had a busy day scheduled and wanted to lie in the sun and sort through matters before it all began.

After her shower, she pulled on her bikini, grabbed a peach from the fruit bowl on her table and made her way outside. She glanced around, her gaze scanning the jungle, wondering whether Cody was waiting, watching . . .

Deciding he was probably asleep, she laid her peach beside her and stretched out on the chaise longue, needing the quiet time to clarify her thoughts and strategize her next move.

As her lids drifted shut, the sound of a ringing phone pulled her from her slumber.

Artie?

She jumped from her chair and rushed into her cabana. Breathlessly she said, "Hello."

"Good morning."

Her heart hammered. The deep masculine voice turned her knees to rubber.

"Good morning," she whispered in return. Her thighs clenched with heated memories as his seductive voice played with her libido.

A pause, a heavy sigh, and then, "I miss you, babe."

As her sex fluttered with need, it occurred to her that Cody was making the call that Artie should have been making.

"Then maybe you shouldn't have snuck out this morning."

He chuckled. "I can't wait to hold you again."

She clutched the phone tighter, her pulse skyrocketing. A riot of emotions raged inside her. *"Cody . . ."*

"Why don't you take the phone and go back outside."

Her glance shot to her open door. "Cody, are you watching me?"

"Yeah. I told you I would be." Arousal edged his voice.

Abby stepped out into the sunshine and glanced toward the hilltop. "Where are you?"

Instead of answering, he said, "Go lie back on your chair."

She immediately obliged. With a quick decision, she decided right then and there to seize this day, this moment and this man, to temporarily shelve her worries in the far corners of her mind to sort through later.

"Now stretch your legs out."

"Like this?"

"That's a good girl, Abby." His tone was low, husky. "Only problem is, you're still dressed. I want you to take your bathing suit off."

She drew a sharp breath and murmured low, "You're a very naughty boy, Cody."

"Yeah, I know." The amusement in his tone tugged at her insides.

Abby laid the phone beside her and slowly peeled her bathing suit off. She could hear Cody's low growl of longing when she brought the phone back to her ear.

"Is that better?" she asked.

"Not quite."

"No?"

"Your legs aren't spread."

"Oh, right." Abby widened her legs, taking note of the sticky wetness between her thighs. Goddamn, she was turned on. She heard a rustling sound that made her wonder what was going on. She tried to keep her voice level but failed. "Cody, what are you doing?"

"My cock is hard, Abby. I'm stroking it."

Oh. My. God.

She brought her hand to her throat and swallowed, trying to keep some semblance of control.

"Do you like knowing I'm rubbing my cock while I watch you?"

"Oh, yeah," was all she managed.

"Your breasts are beautiful, sweetheart. Will you touch them for me?" Abby crooked her neck, positioning the phone on her shoulder in order to free both hands. She brushed her thumbs over her nipples and arched into her touch.

"Mmm," she moaned. "That feels so good."

Cody's breathing deepened. He gave a lusty groan, and she could hear him work his hand over his cock in double time.

"Very nice," he murmured. "Now pinch your nipples. I want them red and swollen."

Abby pinched herself hard and gave a little yelp. Flames licked over her. She was so turned on, she began shaking.

"You see that peach beside you, baby?" His soft voice caressed her flesh, and she could feel color rising on her cheeks. "I want you to take a bite and drip the juice all over your nipples. Get them nice and slick for me, and then imagine me licking them clean."

Her entire body heated from the inside out. She bit into the peach and then dripped the sweet nectar over one plump nipple. When she heard him suck in a deep breath, she widened her legs and drizzled the peach juice over her clit. The cool liquid stimulated her nerve endings. The combination of sweet peach and arousal reached her nostrils.

"Fuck . . ." Cody bit out.

"Do you like that, Cody?" she murmured, reveling in the sensations. Becoming dizzy with desire, she dropped the peach and stroked herself. Good God, she was desperate to ease the tension inside her.

"Put your fingers inside your pussy for me," he said in a strangled voice. "I want you to climax with me. Then I'm going to come down there and lick up all your sweet peach cream."

His sexy words brought on a shudder, such that her entire body trembled from head to toe. Never had she done anything so wild and wicked. No, she corrected herself, that wasn't exactly true. Ever since she'd met Cody, she'd been doing lots of things that were wild and wicked. Things that she wanted to continue to do . . .

With need consuming her, she pushed two fingers inside her while her thumb worked her clit. Her hips rose from the chair and her sex muscles clenched. The action drew her fingers in deeper. She took deep, gulping breaths while her throat tightened with pleasure.

She heard him groan. "That's a girl; come with me, baby." His coaxing voice brought on her climax.

Her sex pulsed and spasmed with her release. She tossed her

head to the side and cried out Cody's name while she rode the waves of pleasure.

After a long moment, when she gulped for air, Cody's husky, labored voice brought her back to him.

"Stay put, Abby. And keep your legs open."

Less than two minutes later, she felt Cody's presence in front of her. She opened her eyes to see him standing over her, dressed in bathing trunks and a blue T-shirt, looking like sex incarnate. The intense look on his face nearly stopped her heart.

His nostrils flared as he dropped to his knees. His eyes swept over her, taking in her spread legs. "You have the prettiest pussy I've ever seen," he whispered in a tone that was alarmingly tender.

They exchanged a look before he buried his face between her thighs. The soft blade of his tongue found her clit. She felt his body tremble. "You taste delicious," he murmured. His long, intimate strokes immediately brought on another orgasm. He inserted a finger, and that was all she needed to shut down her brain. Fire whipped through her blood. Her hot juices flowed endlessly into his mouth.

"Mmm. I love how responsive you are." His voice ended in a soft whisper.

She glanced down at him. The way his dark eyes smoldered when they met hers made her breath catch.

His fingers continued to idly stroke her clit. "You're a wild woman, Abby Benton." Mesmerized, she watched Cody stand, come up beside her and place the sweetest, softest kiss on her mouth, a kiss so tender and passionate it touched something deep inside her.

"I just think you bring that out in me," she rasped, swallowing hard.

He grabbed her hand and tugged her out of the chair. "Let's go inside and get something to drink." Abby gathered her belongings and followed him into her cabana. He grabbed two bottles of water from the fridge while she dressed. He spotted her agenda and turned to her. "You really are a planner, aren't you?" When she nodded, he asked, "So what's your plan for the rest of the day?"

Abby glanced at the clock. "I have a hot-stone massage booked in ten minutes, then a late lunch with the girls." She winked at him. "Even though you already told me it's not your thing, would you like to join me for a couple's massage down by the ocean?"

Couple's . . .

The gravity of that one word hit her hard.

"I guess. Then maybe we can take a swim."

She saw the mischief in his eyes and wondered what he was up to.

Less than ten minutes later they found themselves sprawled out on a massage table, merely a foot separating them, with only their bathing suits on. When the seductive scent of vanilla oil reached Abby's nostrils and the first warm rock touched her back, she moaned in delight.

"Mmm, that feels so good," she murmured, licking her dry lips.

She turned her head and watched Cody's eyes widen. He pitched his voice low and whispered, "You'd better stop making sexy noises, Abby, or I won't be able to control myself."

If that wasn't an invitation to tease him, she didn't know what was. She shifted restlessly and continued to moan, deciding it was time for her to have the upper hand for a change. She lowered her voice to match his. "Oh, my, that heat goes right through me. It makes me feel all hot, tingly, and . . . *wet.*"

Cody growled. "Abby, you do know you're going to pay for that, right?"

His seductive tenor played havoc with her hormones. She flashed her lashes at him as shivers of pleasure raced down her spine. For the next thirty minutes she moaned, purred and mewled, until the fire in Cody's eyes became explosive.

Just as the massage came to an end, she murmured, "Mmm, I do believe that feels better than sex."

"We'll see about that."

Cody threw the sheets off, grabbed her by the arm and hauled her away from the massage table and into the water with him.

She gasped. "Cody, what are you doing?"

"Proving to you that a massage does not feel better than sex. Now, follow me."

Anxious to see what he had in mind, Abby swam out to the rocks with him. They were tucked out of sight, away from the beach, but easily viewable from the hilltop. As they climbed from the water, she glanced around, realizing they were in the exact same location as the couple they had spied on yesterday. She grinned, understanding his earlier mischievous look, and what he was up to now. Cody obviously had this planned all along. Out of nowhere a burst of warmth brought on a shiver. It touched her deeply that he brought her here on purpose so he could play out her secret desires, her darkest fetishes.

Cody grabbed her, hauled her to him and locked his arms around her waist. He planted a hard, ravenous kiss on her mouth then inched back to catch her eyes. He cocked his head. "Is that better than a massage?"

As the air crackled with sexual energy, she tried for casual. "Not even close," she managed through the haze of lust.

Cody's eyes darkened. He unhooked her bathing suit top and turned his attention to her breasts. The soft blade of his tongue flicked over her nipple, hardening it, and it was all she could do to stifle a heated moan. When his thumb scraped over her aching bud, she briefly closed her eyes against the erotic sensations.

"Is that better than a massage?"

She drew a deep breath and looked past his shoulder, going for bored. "It's debatable . . . ," she said, humoring him.

Growling, Cody dropped to his knees and dragged her down with him. Hastily, he pulled her bikini bottoms from her hips and widened her legs. He nuzzled her pussy, inhaled her aroused scent, and then gifted her with one long, luxurious stroke of his tongue. As his mouth moved over her clit, she nearly erupted.

Oh, Lord . . .

He cast her a knowing glance. "How about that, Abby? Does that feel better than a massage?"

Her heart pounded erratically. She made a sexy noise and shifted. "I'm not sure. The jury is still out."

With that Cody tore his clothes off and grabbed a condom from his bathing suit. She bit her lip and watched him, taking pleasure in the sight of his gorgeous, naked body. Without drawing out the foreplay, he quickly rolled the condom on, spread her legs wider, and in one swift movement drove his cock all the way up inside her. She gasped as his fullness stretched her wide open. Moisture pebbled his flesh as he furiously pumped in and out of her. When she shut her eyes in surrender, he said, "Look around, babe. I bet someone is on that hilltop watching me fuck you."

Jesus . . .

Her pulse kicked up a notch and her pussy muscles clenched with the approach of an orgasm. Just knowing others might be watching filled her with raw lust. Frantic, she clawed at his back and grabbed his ass, driving his cock deeper into her cunt. Moments before her orgasm hit, Cody stopped pumping and gave her a devilish grin. One sexy brow rose in amused awareness. "Now, tell me, sweetheart," he said, having brought her to the edge only to keep her there, hovering like a damn hummingbird, payback for all her teasing, she assumed. "Does this feel better than a massage?" His voice was rough with emotion, and she sensed it took all his effort to maintain his control while he played with her.

Frazzled, she muffled sexually frustrated curses under her breath. Cody laughed in response, which reminded her how much she loved the easy intimacy between them.

In desperate need of an orgasm, she drew a shaky breath and conceded defeat. "Yes, yes, of course this feels better than any massage," she burst out. "Now, make me come, goddammit!"

Chuckling, Cody unleashed himself on her, pumping and pushing deep, giving her exactly what she needed as she lost herself in him, body and soul.

Seconds later she tumbled into an orgasm. Her hands tightened around his back. She held him to her, never wanting to let him go.

Cody threw his head back and groaned. She felt his cock throb deep inside her and knew he was joining her in release. Everything about their coupling felt so right, so perfect, that a myriad of emotions rushed to her heart. She found his mouth and kissed him with all the passion inside her.

After a long moment, Cody rolled to his side and gathered her into his arms. It felt so nice to be held by him. When her breathing finally regulated, she traced her finger over his mouth and shot him a questioning glance. "Hmm, what makes me think you had this seduction orchestrated all along?" she teased.

He feigned innocence, softening the angles in his face. "I have no idea why you would think that."

Abby laughed and snuggled in tighter. As the warmth of the sun beat down on them, scorching their bodies, she let her eyes drift shut and listened to his heartbeat settle into a steady rhythm.

Cody tangled his fingers through her hair. His voice dropped to a whisper. "We'd better get out of the sun before we burn to a crisp." Taking her by surprise, he whacked her ass.

"Umm, did you mean for that to turn me on, Cody? Because it did."

He laughed. "You're insatiable."

Cody sat up and retrieved their clothes. As they dressed, Abby looked out over the aquamarine water, listening to the gentle, soothing sound of the waves lapping against the rocks. "God, it's just so beautiful here."

Cody gestured with a nod. "It looks like there is a scuba-diving excursion taking place."

Abby shaded the sun from her eyes. "Where?"

Leaning in close, Cody pointed. "Way out there."

Surprised, Abby said, "How did you spot that? I can barely see the boat."

"From years of training, I guess."

"It sounds like fun. Maybe I'll try."

"Just be careful you don't drown. I won't be there to rescue you this time."

She laughed. "You won't come?"

Cody shook his head. "Malik is always trying to get me to go, but I don't want to."

"Don't you like snorkeling, or scuba diving?"

He shrugged. "I guess I do. Or I used to, anyway."

"So why don't you go? You have a great eye for spotting things. Hey, you even rescued me when I was drowning." She winked at him.

He rolled his eyes and brushed his thumb over her mouth. "I don't go because I think Malik is up to something."

Abby made a face and shook her head in agreement. "He is a wily old man, isn't he?"

"Wily? That's not the first word that comes to my mind."

Abby tilted her face, drinking in the tropical sun, thinking about how quickly her vacation was flying by. She also considered how much she loved the O Spa. It was definitely an oasis of pleasure, she mused. Lots and lots of pleasure. The thought of going back to a snowy Chicago and life as she knew it made her shiver, and not in a good way.

"So, what will you do when you leave here, Cody? Will you go back to the military?"

"No," he answered quickly.

Abby took a moment to think about Cody's unique skills, and the way Mr. Malik pressed him to partake in the water activities. She then thought about Mr. Malik's cryptic words to her. The truth was, if she hadn't ventured off her beaten path, she never would have discovered Cody.

"So, why do you think Mr. Malik is trying to get you to go on the excursions?" she asked.

"My guess is that he's trying to guide me. Help me figure out my future."

"Search and rescue?"

He nodded. "Smart girl."

"I think you'd be great at that, Cody. You already watch over everyone like you're a guardian angel."

"I thought we established that I'm really the devil in disguise."

She chuckled. "Yes, we did, didn't we? But I think you're both." When her stomach grumbled she suddenly remembered her late lunch with the girls. "Oh, shoot. I have to run," she said, rubbing her belly.

"What's up?"

"I have lunch plans with the girls."

His eyes darkened when they locked on hers. "Break them."

God, when he looked at her like that, her skin came alive. "I can't."

He brushed his lips over hers. His heat wrapped around her; his devilish smile turned her insides to molten lava. "Are you sure you want to go? Don't you know great things can happen when you break your plans, sweetheart?" he whispered, enticing her salacious libido with his body.

As tempting as that was, she'd promised her friends she'd be there. "I really can't, Cody."

He took a long moment to study her. "Do you ever break your plans, Abby?"

After a moment of hesitation, she shook her head and said, "No."

He gave a resigned sigh. "So what's on your agenda later, then?"

She cocked her head. "You're on my agenda later." That brought a smile to his face.

"Oh, yeah?"

"Yeah."

"When and where?" he asked.

"Oh, I'm pretty sure you'll have no trouble finding me," she teased. "You always know where to look."

SIX

With Abby off at lunch with her friends, Cody grabbed a quick bite to eat and then walked restlessly around the resort, his thoughts preoccupied with the feelings Abby roused in him. Grinning madly, like an escaped mental patient, he thought about how quickly they went from strangers to lovers, and his heart swelled. He eventually made his way into the pool hall, looking for a distraction. He found one.

"Hey," Cody said, pleased to see Ryan bent over the pool table, especially since it was still daylight and Ryan wasn't known to venture out during the day. "Rack 'em up."

"Hey, Cody. What's up?" Ryan asked.

Cody shrugged. "Just wasting time until I can get off this godforsaken place. You?"

Ryan mimicked his shrug. "Same here. Haven't seen you in a while."

"I've seen you," Cody said. "With Lauren."

That brought a goofy smile to Ryan's face. Cody took that moment to pry for information. "So, tell me, do you know anything about her friend Abby?" he prodded.

Christ, just saying her name out loud had his heart racing. She was so damn sweet, open, honest and eager to experiment sexually. Her zest for life, her enthusiasm, and how she saw beauty in everything around her had awakened his senses, and for the first time in a long time, he felt alive. Rejuvenated. Free. The truth was, Abby had eased herself past his wall of defense and right into his heart. From her responses to his intimate touch, to the way she encouraged him to open himself up to her, every instinct in his body told him that she felt the same way. That he wasn't merely a passing interest to her.

Ryan grabbed the triangle and centered it. "Lauren mentioned that when they leave here, Abby expects to get engaged to her boyfriend. Apparently, Lauren and Danielle are hoping that after some time away from her soon-to-be fiancé, and after drinking the magic elixir—which you and I both know is bogus—Abby will see that getting engaged to this guy isn't what she really wants. She's not known to divert from her plans, but both girls think she'll see things differently after her time here."

Cody's stomach did a nosedive.

She plans on getting engaged.

What the fuck?

Engaged?

That one word kept drumming in his head. Was Ryan serious? Abby had plans to get married? He swallowed as confusion and anger came at the same time.

With his mood blackening, his eyes fixed hard on his friend. "She's getting engaged?" he asked, his voice full of disbelief.

"I guess. I don't remember Lauren's exact words, but she wants Abby to have a wild time while she's here and indulge in an affair with a passionate guy. Something like that, anyway."

Emotional turmoil swept through him.

Was this why she encouraged him not to hold back with her? So she could have an affair with a wild, passionate guy?

He frowned in concentration. Was this thing between them nothing more than a vacation fling to her? A wild ride before she got engaged?

Jesus fucking Christ!

He shook his head in total disbelief and muttered curses under his breath as realization slammed into him. Perspiration broke out on his forehead, despite the chill settling in his bones.

Tense silence lingered until Ryan broke the balls. Cody watched Ryan work the table. Ryan was speaking, he knew, but Cody couldn't seem to follow the conversation.

Jesus H. Christ. He was a fucking idiot.

He rubbed his temples. Here he thought Abby was sweet, honest, open—and all the while she'd kept her future plans from him. Now he knew why he'd sensed she was holding something back earlier. He might have allowed himself to believe things had changed for her, if he hadn't already established that she *never* broke her plans.

Goddammit, he knew better than to let her past his barriers, but did that stop him? Hell, no! His resolve had melted like hot butter at her first sweet touch. He braced his hands on the edge of the pool table and worked to sort through things, while trying to ignore the pain twisting his heart. He never should have opened himself up. It only allowed hurt inside. Hadn't he learned this painful lesson already? He should have just left it at sex. Nothing more.

As he picked up his pool cue, he felt his insides turn to ice and he knew what he had to do. He drew a breath, centering himself. It was time to put her out of his head, and his heart, and forget he ever met her.

After a late lunch with the girls, Abby made her way back to her cabana. As her gaze strayed to the mountaintop, she wondered whether Cody was watching her.

Cody . . .

Her heart beat at double time just thinking about him. Now that he'd unlocked her fantasies and turned himself loose on her, how could she ever go back to being content with Artie? Back to being a good girl with a mapped-out future?

She couldn't, and she damn well knew it.

Before she met Cody she thought she'd had everything her heart desired, just not what her libido desired. Cody had opened her eyes, and her heart, and showed her that she had neither.

She took a moment to think about her advice to Danielle. Over lunch, she'd told her friend to talk to Ethan, to let him know how she felt, to be honest with him, even though Abby hadn't been completely honest with Cody herself.

Now she knew it was time to take her own advice. She needed to tell Cody how he made her feel, to take their relationship to the next logical stage and tell him everything about her, including her future engagement.

Abby stepped into her cabana and checked her phone for messages. Nothing. She knew she had to talk to Artie, but she needed to talk to Cody first. She hovered near her doorway and waved her arms around, hoping Cody was watching from afar. After minutes slipped by, and he'd yet to show, she decided to go looking for him.

She tried his cabana first, and then made her way to the hilltop. She stood on the cliff overlooking her private cove. Disappointment settled in her stomach when she discovered that her guardian angel wasn't perched on the cliff, overlooking the resort. "Where the heck is he hiding?" she murmured.

Just then Mr. Malik came up behind her. "Abby, I see you've ventured off the beaten path. Have you found what you were looking for?"

She smiled and suspected he knew far more than he let on. "I believe I have," she said, her mind racing to Cody.

"Then the magic elixir is working for you?"

"Yes," she said, a sudden believer in the magic of the elixir, the magic of this island. She'd come to understand that she needed to venture off the beaten path before she found her true heart's desire.

She took a moment to think about Cody and his deepest desires. He'd said he wanted solitude, but like her, she suspected that what he *thought* he wanted and what he *really* wanted were two different things.

"Do you feel the chill in the air, Abby?"

She shot him a perplexed frown. It had to be at least one hundred degrees outside. Before she could answer, he said, "I find the only thing to take the chill out of the bones is the sauna." With that he turned and disappeared into the jungle.

She suspected Mr. Malik was giving her some sort of secret message. Deciding to listen, she climbed from the mountain and made her way to the sauna, the same sauna she'd made love in with Cody. She cracked the door, peeked inside and spotted Cody. His arms were braced on the wall. Her mouth salivated and her libido roared to life as she took in his beautiful naked body. God, she wanted him, today, tomorrow, forever.

Giving in to the impulse, she made short work of her clothes and quietly slipped inside.

Moving toward him, she made no attempt at discretion. "Cody," she whispered, pressing her chest to his back. "I waited for you, but you never came, so I thought I'd come find you instead." She circled her arms around his waist, needing the intimate contact, loving the new closeness between them.

When his body stiffened, she tensed as well. Her heart started pounding in her chest, and her stomach knotted.

Without turning to face her, he bit out, "Abby. You need to leave."

The coolness in his tone took her by surprise. She ducked under his arm and came around to face him. When she saw the pain and ice in his eyes, she knew something was wrong.

She held his gaze. "What is it, Cody?" she pressed, refusing to let him bury his emotions again, to go to that place where he shut the world out, shut her out.

"I just want solitude, Abby. I already told you that. It's my deepest desire, remember?"

Anger coiled in her gut. Why was he doing this? Why was he pushing her away and denying the connection they'd made? "That's bullshit, and you and I both know it." She widened her stance and held her ground. "I'm not going anywhere until you talk to me. I'm not giving up on you, or what's between us."

For one agonizing minute, he stood there staring at her. Then, his expression wary, he said, "No? Maybe you should be talking to your fiancé about this instead of me. Heck, maybe you should even be fucking him instead of me, too."

She drew a surprised breath.

Cody scoffed. "Yeah, that's what I thought." He stepped back, leaving cold where there was once heat. "Don't you have plans to make, Abby? And since I know you never break your plans—"

"Cody, wait." Oh, God, she couldn't lose him now, not when she'd just found him. "He's not my fiancé."

Cody shook his head. "Okay. Your soon-to-be-fiancé, then." He grabbed his clothes and reached for the door handle.

"Someone recently told me that great things can happen when I break my plans."

Her words stopped him; he turned back to face her, his eyes moving over her face. "Meaning?"

"Meaning, my plans have changed," she rushed out. "Yes, I was planning on getting engaged. I can't deny that." When Cody narrowed his eyes and waited for her to go on, she said, "You see, Cody, when I came to this island I had my future all mapped out, but I was on the wrong path. You showed me that." She took a step toward him and grabbed his hand. "I was also ready to live a life without passion, believing passionate men existed only in my novels, but after what we shared, after you opened up and showed me that wild, passionate men really do exist, I knew I couldn't go through with it. I veered off the beaten path, and what I found"—she stopped to jab her finger into his chest—"made me realize that I never really had what my heart desires."

His face softened. "And now?"

"And now I have what my heart desires and what my libido desires, too," she said, hoping to lighten the mood.

He moistened his lips. "I'm what your heart and libido desire?" he asked, his eyes darkening with need.

"Hell yeah!"

He shook his head, still holding back. "Abby, are you serious? Because I couldn't take it if you weren't."

"I have no intentions of getting engaged, Cody." When she still felt his reserve, she rushed on. "Ever."

He frowned and seemed to take an extra-long time to contemplate that. Then, after a moment he said, "Not ever?"

"No."

"Really?" He blew a heavy sigh, and paused before adding, "I'm sorry to hear that."

She shot him a confused look. "What? Why?"

"Because someday if I ask you to marry me, I'd want you to say yes."

She threw her head back and laughed out loud, her heart soaring with joy. "Oh, I will, on one condition."

Cody pulled a condom from his swimsuit, and then dropped

his clothes onto the floor. He stalked closer to her. His eyes grew dark with lust; his breath grew shallow. "What's that?"

She tapped his chest. "I don't want you to bury anything in here anymore."

Cody scooped her up in his arms and laid her out on the cedar bench. He tapped his chest. "I won't bury anything in here." He climbed over her, quickly sheathed his cock and positioned it at her entrance. His mouth twitched. "But I sure as hell plan on burying something in here. Daily." In one quick thrust, he drove into her.

"Oh, God, that feels so wonderful," she cried out as he sank his cock all the way up inside her.

She raked her fingers through his hair and caught his glance. Everything in her reached out to him, and what they'd found together. "I guess the elixir really did work for me, Cody. All my desires are fulfilled."

"Mine, too," he murmured. "I guess it wasn't really solitude I was looking for, Abby. It was love, life and laughter. And you gave it all back to me." As he pumped into her, making sweet, passionate love, he brushed her hair back and said, "You were wrong earlier, calling me your guardian angel after I rescued you." His lips found hers for a slow, simmering kiss, and then he said, "Because, Abby, sweetheart, it was you who rescued me."

EPILOGUE

Malik

Malik stood on the makeshift tarmac, ready to greet the three high-powered New York City CEOs as they exited the aircraft and began their two-week stay. He rubbed his goatee and took his time to let his gaze rake over each man, studying every detail, and strategizing his plan of action.

Although all three men had come to the island to unwind and destress, Malik knew they were all going to find more than just a little R & R while on vacation, especially since the Playhouse Palace models were on the exclusive island for a tropical sun and sand photo session.

He turned his attention to Danielle, Lauren and Abby, along with their partners, Ethan, Ryan and Cody, as they all prepared to board the plane and begin their lives together. The men were free to go now that they had fulfilled their rehabilitation obligations and were considered healed by their superiors.

After a round of handshakes, hugs and thank-yous, Cody spoke up. "How did you know?" he asked, furrowing his brow. "How did you know what we all wanted and needed?"

Malik spread his arms wide. "It wasn't me, my child. It was the magic elixir."

"You certainly made a believer out of me," Cody said, laughing as he pulled Abby tighter into his embrace. "To the elixir," he said loudly and glanced at his friends.

"To the elixir," they all joined in.

After the three couples boarded the plane, Malik walked his new guests to their cabanas and extended a dinner invitation before making his way back to his own quarters. He had to admit, he was most pleased that his last guests had all fulfilled their sexual desires, as well as their hearts' desires, but little did they know that the magic elixir had had nothing to do with it. Their strength to heal and seek out their deepest desires had come from within, with a little bit of guidance from him, of course.

Malik walked to his tap and poured himself a glass of cold water. He held it up in salute, stepped up to his open window and watched the plane take off. "To the elixir," he whispered, his words floating away on the breeze.

ABOUT THE AUTHOR

A former government financial officer, **Cathryn Fox** graduated from university with a bachelor of business degree. Shortly into her career, Cathryn figured out that corporate life wasn't for her. Needing an outlet for her creative energy, she turned in her brief-case and calculator and began writing erotic romance full-time. Cathryn enjoys writing dark paranormals and humorous contemporaries. She lives in eastern Canada with her husband, two kids, and chocolate Labrador retriever.